GUILT STRIKES AT GRANGER'S STORE

Also by Terry Shames

Samuel Craddock mysteries

A KILLING AT COTTON HILL
THE LAST DEATH OF JACK HARBIN
DEAD BROKE IN JARRETT CREEK
A DEADLY AFFAIR AT BOBTAIL RIDGE
THE NECESSARY MURDER OF NONIE BLAKE
AN UNSETTLING CRIME FOR SAMUEL CRADDOCK
A RECKONING IN THE BACK COUNTRY
A RISKY UNDERTAKING FOR LORETTA SINGLETARY
MURDER AT JUBILEE RALLY *

* *available from Severn House*

GUILT STRIKES AT GRANGER'S STORE

Terry Shames

SEVERN
HOUSE

First world edition published in Great Britain and the USA in 2023
by Severn House, an imprint of Canongate Books Ltd,
14 High Street, Edinburgh EH1 1TE.

severnhouse.com

British Library Cataloguing-in-Publication Data
A CIP catalogue record for this title is available from the British Library.

ISBN-13: 978-1-4483-1127-9 (cased)
ISBN-13: 978-1-4483-1126-2 (e-book)

All Severn House titles are printed on acid-free paper.

MIX
Paper from
responsible sources
FSC
www.fsc.org   FSC® C013056

Typeset by Palimpsest Book Production Ltd.,
Falkirk, Stirlingshire, Scotland.
Printed and bound in Great Britain by
TJ Books Limited, Padstow, Cornwall.

Praise for Terry Shames

About the author

Award-winning author **Terry Shames** is the author of nine previous Samuel Craddock mysteries. As well as winning the Macavity Award for Best First Novel, *A Killing at Cotton Hill* was also nominated for The Strand Critics Award. *The Necessary Murder of Nonie Blake* won the RT Critics Award for Best Mystery. Her books have also been nominated for Left Coast Crime Awards for Best Mystery.

Terry grew up in Texas, and her Samuel Craddock series is set in the fictitious town of Jarrett Creek, which is based on the fascinating people, landscape, and culture of the small town where her grandparents lived. She is a member of Sisters in Crime and on the board of Mystery Writers of America.

www.terryshames.com

ONE

'Samuel! I need help.'

I'm eating breakfast on Thursday morning and I almost drop my cup of coffee. I've been dating Wendy for a couple of years and have never heard her voice so frantic. 'What's happened? Where are you?'

'I'm home. But it's Allison. Apparently she's in jail in Mexico. I don't know what to do. Is there any way you can find out anything?'

There's always some drama with Wendy's wayward daughter, Allison. She seems to attract trouble that Wendy has to deal with, usually involving funds. Although I'll do anything I can to help for Wendy's sake, in this case I'm not sure what I can do. I'm chief of police, so people think I have all kinds of powers that I don't necessarily have. But I'll do my best.

'OK, let's take this a step at a time. Where in Mexico?'

'Monterrey.'

Not far over the Texas border. 'How did you find out she's in jail?'

'She called Jessica.' Jessica is Wendy's younger daughter, the one who inherited the good sense. 'She told Jessica to keep it secret from me, that she didn't want me to come down there. But of course Jessica told me. She called this morning before she left for work. I think I should go to Allison, but . . .' She trails away in a sob.

'Look, I'm coming over. Sit tight. We'll figure something out.' She lives a half-hour away, in Bryan-College Station.

It's a problem for me to leave. I'm expecting the man who bought my bull to come and pick him up. I keep a small herd of Hereford cows in a lot behind my house, and I've bought a new bull that will be delivered next week. I hate to lose this bull. He's a fine one, in top condition, and has a steady disposition. But you have to rotate in a new bull every few years to avoid genetic problems in the herd.

I call the buyer and tell him something has come up and ask if he can delay his trip for a couple of hours. He's been an amiable man to deal with and he says that won't be a problem. 'Gives me time for another cup of coffee.' My kind of man.

I also call my deputy, Maria Trevino, to tell her I've got to make a quick trip to Wendy's.

'Everything OK?' She likes Wendy.

'Something has come up.'

Wendy is watching for me and flings open the door before I'm up the steps. She flies into my arms, almost knocking me down. I hug her, feeling the tension in her body.

'I'm so glad you're here,' she says.

I've brought my dog, Dusty, who is Wendy's biggest fan, and Dusty dances around, yelping with delight. Wendy crouches down and hugs him so he'll calm down. 'You're a good boy,' she murmurs.

She stands back up. 'Thank you for coming. I hope it didn't interfere with work too much.'

I put my arm around her and we go inside. 'I can always make time for you.'

She shivers. 'I'm about to have a nervous breakdown. I don't know what to do. What is wrong with that girl? Why is she always in trouble?'

We've had this conversation before, and I still don't have anything to offer. Wendy calls her a free spirit, but I think of her as somebody who needs to grow up. Not that I'd say that to Wendy. Whatever problems they have between them, Wendy is fiercely protective of her daughters.

We sit at the kitchen table with coffee. Dusty flops at Wendy's feet. 'Jessica said Allison was allowed one call, and she called Jessica because she knew Jess wouldn't yell at her. She said she was in an auto accident and didn't have any insurance.'

'That's not good,' I say. But it's not unusual for Allison, who is careless of consequences.

'She said they're treating her OK, but that they're making a big deal out of the accident.'

'Was someone hurt?'

'She didn't say. Samuel, is there anyone you can call to find out what's going on?'

I've been thinking about it on the way over, and it seems like the best idea is for me to call the Department of Public Safety and find out what they recommend. And maybe contact the US Consulate. But it might be better if Wendy did that. And there's another step she needs to take. 'You need to talk to a lawyer. Maybe somebody who's got contacts in Mexico.'

She manages a smile. 'I don't know why I didn't think of that. I was just so rattled. But do you think I should go down there? I really want to.'

'Lawyer first. The lawyer can advise you about that. I wouldn't run down there too fast. You may be wasting your time.' She starts to protest, but I take her hand. 'I know you're worried, but you need to be calm.' I doubt her running off to Mexico would help.

'But why did she call Jessica and not me? I'm her mother!'

'She might be embarrassed. Did she ask Jessica to help her?'

'Jessica didn't say.'

'Did Allison say whether she was alone in Mexico?'

Wendy bites her lip. 'I'm so stupid. I didn't think to ask.'

'You're not stupid, you're upset. Let me call Jessica and see if there's more.' More that she didn't tell Wendy. 'Do you know a lawyer you can call?'

She looks doubtful. 'Only the man who handled the probate when James died.' James was her late husband, who died of a heart attack several years ago.

'Call the lawyer and see if he can recommend someone.' That will keep her busy. Unless someone was hurt in the accident, this shouldn't take too long to sort out.

My phone rings and I see that it's Maria. Uh oh. She knows where I am and she wouldn't call if it wasn't urgent. She's got enough experience now to handle most things herself.

'What's up?'

'Trouble at the feed store.'

'What kind of trouble?'

'Mark Granger was assaulted.'

'Really, what happened? Is he hurt?'

'Not too bad. Just roughed up. I thought you'd want to know.'

Melvin Granger, longtime owner of Granger's Feed Store, had a stroke a few months back that left him bedridden. His son, Mark, moved back from Houston to take care of his daddy and run the feed store. But a few weeks ago, Mark let it be known that he had Big Ideas for the store. After all these years of Melvin Granger running a basic feed store – a place farmers around Jarrett Creek counted on to buy their animal feed, and supplies related to raising stock and agriculture – his son decided to expand the store to include a gift shop, of all things.

I know a few people have been annoyed at the idea of Mark Granger modernizing the store, but I didn't expect anybody to attack him over it. 'Did you call the sheriff?'

'I did, but I told him I didn't think there was any need for him to come in.'

I finish the call and tell Wendy I have to go. 'A little trouble in town. Call me as soon as you've talked to the lawyer, and I'll get in touch with the DPS and see what they recommend.' I whistle up Dusty, and we head back to Jarrett Creek.

Granger's Feed Store is on the south side of town, right outside the city limits, across from the Best Value Motel. It's a hulk of a tall wooden building, without any kind of embellishments except its big sign on the roof. Converted from an icehouse many years ago, the original structure was built on high concrete pillars to facilitate loading ice onto wagons, so you have to walk up a short flight of stairs to the store.

I pull in next to Maria's car and the ambulance. When I get out, I tell Dusty to stay close. Not that he listens. He'll probably sneak off into the storage room in back and try to scare up a rat.

When I walk up the stairs and into the store, the EMTs are crouched down talking to Mark, who's propped up against the front counter. He looks dazed, as he well might, considering the cut above his eye.

My eyes sweep the cavernous room, with its shelves loaded with feed supplements, over-the-counter animal medications, cleaning supplies, and paraphernalia for dealing with big animals. Huge, open sacks of feed are propped along the walls and on the ends of the counters. On one wall there are pegs hung with collars, reins, harnesses, and switches.

Maria is standing nearby, next to an angry-looking young

woman with her arms crossed. Dusty rushes over to Maria. She's his favorite person. Apparently sensing that the young woman next to Maria is unhappy, he skirts clear of her. Maria reaches down and fondles his ears, although it's an absent-minded gesture.

She steps over to me. 'You made good time. The ambulance just got here.'

Mark groans and shifts his weight. He looks the image of his daddy, medium build with sandy hair and piercing blue eyes. Melvin always wore overhauls, though, and Mark's in blue jeans with a blue button-down denim shirt.

'Mark, what happened?' I ask.

'It's pretty obvious he was attacked,' the young woman with Maria snaps.

I'm surprised at her annoyance. 'I'm sorry, I don't recognize you.'

'I'm Mark's sister, Chelsea.' She looks like her late mamma – petite and pretty, with silky brown hair that she wears in a ponytail, and intense blue eyes. But she's pale with distress.

I introduce myself. 'Chelsea, did Mark tell you who did this?'

She shakes her head, gazing at her brother and holding back tears. She has a stubborn set to her jaw, also like her mamma.

'Who found him?'

'I did. I just got into town last night and we were supposed to meet at eight a.m. so he could show me his plans for the store renovation. When I got here, I found him on the floor.' She squeezes her eyes shut. 'I told him it was a bad idea to shake things up.'

'Maybe, but it's hard for me to imagine someone beating Mark up because they don't want the feed store to be changed.'

'Well, somebody is upset about it,' she says.

Before I can ask what she means, Mark groans again.

'Let's get you to the hospital,' one of the ambulance drivers says. He looks awfully young, but he speaks with authority. 'They'll want to make sure you don't have a concussion.'

'Fellows, can I speak to the victim for a moment?'

'We have to go get the cart, so have at it,' the driver says.

I hunker down next to Mark. 'Mark, do you have any idea who attacked you?'

'No.' His voice is faint. 'They were waiting inside when I

got here. They jumped me from behind. Hit me on the head. When I fell down, they kicked me.'

'They?'

'There were two of them. I think.'

'Can you give me any description at all? Did you see their clothes? Shoes? Were they tall? Short?'

He shakes his head. 'I almost lost consciousness when they hit me.'

'How'd you get the cut on your forehead?'

'Hit it when I fell.'

'Did your attackers say anything?'

'Yeah. One said I had no business here. He said "get out."'

I was wrong thinking that no one would be angry enough to take an aggressive stand against the renovation. 'Have you had any run-ins with anybody lately? Any threats?'

'Couple of weird phone calls.'

'From whom? Men? Women?'

'Men, but they didn't identify themselves.'

I have more questions, but the EMTs are back with their portable stretcher and they shoo me away. I tell Mark I'll come to the hospital later.

After they leave, I ask Chelsea if she'll come down to my office so I can take a statement.

'I'll drive you down and bring you back to your car when you're done,' Maria says.

'Do you have coffee there?' Chelsea asks. Her expression has softened.

I tell her we do and that I'll stop and get some pastries on the way.

Before we can get out the door, a gray-haired man comes in that I recognize as a farmer from out east of town. He looks confused when he sees so many people standing near the cash register. 'Melvin around?' he asks.

Chelsea seems at a loss for words, so I tell him about Melvin's stroke. 'His son has been minding the store. Can we help you?'

The farmer frowns at us as if we don't look competent to deal with his needs, which we aren't. 'I know exactly where the feed is kept. If you don't mind, I'll go get a sack and you can put it on my account.'

'Good idea,' I say.

He walks back into a room behind the front counter and comes back in a minute with a big bag of feed slung over his shoulder. 'I hope Melvin is OK,' he says as he lowers the sack to the floor.

I've walked around behind the counter. On a shelf below the cash register, I see an account book, which I haul out onto the countertop. The farmer watches, and when I open the book he says, 'It'll be under my name. Jeff Dolby.'

I'm relieved to see that the accounts are in alphabetical order, and Dolby's account is right there. 'I'm sorry, I have no idea how much to charge you,' I say.

He gives a short bark of laughter. 'I could tell you any kind of lie, I guess.'

'You could,' I agree.

Chelsea mutters something and he looks over at her. 'You look just like your mamma,' he says. 'Anyway, if you'll look, you'll see I always buy the same thing and I get charged the same amount. And I always pay when the bill comes,' he adds, shooting a pointed glance at Chelsea.

As soon as he leaves, I say to Chelsea, 'What do you want to do? People are going to come in. You prepared to tend the store?'

She looks shocked, but then shrugs. 'I guess. There's nobody else to do it. If I have a problem I can call Daddy. He can't come down, but at least he can give me instructions on what to do.'

We leave a note saying she'll be back in an hour.

TWO

At around nine a.m. at headquarters Chelsea, Maria, and I sit down with kolaches and coffee. Chelsea gives her full name as Chelsea Hampton. So she's married, although I don't see a ring on her finger. Maybe divorced.

'OK, Chelsea, I need some details. When you found Mark, was he conscious?'

'Barely. He was lying on the floor. I helped him sit up.'

'Did he say anything at all that he didn't tell me?'

'No, he could hardly talk. Dammit!' She pounds a fist in her hand. 'I can't believe my brother put himself in this position. He's not careful.'

Her words don't make much sense. What position?

'I'm sorry. I don't know what you mean. Careful about what? You mean renovating his daddy's store?'

She catches her lower lip between her teeth, looking distressed. 'He's always been careless about stepping on people's toes. People here may not want change. I mean, clearly they don't. He didn't ask anybody, he's just charging ahead with this bright idea.'

'You said he's not careful. It sounds like he's had problems in the past.'

'He lived in Houston after he got out of college. He and his business partner bought a store that was a local grocery store and turned it into a discount clothing store and people in the community were really angry. They were trying to figure out a way to buy the store and continue having a grocery when he came along and bought it.'

'So you think it's possible someone doesn't want him to change the feed store, and they attacked him?'

'Yes.'

'You might be right, but let's not jump to conclusions. Why would anyone care? Your brother said he'd had a couple of threatening phone calls. You know anything about that?'

She shakes her head. 'Like I said, I got here last night and we've barely had time to talk.'

'You came to help with your daddy?'

She hesitates. 'Yes. That's right. We have a caregiver for him now, but he gets restless, and Mark said he feels like we ought to be around for him. Mark didn't exactly ask me to come, but he said it would be nice if I did.'

'I'm sure your daddy appreciates it.' I get up. 'I'm going to the hospital to have a talk with Mark and see if he can remember any more about the attack. Meanwhile, are you certain you can take care of the store until he's back on his feet, or do you want me to ask around if there's someone you can hire to do it?'

'I guess I'll have to. We can't really afford to hire anybody.'
She looks worried. 'Do you think I'll be safe there?'

'I'll arrange for someone to stop by in the mornings when
you open up. Meanwhile, I'll go back with you now. I want to
take a look around.' I want to see if whoever attacked Mark
was careless and left any clues.

On the way to the store, my bull buyer calls to say he'll be
at my place in thirty minutes.

At the feed store, there are two people waiting for Chelsea
to open back up. I tell them what happened and that they
need to work with her. 'She just got in town last night and
doesn't know the store well, so please be patient.'

One of the men shows Chelsea how to use the ancient cash
register, and while she works to take care of her customers, I
walk around the front of the store and then back to the storage
room to see if anything has been disturbed. It's a long shot, but
it's possible that Mark caught someone trying to steal
something.

It's hard to tell if anything has been disturbed, since I don't
know what it looks like normally. It seems orderly. I wonder
what Mark has in mind with his changes. When I leave the
store, I take a look around the outside. Again, there's nothing
to indicate who might have lain in wait. Even if there were
footprints, they could be from anytime.

But I notice that at the back of the property there's a house
on the other side of the fence. I'll pay whoever lives there a
call later to see if they saw or heard anything.

When I get to my place, Jay Baumann, the man buying my bull,
is getting out of his truck. He's an amiable man. I met him when
he came over from near Waco last week to examine the bull.

'I don't mind telling you I hate to lose this one,' I say, as he
and his helper load the bull into the trailer. 'He was easy to get
along with.'

Baumann grins. 'I'll make sure he has a feather bed and a
nice pillow,' he says. We laugh. 'I can see he's pretty calm.
That dog could upset some bulls.' He nods toward Dusty, who
as usual is dancing around, excited about the action of loading
the bull. 'At least he doesn't bark.'

'That's pretty much the only thing I've managed to teach him.'

The hospital in Bobtail is small, but it's efficient, and I always feel like people are in good hands.

Mark looks considerably better than he did two hours ago. His face has been cleaned up and bandages applied where necessary, and he doesn't look so shocked. The nurse who sent me to the room told me Mark didn't have a concussion, but he did have two bruised ribs. 'He'll be out tomorrow. The doctor wants to keep him overnight for observation.'

'Mark, how are you feeling?'

'Like an idiot. How could I let myself be jumped like that?' His voice is strained.

'Did you see a car when you arrived?'

'No, they must have come on foot. Or maybe parked around back.'

'They could have parked down the road or in the motel parking lot.'

He grimaces. 'I sure didn't expect to be roughed up here in Jarrett Creek. I grew up here. I know things have changed everywhere. People are more brutal and angrier. But I didn't think Jarrett Creek would be part of that.'

I know what he means. It seems like the last couple of years the state of the world has darkened. There's no reason for Jarrett Creek to have been affected, but maybe I'm naïve to think that.

'Have you remembered any more about what happened? Anything you noticed? A certain smell? The two guys say anything to each other?'

'I think the guy who did the dirty work was wearing boots. A couple of the bruises feel like they were made with a poker.'

'So only one of them actually attacked you?'

'It seems like the other one was standing by.'

'But you didn't see anything.'

'Nothing.'

'Did he sound young? Old?'

Mark squints into the distance. 'I want to say not young, but I don't know why.'

'That's good enough. Mark, you said you'd gotten a couple of threatening phone calls. Could it have been the same person?'

'It makes sense, but I didn't take the calls seriously so I didn't pay much attention.'

'What did the person who called you say?'

He chuckles and then winces. 'Damn, those ribs hurt. He said something like, "We don't need you and your big ideas. Leave well enough alone."'

'How many calls were there and when did they come in?'

'Two. Just last week. I don't know why they waited so long. I've let it be known for a few weeks that I planned to make some changes.'

'Your sister was pretty upset.'

He waves his good hand. 'Yeah, she's always protective. Overprotective, really.'

'Your sister doesn't seem to be too excited about the renovation.'

He shrugs and looks annoyed. 'Chelsea is mad at the world. She's taking it out on me.'

'What does your daddy think of modernizing the store?'

He looks uncomfortable. 'I haven't actually told him. I was afraid it would be a problem for him. I just told him we were fixing things up a little. I guess now I'll have to break it to him since he'll want to know why I got jumped.'

'Better do it soon. He's going to find out.'

He looks gloomy. 'I don't understand it. People know me here. They're friendly. I mean, maybe not everybody is happy with the changes I'm proposing, but I was surprised anybody would take it this far.'

'Have you phoned your daddy yet to tell him what happened this morning? Did he have anything to say?'

'I didn't tell him, but you can bet Chelsea will.'

'He needs to know. Your sister will have to handle the store while you're laid up.'

'Damn, I didn't think about that. She's going to hate it.'

'Why?'

'She's pampered. Married a rich guy out in Lubbock and, except for raising a couple of teenage boys, I don't think she does much of anything but get her nails and hair done.'

'You sound resentful.'

He looks embarrassed. 'Maybe I am. Things haven't been easy for me.' He shifts in the bed and looks away from me.

'What do you mean?'

'People have told me they admire me for coming back to take care of my daddy and his business, but they don't know the whole story. There's more to it.'

He sighs and glances around the room as if looking for an exit. I wait for the rest.

'During Covid my business went belly up. I had a clothing store and my partner and I couldn't keep it afloat. I had to declare bankruptcy a few months ago.' He huffs. 'For a while there I thought maybe I'd be homeless.'

'Wouldn't your sister have helped you?'

'I didn't ask. Can you imagine me telling her I'd gone bankrupt and asking her for money? She'd never let me forget it.'

Maybe it's a sibling thing.

'So you came back here to lick your wounds.'

'Yeah.' Gloom has descended. 'And got some fresh ones.'

THREE

On the way back to headquarters that afternoon, I stop to see how Chelsea is doing with the store. Contrary to what Mark said, she seems to be fairly cheerful, bantering with a couple of customers. Dusty has come with me, but heads for the storage room. I hope he doesn't get into a bag of dog food.

When everyone leaves I ask Chelsea how it's going.

'I'm actually glad to have something to take my mind off things.' She crosses her arms and leans across the counter. 'When Mark called, I was glad to have an excuse to get out of town. My husband and I are having some problems. But I left my two teenage sons behind, and I'm feeling guilty.'

'How old?'

'Chris is fifteen and Trevor is twelve.' Her voice wobbles at the end. 'I know Chris will be fine. He'll be glad to get rid of me. You know, teenagers. But Trevor . . .' She sighs. 'Chris and his daddy get along well, but Trevor is a mamma's boy. I should have brought him.'

'Is your husband good to him?'

'Oh, yeah. They're actually Conrad's kids by a previous marriage. But we married when the kids were little, so the kids are mine, too. I'm not worried that he'll mistreat them. Just whether or not he'll do the little things, you know? The mom things?'

I nod. 'I went to the hospital and saw your brother. Have you told your daddy what happened to him?'

'Not yet. I hate to. He's not in any shape to be upset. I may close up early so I can get on over to see him. I think it's best if I tell him while the caregiver is there. She's good with him. Knows how to handle him.' She sighs. 'I should have called Mark to see how he's feeling. Now I feel guilty about that, too.'

'I'm sure he'd appreciate a call, but his wounds were superficial. He's going to be fine.'

'I was really upset at the way he looked. I hope he'll see reason now and give up this crazy plan. I don't see how it's going to work.'

He didn't seem likely to, but I'll let them hash it out.

I pull Dusty out of the back room, where he seems to have found something interesting to sniff out.

I go directly to see Melvin. I've been wanting to call on him anyway, and his son's attack is an additional reason to go. But the caregiver, a stern woman named Mrs Sholtz, answers the door and says he's sleeping and I'll have to come back another time. She's not someone to argue with.

Remembering that I want to question whoever lives behind the feed store to find out if they heard or saw anything suspicious early this morning, I head over there.

The house is near where Truly Bennett used to live before he left for west Texas, in an area that used to be called Darktown, but in the past decade has become more of a mixed neighborhood. No one answers the door, but a furious dog is barking inside. I'm glad I left Dusty in the truck.

I hear a lawnmower out back, so I walk around the side. The man mowing the lawn gets that alert look that Black people get when they are approached by a white man, especially the law. He's an older man, tall but a little stooped, wearing baggy khaki pants and a white undershirt, and a straw hat against the heat. He cuts off the mower and ambles over to me.

I take my hat off and introduce myself.

'I know who you are,' he says, with a slight smile. He says his name is Carlton Jones. 'What can I do for you?'

'Mr Jones, I'm hoping you can help me with some information. There was some trouble at the feed store.' I nod toward the store.

He waits, not suspicious exactly, but on the alert.

'I wonder if you happened to hear or see anything unusual early this morning?'

He removes his hat and fans himself with it. 'Let's step onto the porch into the shade,' he says.

I follow him, glad to get out of the sun.

The dog is still barking, and Jones walks over to the door and in a firm voice tells the dog to be quiet. I'm impressed that it worked.

He squares a look at me. 'I don't want any trouble,' he says. 'What happened?'

'Mark Granger was attacked.'

'That's Melvin's son. Is he OK?'

'Just roughed up a little bit. Did you notice unusual activity this morning, sometime before eight o'clock?'

'No, sir. I needed to go to the grocery store before it got too hot, so I left before eight.'

Late afternoon we have a recurring problem to deal with. Pigs have gotten into Mrs Bedichek's vegetable garden, so I have to go help the owner of the pigs, Sandy Morton, to round them up.

Sandy grew up in Jarrett Creek and moved to East Texas, where he lived for many years. When he retired, he moved back here and for some reason decided to take up raising pigs. The problem is that the pigs seem to be cleverer than Sandy. Or maybe he's lazy. At any rate, they find ways to get out and raise havoc, either getting on the road and stopping local traffic, or invading neighbors' yards.

We have a hard time rounding them up. They have no intention of leaving the nice garden where they've chomped on half the green beans and pulled out plants that are going to seed. Maybe because it's late summer and most of the vegetables have been harvested, Aleta Bedichek is more philosophical about the raid than I might have imagined. In her fifties, she teaches school at Jarrett Creek High, and I suspect she's learned a bit of patience over the years. She gets out in the garden with Sandy and me and shoos the pigs out the gate.

When Sandy finally has the five of them in the back of his pickup, she says to him, 'Sandy, you're lucky I'm sick of green beans and the rest of the garden is ready to plow under. If those pigs get in my fall garden once I've planted it, I'm going to be eating pork chops for a long time.'

Sandy is a heavy man, perspiring from the effort of chasing the pigs around the garden. He looks at his five well-fed pigs and shakes his head. 'I'm beginning to think they're more trouble than they're worth.' He offers to pay her for the damage, but she declines.

'Use the money to get a better fence,' she says.

After he's gone, she says to me, 'It's lucky my husband is off fishing. He wouldn't have been so easy on Sandy.'

When I get home from work, I call Wendy to see if she's found a lawyer. 'I have. He got right on it. Turns out Allison was assigned a Hispanic lawyer in Monterrey. We don't know whether he's any good, but he asked for money and my lawyer advised me to send it.'

'Is there a lot of money involved?'

'Doesn't seem like too much. The lawyer I've hired here says one of the worst things you can do in Mexico is get in an accident – that the whole prison system there is on the take and if you have an auto accident they really go after you.'

I hope they don't get too greedy. Wendy has enough money to live comfortably because although her husband was never much of a success, he carried a substantial life insurance policy.

But I know she'd pay whatever it takes to get her daughter out of trouble, and that may end up being expensive.

'Do you know what Allison was doing in Mexico?'

'I didn't even know she was there.'

'What does your lawyer advise about you going down there?'

'He says forget it, that I need to be patient.'

I'm relieved to hear that.

She gives a little laugh. 'He's probably right. I can see myself going to the jail and asking to see her and getting hysterical if they wouldn't let me. For all I know, they'd throw me in jail, too.'

'Then you need to follow the lawyer's advice.' I shudder to think of Wendy or her daughter in prison in Mexico. I've heard stories, and I'm truly worried, but it's best to keep that to myself for now.

Wendy's relationship with her daughter is dicey. Allison is what she calls a free spirit – sort of like Wendy – and in the rare moments when Allison is in town, they usually end up arguing. I've only met her once. She looks a lot like Wendy, pretty with soft brown eyes and untamed, curly hair. But she's skittish and I've wondered if she's into drugs, although I've never asked Wendy and she never volunteered.

'Look, let's have lunch tomorrow to discuss it.'

'Maybe the lawyer can come, too.'

We arrange to meet at Bosco's at noon.

I hang up, feeling alarmed. I have a hunch there's more to the story than we're hearing. I had the impression that when an American is jailed, especially near the border, money usually exchanges hands and there's a quick release of the criminal. Why hasn't that happened? I wonder if this is a situation I should get Maria involved in. I speak a little Spanish, but Maria is Hispanic and is fluent. I didn't ask Wendy if Allison speaks Spanish. We'll talk about it tomorrow.

FOUR

First thing Friday morning, I call the Department of Public Safety headquarters in Bryan and tell the crisp-voiced young woman who answers that I need some information about a citizen in trouble in Mexico. In the past, I would have called my old friend Luke Schoppe, but he's retired, and is dealing with cancer and I hate to bother him.

'You'd be better off talking to somebody in one of our border offices. Let me get you a name.'

She comes back in a minute with a name and number. She may not be warm and fuzzy, but she's efficient.

I reach Rolando Flores in Brownsville. He apparently doesn't do small talk and abruptly asks what I want from him.

'What does the DPS do if an American is jailed in a Mexican prison, specifically Monterrey?' I ask.

'Jailed for what?' He sounds impatient.

'Car accident.'

'You mean somebody stupid enough to be driving in Mexico without Mexican auto insurance?'

'I don't know the details.'

'All I know is that in Mexico, if you fail to have auto insurance and you get in an accident, you'd better be able to pay for damages on the spot, or you get thrown in jail.'

'If there are injuries, how much money are we talking?'

There's silence for several seconds, and then he barks, 'Did somebody get killed? That's a whole 'nother order of business.'

'I don't know.'

'Well, what do you know?'

'Very little. My girlfriend's daughter was the driver, and getting information has been impossible.'

'I'll bet. My advice? Your friend needs to get a Mexican lawyer. And get in touch with the US Embassy. And you need to find out how bad the accident was. If somebody was killed or hurt bad, you're looking at a big problem.'

As blunt as he is, he's right: we need to know how bad the accident was.

'I appreciate the help. My friend is worried about her daughter.'

'She should be.'

I'm on time getting to the restaurant in Bryan, but Wendy is already waiting for me, along with a man in a business suit. He gets up and introduces himself as Wendy's lawyer, Chuck Hernandez. He's a portly man with a buzz cut and a friendly smile.

Wendy has secured us a booth, and we sit with the two of them across from me. I'm alarmed by the way Wendy looks. Her face is drawn, her eyes dull. But more to the point, her whole demeanor is different. She's usually in charge – peppy and with an impish grin. That's all gone. She sits down, and when she puts her hands on the table in front of her I see that they're trembling. I reach over and put a hand over hers. She grabs onto my hand with both of hers, holding on as if I'm a lifeline.

'I hope you can get information on what's going on with Wendy's daughter,' I say to Hernandez.

'I made some calls this morning,' he says. 'I did it first thing because the weekend is coming up and their offices will be closed. But when I tell you what I found out, you will understand why it's not as straightforward as one might hope.' His words are measured, as if he's speaking in front of a judge. It's clear he's already told Wendy what he's going to tell me. She looks over at him, sitting next to her, with a look of despair.

The waiter comes and we tell him we'll order soon, and to bring us a glass of wine, white for Wendy, red for me. Hernandez orders a martini.

'Now,' I say to Hernandez, 'What do you mean "not straightforward?"'

He clears his throat. 'It seems that Allison had the misfortune to rear-end a car that carried a high-ranking legislative member's wife,' he says.

'Was the woman hurt?'

He hesitates. 'It's hard to say. There are conflicting answers to the question.' He draws a breath. 'But according to Allison's lawyer, Señora Rojas is a vindictive person.'

'What do you know about the lawyer? Was he assigned by the court? Is he reputable?'

'His name is Enrique Orozco. He was assigned by the court and, as far as I can tell, he's legitimate. I looked him up and he's in the register for attorneys in Mexico. But he's young, and it would be better if Allison had someone with experience. And who knows why they chose him as her attorney? It could be that he's in someone's pay.'

'Can we replace him with someone we choose?'

'I think it's a good idea to try. Whether the court will accept it, I don't know. But I think we might get more help from someone who is independent of the court system.'

'Let's do that right away. Can you do it?'

'I'll make some calls.'

'Now, you said this woman who was in the other car is vindictive. They can't just hold Allison because the woman is mad, can they?'

'I'm afraid they can. Her husband has influence with the police commissioner, and the commissioner holds all the power over how justice works in the city.'

'Are you sure it was just a fender-bender?' I ask.

'Details are vague.'

I'm getting impatient with his hesitation. 'What do you mean vague? Isn't there a police report?'

He splays his hands out in front of him. 'There should be. Unfortunately, I believe that Allison has stepped into a political battle between two factions. One thinks the police are too lenient on Americans who come to vacation in Monterrey, and the other thinks Americans should be welcomed because they spend a lot of money.'

A political situation. Just what Allison needs. 'What kind of physical situation is she in? Is she in danger? Is she getting adequate food and a safe place to sleep?'

'That's the only part of this that is hopeful,' he says. 'I'm told that she is in a facility where she has a room to herself and is receiving better treatment than is often afforded criminals.'

'Criminals?' Wendy says. 'You're calling her a criminal?' Her voice is shaking with rage.

'Mrs Gleason, your daughter did, in fact, commit a crime. Admittedly, had she been a Mexican national, most likely she would have been fined on the spot and let go. But let's focus on the positive part. That she's being treated better than one might fear.'

'What do you mean a room? Is she in a cell?'

'I asked the same thing, but again, the answer is vague. He did say it wasn't the regular prison.'

'If it's money they're after, how much do you think they want?'

He sighs and looks down at his hands, which he's knitted together on the table in front of him. 'As I said, it isn't that simple. The woman in the other car hopes to make an example of Allison as an American who came to town and treated the law casually. Unfortunately, Allison failed to get automobile insurance, which does make Señora Rojas's case more compelling.'

I sit back, shaking my head. How could Allison be so careless? Everyone knows that in Mexico you absolutely have to have car insurance. 'What was she doing in Monterrey? Had she been there long?'

'I don't know that, but she likely wasn't there long. Many young people go over the border to Monterrey to have an evening of entertainment, and spend only one night. Monterrey is a beautiful city and they feel safe there. And it's easy to get to, a couple of hours from the border.' He turns to Wendy. 'If it's any consolation, Allison is not the first young person who didn't bother with insurance.'

The waiter comes back and we order. I can see that Wendy doesn't have any interest in food. She orders a Cobb salad, while Hernandez and I get hamburgers.

'Was Allison traveling with anyone?'

Hernandez leans forward, elbows on the table. 'Good question. I don't know. It's hard to imagine a young woman going there alone. If she was by herself, I fear there's more to it.'

'Like what?' Wendy asks.

'Like she was there to buy certain products,' he says carefully.

'Drugs?' I ask.

He nods.

Wendy has bowed her head so that I can't see her face. 'Wendy,' I say. 'Do you know anything about this?'

She raises her head. Her expression is bleak. 'I wouldn't put it past her.'

The waiter brings our food. Hernandez puts a half-bottle of ketchup on his burger and fries before he takes a bite of his burger.

Wendy pokes at her salad. 'You've done a lot this morning, Mr Hernandez, and I appreciate it.'

He chuckles. 'You were lucky. My court appearance got canceled, so I had time.'

'Is it possible for me to talk to Allison?'

'Um, there seems to be a problem.'

'What problem?'

He cuts his eyes in my direction. There's something he doesn't want to tell Wendy. 'I don't know if this is true, but Orozco said Allison doesn't want to talk to her mother.'

Wendy throws the fork down. 'Oh for heaven's sake. Why am I even bothering?'

Hernandez puts a hand on her arm. 'Mrs Gleason, Wendy, like I said, I don't know if it's true . . .'

'I know it's true,' Wendy says bitterly. 'She'll do anything to spite me.'

Wendy groans. I can imagine how terrifying it is to think her daughter is in a situation where she can't talk to friends or family.

'Here's my plan,' Hernandez says. I like his reasonable demeanor. 'I'll ask Orozco if Allison will talk to me. And meanwhile, I'll try to get the name of another lawyer who can take the case.'

'And let's try to find out if there was anyone else in either car,' I say.

'I've got a call in to a former colleague from law school,' he says. 'He doesn't live in Monterrey, but he has family there and his father is well-connected.'

'The sooner, the better,' I say.

Wendy and I linger after Hernandez leaves and I try to

comfort her the best I can. 'Hernandez seems competent,' I say. 'And we've got a plan.'

'I just keep thinking of her in jail.'

'Try to stay positive. Hernandez seems to think they're using her as a pawn, and if that's the case, they're going to want to keep her in good condition. It wouldn't do to trot out a woman who has been mishandled.'

'I guess that's comforting.' She can barely manage a smile.

I've just gotten home when Loretta pops by. She's my neighbor down the street. She may be a 'senior citizen,' but she has more energy than most young people I know. She usually comes over every couple of mornings bearing baked goods, but the last couple of days I haven't seen her.

I invite her in, but she says she can't stay. 'I'm in hurry to get down the church. Ida Ruth and I are in charge of the bake sale this weekend and there are lots of last-minute things to do. If I know Ida Ruth, she's already down at the church, tapping her foot, wondering when I'll get there. I came by to tell you I better see you there spending a good bit of cash.' It's a fundraiser for the band, and I'd just as soon give them a check as go there, but she insists that it's important for me to show up in person. 'People need to see the police chief supporting our sale.'

'What do I need with baked goods?' I ask. 'You keep me supplied.' I'm teasing her, but she takes it seriously.

'Just because you buy the baked goods doesn't mean you have to eat them,' she says.

In the evening my next-door neighbor Jenny Sandstone has invited me to dinner with her friend Will Devereaux. They've been seeing each other for quite a while, but neither seems in a hurry to get married. I don't ask because Jenny doesn't like being quizzed – although she doesn't seem to see the irony in the fact that she readily fires questions at me.

We are enjoying a bottle of good red wine. She introduced me to the wonders of wine a few years ago. I've never gotten the hang of white ones; I prefer red. We're sitting out on her deck. It's hot, but there's that feeling of fall in the air that you sometimes get at the end of August. Not cool exactly, but the sharpness of the heat disappears in the evening. Will has brought appetizers, some kind of puffy cheese thing and stuffed mushrooms. Will likes to cook, which is a boon for all who know Jenny. Before he arrived on the scene, her 'cooking' consisted of cheese and crackers and whatever she could buy at a grocery store that could be heated up.

Dusty is sprawled out next to the table, content to be among friends.

Over drinks, Jenny and Will regale me about their latest cases. They both work as lawyers in Bobtail, but on opposite sides. Jenny is a prosecutor who works for the DA, and Will is a defense attorney.

Jenny asks about the proposed renovation at Granger's Feed Store.

'I understand Melvin Granger's son is bringing the feed store into the modern world,' Jenny says.

'I don't know if he knows what he's doing, but I talked to Loretta, and she seems to think it could be a success.'

In fact, I had an argument with Loretta about it. There was a time when she would have been horrified at the proposed change to Granger's Feed Store. She likes things to stay the way they are. But ever since she got herself a new hairstyle and started wearing slacks, she has revised her opinions about new ideas. Now she's one hundred percent on the side of progress.

I told her I doubted there would be enough business to justify all the work Melvin's son is considering.

'I wish you'd stop being so negative,' she said. 'It's that kind of thinking that will keep people from accepting the changes. I think what the boy is doing is going to be good for the town. Bring in some outside money. And it will be convenient to be able to buy nice hand creams and lotions and soap right here in town instead of having to traipse off to Bobtail.'

'She's right,' Jenny says, when I tell her Loretta's opinion. 'If Granger's son puts up a good sign and paints the place, people driving through town will stop. You get people going back and forth between Austin and Houston, and this is as good a place as any to stop and stretch their legs. And why not do it at the gift shop?'

'You put it that way, maybe you're right,' I say.

I do know that if Loretta is in favor of it, that's a big plus for the store. Ever since she disappeared and everyone thought she had been killed, she's been a celebrity. I'm not sure why that made her opinion on things more valuable, but I'm not inclined to judge. Let her enjoy her position.

When we sit down to dinner – Will has made a fine goulash – Jenny says, 'I invited Wendy tonight but she said she couldn't make it. I got the feeling something's going on, but I didn't want to ask her.'

I knew Wendy had been invited tonight, because she told me, saying she couldn't face socializing. I asked if it was OK for me to discuss Allison's situation with them, since they might be able to shed some light, and aren't likely to gossip. She said that would be OK, that anything they could add would be helpful.

I explain the problem, and Will shudders. 'It's the political element that's alarming. Usually these things can be dealt with right away with a little cold, hard cash, but it sounds like they've got an agenda.'

We're just starting in on Will's chess pie when my cell phone rings. I glance at it and see it's Billy Crewes. He's chief of the volunteer fire department.

'I need to take this,' I say.

I walk away from the table. Dusty jumps up and follows me, watching while I take the call, as if he needs to hear what's being said.

When I say hello, I hear a lot of commotion in the background. I have to repeat my greeting, and then Billy's voice comes on, loud and authoritative. 'Chief Craddock? There's been a fire here at the feed store.'

My stomach clenches. The place is all wood. 'Has it been put out?'

'Yes, we got to it in time.'

'Is there much damage?'

'Just some scorching. We were damn lucky. Guy who lives behind the store saw the flames before they could get too far along. But that's not the problem.'

By the strain in his voice, I almost know what he's going to say before he says it.

'There's a body here. Looks like he was killed in the last few hours.'

'I'll be right there.' I tell him to call the Highway Patrol and the sheriff's office in Bobtail. 'Keep everybody away so you don't contaminate the scene.'

'I already called them, and unfortunately it's a little late to worry about the scene.'

I tell Jenny and Will why I have to leave. Jenny says, 'I'll take Dusty to your house.'

FIVE

The scene outside the feed store is one of controlled chaos. The Jarrett Creek volunteer fire team has been joined by a crew from Bobtail and they are still hosing down the outside back wall of the storage room where the renovation is going to take place.

I go upstairs into the store, where Billy Crewes greets me, looking harried. 'The fire started inside,' he says, 'but we got it put out right away. It was only afterwards that we found the body.'

'What time did you get called?' I ask.

'A little before eight. We were just sitting down to watch TV after supper,' he says. 'Still some daylight.' He's a scrawny guy, baby-faced, looks like he just got out of high school, although I know he's in his thirties.

'Have you notified the owner?'

'Haven't had time.'

'I'll take care of it.'

I put in a call to the Granger residence, and reach Chelsea. I tell her what's happened and she says she and Mark will be here right away, that Mark is just finishing his dinner.

The wooden floor squeaks as Billy and I walk toward the back storage room. The entrance to the room is stacked with boxes

and more large sacks of feed. Billy said they moved them so
they wouldn't get too water-logged. We can barely get by them
and into the room where all this stuff is usually stored. The air
is musty with the smell of grain, the familiar tang of oats and
mash. But there's also the smell of blood, tangy and metallic.

The lighting is dim and it's hard to make out details, but I
see what Billy meant when he said it was too late for the scene
to be secured. The floor has been thoroughly washed down in
the process of putting out the fire, leaving a bright sheen over
it. Firefighters have trampled all over the room, so damp footprints cover the floor.

The reason they didn't notice the body is that it's in a heap
to the right of the entry, looking like a pile of clothing. The
fire, across the back wall, would have drawn their attention
first. Although it's possible the fire started accidentally, my
best guess is that somebody started it deliberately, intending
for the whole structure to burn down, taking the body with it.

I'm not sure what good it is, but I ask Billy to help me bring
in a couple of chairs from behind the counter in the front room
to string yellow tape to establish a perimeter. At least the body
needs to be protected.

I hear a commotion out in the front room. Mark Granger has
arrived, looking distraught. I tell him about the body that
has been found. 'I'm going to have to ask you to wait
downstairs.'

Mark is still bearing a bandage on the cut above his eye.
'Why is this happening?' he asks.

'We'll figure it out,' I say. 'Hang tight.'

I go back into the storeroom and put on booties and gloves
and crouch down to take a look at the body. There's blood on
the floor at the back of the torso, still tacky, but that may be
due to the water from the hoses. The man is facing away from
me, and I don't want to move him until the medical examiner
gets here, so I lean over to peer at the face. I don't recognize
him. He's a man in his fifties, hefty, with short-cropped light
hair. He's wearing jeans and a black T-shirt with some kind of
logo on the front that I can't see. Once the medical examiner
gets here, I can get him turned over.

From the back, it's pretty obvious what killed the man. There's a gunshot exit wound in the vicinity of his heart. There should be a bullet in the wall, unless the killer took it with him when he left. Or she. That's Maria, talking in my mind, admonishing me not to take anything for granted. I wish Maria was here. She had a couple of days off and has gone to San Antonio to see her family.

'Any idea what started the fire?' I ask Billy.

'Whoever set it didn't bother trying to make it look spontaneous. There were gasoline-soaked rags along the wall. I guess they figured since this building was wood, it would go up fast. If it hadn't been for the guy who saw it and called it in, they would have been right.'

'Who called it in?'

'Name is Carlton Jones. I asked him to wait outside. I figured you'd want to talk to him.'

'I do. I'm glad you asked him to wait.'

Outside Jones is standing off to one side, watching the action. He's getting more than his share of excitement. 'Mr Jones, looks like you saved us some trouble,' I say.

He nods, his face concerned in the glow from the lights the firefighters have strung up. 'It was by chance I saw the flames. I went out to the yard just before eight to chain up my dog and saw a light coming from here that I don't usually see. So I stepped to the back of the property and smelled the smoke. I called the fire department number and then hustled over here to see if there was anything I could do.'

'When you got here, did you see anybody hanging around? Somebody who might have set the fire?'

'No, sir.' He peers at me. 'You mean it was set deliberately? I thought maybe it was somebody being careless. You know, leaving oily rags around or the like.'

'It appears that someone set it to cover up another crime. We've found a body inside. That's why I need you to think back if you saw anything odd.'

He shakes his head. 'I'm afraid I was more interested in the fire than the surroundings. You can see that my property butts up in the back here and I have a wooden fence, so I was worried the fire might get out of hand. I have to say those volunteers got here fast.'

I thank him for his quick thinking and tell him he can go home. 'I may have more questions, but that's it for now.'

Highway patrol officers have arrived. I vaguely recognize one of them, but can't remember from where. He gives his name as Arnold Mosier. That triggers the memory from a few years back when my friend Jenny Sandstone was in an accident and he was especially kind to her. We shake hands and he introduces me to the other officer, Franklin Bowles.

'You've got a body?' Mosier asks.

I nod. 'Come on upstairs. It's in a back storage room.'

A squad car from Bobtail PD wheels into the gravel lot and the three of us wait for them to join us. I fill them in, and lead the four officers upstairs.

We file into the back room, where I point out the body. 'We're waiting for the coroner.'

Billy Crewes comes into the room and says he can turn over the scene when the police are ready. The firefighters always have jurisdiction over a fire scene, even though it's a volunteer outfit.

'We came to secure the scene,' one of the Bobtail officers says. 'Sheriff Hedges says we need to determine if we should send out a forensics team or if the DPS wants to take it over.' The Department of Public Safety has jurisdiction over homicides in towns like Jarrett Creek with a small police force.

'I imagine the DPS will want it,' I say. 'You want to call this into headquarters?' I ask Mosier.

He goes back to his car to make the call.

When Mosier returns, he looks surprised.

'Forensics?' I ask.

'They said Bobtail can handle it. I wasn't expecting that. We've got a new district manager, Sergeant Reagan, and he doesn't seem like the type to let things out of his control.'

'I'll call Sheriff Hedges and tell him we're on it,' the Bobtail officer says.

But before he can get to his car, Hedges drives up. He gets out of his car and comes over and shakes my hand. 'You know who the victim is?'

'I don't recognize him. When the coroner gets here maybe

he'll find some ID.' I tell him that the DPS said Bobtail could handle the forensics.

'I'll get these two boys to stay the night and guard the scene,' he says, nodding to his officers. 'Forensics can tackle the scene first thing in the morning. Is the medical examiner on his way?'

'He's been called.'

In no time, the ambulance arrives, followed by a young guy who identifies himself as the medical examiner's assistant, Junior Addison. He's new, just hired into the job.

I follow him inside to show him the body. He goes straight to work, and seems competent. I ask him about his credentials and he says he worked in the coroner's office in Houston for a couple of years, but decided he didn't like city living. 'I took a pay cut, but the cost of living is cheaper around here.' While he talks, he's looking over the body, turning the man onto his back. 'Not much doubt what killed him,' he says. 'Unless he was poisoned before he was shot.' He chuckles. Not for the first time, I've noticed that medical examiners seem to have a droll sense of humor.

'Any idea how long he's been here?' I ask.

'Rigor has started in his head and neck, but hasn't advanced . . . so more than an hour, but probably no more than three.'

It's after eight-thirty now, so that means he was killed anywhere from six to eight, when the fire crew showed up. Whoever killed him worked fast, setting the fire right after the murder.

'Any ID on the body?' I ask.

Addison searches the man's pockets, and to my surprise he retrieves a wallet. 'This should help.'

Sure enough, there's a driver's license and credit cards, plus a photo of a woman I take to be the man's wife or girlfriend. His name is Michael Sullivan and he's fifty years old. His address puts him in Belleville, a town thirty minutes south of here.

'Set of keys,' Addison says. He hands me a key ring with several keys on it.

Leaving identification on the body suggests that whoever killed the man thought the fire would consume the body so thoroughly that even the wallet would burn. Or maybe the killer was rattled by what they did and didn't think to check for identification.

I hear raised voices and go to the front of the store. Chelsea Granger has arrived. She and her brother have come upstairs and look to have been squabbling.

Mark is red in the face. 'Chelsea, how the hell was I supposed to know somebody would be murdered?'

'You should have left well enough alone,' she says. I hear the cantankerous tone of a grudge in her voice. 'Daddy doesn't need this. First you getting attacked, and now someone murdered in the store.'

It's late, but I'm not going to wait until tomorrow to question the two of them, so I tell them I'd like them to come down to the station.

When I arrive, I make coffee and they come trailing in, looking sulky, like they're still fighting.

I sit them down. 'First off, the victim's name is Michael Sullivan. Do either of you know him?'

They say they don't.

'I wonder if your daddy knew him.'

'We could ask.'

'You leave it alone. I'll drop by tomorrow and ask him.'

'You know Daddy isn't doing that well,' Mark says. 'You have to choose your time.'

'I'll call first. I already tried to get past Mrs Sholtz once.'

'She's pretty amazing,' Chelsea says. 'Not always in a good way. But she does take good care of Daddy.'

'Mark, have you had any more threatening phone calls?'

He shakes his head.

'Anybody in the store complaining about the changes you're proposing?'

'No,' Mark says, 'in fact, the opposite. People seem to like the idea. I had a couple of ladies come in to tell me they'd like to sell their pickles and jams in the store. Unfortunately, I had to tell them I can't take goods that somebody made in their kitchen. There are laws governing what gets sold and who makes it.'

'That's too bad.' I remember Loretta saying some women

might like to make a few extra dollars selling their canned pickles and jams.

'They were disappointed, but it's possible I can figure out some way to have a food fair or a booth set up in the parking lot.'

Chelsea groans. 'This gets worse and worse. Daddy is going to have a fit.'

'You still haven't told him your plans?' I say to Mark.

He shakes his head.

'Well, we're going to have to, soon,' Chelsea says. 'My brilliant brother has already hired guys to start construction.'

'So you got permits?' I ask.

He nods. 'I asked Mr LoPresto for help, and he guided me through the process.'

Gabe LoPresto has the biggest construction company in the county and does most of the construction work around Jarrett Creek.

'When is work going to begin?'

'They were supposed to start this coming Monday. Will the investigators be done by then?'

'It will depend on what the forensics people say. I'll get back to you tomorrow.'

SIX

I feed and check up on my cows quickly Saturday morning, making sure the new bull is settled, before I go back to the scene of last night's murder and fire. I want to be there when the forensics team arrives.

Usually I can stash Dusty at headquarters with Maria, but she's gone so I have to leave him at home. I don't need him bouncing around at a crime scene. The way he looks at me when I walk out the door without him, you'd think the end of the world had come.

On the way to the feed store, I stop at the bakery to pick up some coffee to take to the two Bobtail officers who were left behind to guard the scene. I'm also bringing some coffee cake that I thawed out since Loretta has been too busy to bake. They are grateful, and even more grateful when I tell them I'll stay until the team gets here, so they can head home.

Before I can get inside the store, I get a call from Arnold Mosier, the patrol officer who went to the dead man's address. He says Michael Sullivan has a wife, Connie, and tells me they notified her last night that he'd been killed.

'She said something interesting before she clammed up. She said she told him it was a bad idea to go over to Jarrett Creek. I couldn't get her to say why, though. She was pretty broken up.'

'Did she say what time her husband left to come here?'

'She said it was a few minutes before six o'clock.'

That further narrows the timeline of when Sullivan was killed. The ME put the death between six and eight, but it would have taken Sullivan thirty minutes to get here, so he can't have been killed before six thirty, and since Jones called in the fire around eight, the murder has to have been committed before that.

I'll go over to question the wife later, and see if I can get her to say more.

I slip on gloves and booties, go inside and take another look at the murder scene in the early morning light. There's nothing new to see where Sullivan's body was lying, except that what I took to be a shine from water on the floor last night appears to be a high-gloss varnish on the floor. All around the perimeter of the room there are little ridges of silt. The floor must not have been cleaned in years, and dust from the feed and from regular dirt in the air had dulled it. I wonder why they bothered to install such a fine floor in what is basically a storeroom?

While I survey the room, I ponder the murder. Why was Sullivan killed here at Granger's Feed Store? I try to imagine someone asking Sullivan to meet them here. How did they get in? Surely the door was locked. I didn't think to wonder about that last night, so I check on the front door. There's no sign of tampering with the lock. Did someone have a key?

The door has a simple lock on it, and might have been opened easily enough with a credit card – something I've heard can be done but have never had the occasion to use. Or maybe they got in some other way. I've never seen another entrance, but that doesn't mean there isn't one. I walk back to the dark rear of the store and, sure enough, I see another door, one that's not apparent at first because sacks of feed are stacked back here. But the sacks have been shoved aside. I try the door, and it opens readily. Likely, Granger hadn't locked the door in years because he had the big sacks stacked back here. But who could have known that? Or was it simply a matter of opportunity? At the open door, I examine the steps. They haven't been cleaned in a long time, and the accumulated dirt doesn't seem to have been disturbed. Still, I'll point it out to the forensics team.

Another question takes me outside. How did Michael Sullivan get here? There was a car key on his key ring. But my squad car is the only one parked nearby. I see a movement and look up to see Carlton Jones behind his house, thirty yards away, leaning on a hoe, watching me. He's got a nice garden in the back of his house, one reason he would worry that the fire would spread back here. He waves and goes back to his work. Looks like he's preparing the garden for fall planting. The only reason I know that is that Loretta told me this is the time of year for that.

The feed store is situated on Highway 36, and I look in either direction along the road and don't see any cars parked on the shoulder.

It's possible Sullivan parked in the motel lot across the street. I'll check it out.

When the forensics team arrives, I tell them about the back entrance, and they say they'll examine it. I ask them how long their investigation will take. 'The owner wants to start some construction work here Monday. Do you think you'll be done with the crime scene by then?'

The head of the team looks around. 'Not much to see here. Maybe we'll cordon off the area where the body was found in case we need any more information, but most of the place won't be affected.'

They set to work taking measurements, looking for a bullet, and scouring the area for other clues. I watch them for a while before I walk over to the motel to see if Sullivan left his car there. But there are only a few cars in the lot, and the desk clerk identifies them as belonging to hotel guests. As I'm winding up, I get a call that takes me back to headquarters.

Connor Loving has called in a dither because someone reported a car in the lake. 'They said it was upside down, partly submerged. I didn't know whether to call a wrecking company or what,' he says. Connor takes directions well, but he's not good at self-direction. That's OK. I suspect I know how the car got there.

'Who called it in?'

'Dooley Phillips. He was on his way to work and saw it. He said he checked, but there was nobody inside.' Dooley owns a boat dock and general store at the lake. I'm glad he saw it early, so there won't be so many gawkers yet.

'Never mind. I'll take care of it. Any other calls from last night?'

'Mrs Somerville phoned to say there was a drunk man singing in the street. I called her and she said whoever it was, was walking down the street, singing loud, but after a minute she didn't hear him anymore.'

Mrs Somerville is almost deaf, so either the man was really loud, or she thought she heard it. Or maybe just needs some attention. 'Go talk to her and see if she needs anything.' Connor is happy to do that. He has a nice way with older folks.

It's almost ten when I get to the lake. A couple of men are standing near the edge of the water where the gray car went in.

I keep knee-high rubber boots in the trunk of my squad car, and I put them on before I head to the site. The gravel and mud are disturbed at the shoreline. The car is far enough into the water that Dooley must have had to wade out to check if anybody was inside.

After a summer of heat, the water is murky with algae.

The two men eyeing the car say they are from out of town. They were on their way to Dooley's marina at the end of the lake, to rent a boat for a week, when they spied the car. They're in their thirties, clean-cut guys who say they're here for a week of fishing.

One says, 'Looks like the car left the embankment up there and must have been traveling fast. It bounced a couple of times.'

He points toward two huge gouges in the soft, graveled beach, which indicate the car must have hit twice and bounced before landing on its roof.

'You got a good read on it,' I tell him.

'I'm an engineer,' he says. 'Odd things like this always get my attention.'

They head on their way, and I wade out to take a look at the car. The windows are wide open. Which brings me to a question. Were the windows open to aid in the sinking of the car? Or was the driver needing some fresh air? Either way, whoever had the accident apparently managed to swim out. But why not call in the accident? And why abandon the car? If I were a betting man, I'd bet this car belongs to Sullivan, and his killer tried to get rid of it. It seems like a risky way to do it. I don't see how they managed to get it up to speed and then jump out before it crashed. I suppose I'm wrong, and it may not have anything to do with Michael Sullivan. Could have been a drunk who careened off the road and wasn't so injured that he couldn't climb out of the car. It will become clearer once we get it out of the water.

I put in a call to Skippy Ryland, who owns the only service station in town that does towing. He sounds skeptical when I tell him where the car is. 'Maybe you ought to call one of those big outfits in Bobtail,' he says. This isn't the first time I've noticed that Skippy is reluctant to take on any but the easiest jobs.

'Skippy, this is a police matter, and I need you to take care of it,' I say.

He grumbles some more but says he'll have a crew out here within the hour to haul out the car.

I think of calling Connor to come out and wait for the truck, but if anything goes wrong, Connor won't have the initiative to handle it. I go back to my squad car to wait, wishing that I'd thought to bring coffee with me.

Thirty minutes later, Skippy's tow truck approaches cautiously, a sign of the reluctance with which Skippy faces most of his jobs. He hauls himself out of his truck. He's a scraggly man, hair hanging down the sides of his face, enormous gut sagging over his belt, jowls drooping to his chin-line. He's brought a helper, a kid who looks sixteen. The kid jumps out of the truck and trots over to the waterline.

'Whoa!' He turns to Skippy. 'Daddy, look at that! We're going to have some job getting that car out of there.' He looks enthusiastic at the prospect.

'Hey, Samuel.' Skippy nods to me and ambles toward where his son is standing.

I walk down with them. 'How you going to approach this?' I ask. 'You turn it over first, or drag it out on its top?'

Skippy looks me up and down. 'I assume the city is going to pay me a good amount to take care of this.'

'We'll pay a fair price,' I say.

He grumbles and spits to one side. 'We'll turn it over first.' Then he calls to his son, 'Cooter, I'll get the truck backed up. You wade out there and attach the hooks.'

Cooter goes back to the truck and puts on a pair of waterproof pants and boots and wades out into the water.

Not only is Cooter more enthusiastic than his daddy, but he does his part of the job efficiently. Skippy positions his tow truck in the water up to the floorboards, perpendicular to the car. Cooter runs chains over the bottom of the car and attaches hooks to the passenger side door just inside the window.

By now we have a handful of people standing by to watch and comment.

'Take it easy there,' one of them calls out as Skippy gets into the truck.

Skippy slowly engages the truck, which grinds and groans as it slowly lifts the car onto its side, with its wheels toward the tow truck.

Cooter then dis-attaches the hooks and runs them over the top of the car, and attaches them to the inside top of the passenger side door.

This time the truck doesn't protest as much, as it has less weight to tackle, and in a couple of minutes the car slams down onto its wheels, bouncing back and forth with the force of its fall. The bystanders clap, as if they're seeing entertainment.

After that, it's a relatively simple job to reposition the truck, attach a hook under the rear bumper, and drag it out of the water. The whole thing has taken under an hour.

Cooter has his hands on his hips, grinning with satisfaction, while Skippy never loses his disgruntled look.

I follow them back to the station in order to have a look inside. A forensics team will have to go over it for fingerprints, but I want to examine it myself.

First, I take a look at the gas pedal to see if it has been jimmied in some way to hold it down, but I don't see anything. The driver must have been in the car and was lucky not to be too injured to swim out.

I had hoped that whoever sent this car into the lake hadn't thought to remove the registration information from the car, but no such luck. There's nothing in the glove compartment. Nothing in the trunk either. But they didn't think of taking the license plate. Or maybe they were in a hurry to get out of there.

Back at headquarters, I run the license plate information and find out quickly enough that the car did, in fact, belong to the shooting victim, Michael Sullivan. So whoever killed him took the risk of sending the car into the lake. A desperate move.

SEVEN

It's already noon. I want to go to Belleville to question the widow of the man whose body we found last night, but first I promised Loretta I'd drop by the bake sale.

I'm glad I left Dusty home, because the place is swarming with people and I suspect more than one of them would share baked goods with him. And he would have been happy to oblige.

Loretta is harried, her cheeks pink with success and over-work. 'At this rate we're going to have to close down early.' She's almost breathless. I never see her this flustered and it worries me. 'Go on, look around,' she says. 'If you want something, you better get it now.' In a lowered voice, she says, 'Buy that sad-looking cake that Claire Booth made. I don't know why that poor woman wastes her time. She's no baker. Nobody will buy it if you don't, and it will hurt her feelings.'

I see exactly which one she's talking about, a cake leaning precariously to one side, with sprinkles trying to cover up for

icing that seems to have mostly run onto the cake pan. I buy
it and a batch of cookies to take to headquarters.

I go over to the table where a couple of women are taking
money and selling raffle tickets. They're raffling off goods from
various local businesses, none of which I need, but I want to
support the cause, so I buy a handful. Several younger women
are in a chatty group nearby. They could be taking some of the
burden off Loretta. I don't want to give them the impression
that I think Loretta isn't up to the task of managing the bake
sale, but I think one of the younger women should offer to help
instead of standing around.

'I wonder if one of you could do me a favor? I need to talk
to Loretta for a minute, but she's in charge and hates to leave
it unattended.'

'Say no more!' one cries. 'I asked her if I could help out,
but she wouldn't hear of it. Come on, Alexa.' She pulls another
woman out of the group. 'We'll insist.'

In a minute Loretta comes over, casting worried glances back
at the pair who have taken over.

'Loretta, let them do it. They wanted to.'

'I know, I know. I just . . .' She sighs and leans in close.
'I'm afraid if they think I'm not capable anymore they'll ease
me out.'

'You know that's not going to happen,' I say. 'They count
on you.' I know she's right, though. We're getting to an age
where we are afraid we'll be redundant.

I steer her to a vacant table and she heaves a sigh when we
sit down. 'I'm going to get us some water,' I say. I come back
with water and a couple of cookies. 'You should eat something,'
I say.

She eyes the cookies as if I've brought her a snake to eat.

'No, they aren't up to your standards,' I say. 'But they won't
kill you.'

She nibbles a bite and I eat one, more to urge her on than
out of hunger.

'Samuel, I heard about that man who got killed at the feed
store. I swear I don't know what this town is coming to. First
Mark gets attacked, and now this man killed. Do you know
who he was?'

'Name is Michael Sullivan. He's from Belleville. You ever heard of him?'

She considers and shakes her head. 'I don't think so. What in the world was he doing here?'

'I'm going over to talk to his widow and find out.'

I know she's itching to get back to work, but I want to make her rest a while longer, so I tell her the details of what happened last night. She is interested, but before long somebody comes to ask her a question, and she escapes.

I drop the cake and cookies by headquarters, where Connor Loving informs me that some of the saddest-looking cakes actually taste the best. He plans to test out his theory, and I leave him to it.

Some sheriffs might consider it meddling for me to insert myself into the investigation by questioning the widow, but when I call Hedges to pass it by him, he says he was hoping I'd ask. 'The officers who broke the news to Sullivan's wife couldn't get much out of her. Said she didn't know what her husband was doing in Jarrett Creek. I was going to send somebody back out there, but I'd just as soon it would be you. Sullivan was killed in your territory. You know your people.'

'Good. I'm on my way.'

Belleville is a thirty-minute drive, southeast on Highway 36, due south of Bobtail. It's a drive-through on the way to Houston, and I've never stopped there, so I don't know much about it. It's a little larger than Jarrett Creek and has a handsome town square that looks like it was the original when the town was built.

On the way to Sullivan's house, I pass homes that look pretty much the same as the ones in Jarrett Creek, but then I come upon a grander section of town, with larger homes that tell of prosperity. And that's where Sullivan's place is located. I wonder what kind of work he did to be able to afford it. It's a grand two-story southern style, with pillars in front, a big porch, and a two-car garage. There's a Cadillac parked in the driveway.

A stout black woman in a black skirt and white blouse, with an apron on, answers the door, her eyes red from weeping. I ask if this is the Sullivan residence, and she says it is, and in answer to my question says her name is June, and she's the maid. This throws me. I don't know anybody around this area who keeps a servant to answer the door. She goes to fetch Mrs Sullivan, and leaves me to wait in a large, plushly carpeted living room.

The room is nicely furnished, but lived in, with a comfortable feel, as if it isn't a room just for show. There's a big TV on one wall, and a sofa and expansive armchairs positioned in front of it. Magazines are casually strewn on tables next to the armchairs, and there's a coffee table with travel brochures and a yellow pad with notes on it. It's tidy, but not fussy.

Before Connie Sullivan arrives, I have a chance to take a look at family photos positioned on a fancy table. The Sullivans look to have had two children, a boy and girl. There are high school and college graduation photos, and then photos of a baby, probably a grandchild. There's a photo of Michael Sullivan and his wife in front of a building that looks like it's somewhere in Europe.

The woman who appears behind June is petite, wearing a gray dress and pearls. The only evidence that she's been crying is a little puffiness around her eyes.

I introduce myself and tell her I'm chief of police of the town where her husband was killed.

'I'm Connie Sullivan.' She offers a hand to shake. In a quiet voice, she says, 'June, would you bring Chief Craddock some coffee?' She looks at me. 'Or would you rather have iced tea? I guess since Paddy always drank coffee, I assume all men do.' Her smile is gentle and sad.

I tell her coffee will be fine.

'Mrs Sullivan, I'm sorry for your loss. I know it's a hard time, but I need to ask you some questions. The earlier I ask them, the more likely I am to find out what happened to your husband.'

'I understand and I'll do my best to answer, but honestly I don't know what I can tell you.'

She gestures to one of the armchairs, and I sit down, with her taking a corner of the sofa near me.

'First, let me ask you. Your husband's name is Michael?'

'Yes, his middle name is Patrick, and when his brother was

a child, he couldn't say Patrick so he said Paddy, and the family started calling him that and it stuck.'

'What kind of work did your husband do?'

'He's a building contractor. He mostly does commercial buildings and mostly in Bobtail.' She smiles a wan smile. 'You probably want to know why we live here rather than in Bobtail. I was born here and I love this town and Paddy was fine with living here. He indulged me.' The last is said with a shaky voice.

'Mrs Sullivan . . .' I begin, but she waves me off.

'Please call me Connie. I'm not used to formality.'

'Connie, do you have any idea what your husband was doing in Jarrett Creek?'

She puts a hand to her pearls, as if they will give her strength. She shakes her head. 'I have no idea. All I know is that he got a call after he came home from work and he said he needed to go out to check on some work. But . . .' she swallows, '. . . I know this will sound funny, but I thought he was lying. Paddy never lied to me, and I don't know why I thought he wasn't telling me the truth. Maybe he looked guilty.' She gives me a questioning look.

June comes in with coffee and a tray of cookies.

'Please help yourself,' Connie says.

I'm glad to see the coffee. I can use it. I tell her I just came from a bake sale and can't face any more cookies. Trying to set her at ease with small talk.

She takes a cookie, but sets it down. She's moving like she's on automatic.

'Connie, had your husband gone to Jarrett Creek recently for anything? Is it possible he was talking to someone about a construction job?'

'I suppose it's possible, but I don't think so. And if he went there recently, he didn't say. I don't know if you're aware, but Paddy was from Jarrett Creek.'

'No, I didn't know that. He grew up there? When did he leave?'

'When he went to college. He went to Texas Tech, and while he was there his folks moved to Houston, so he never went back to Jarrett Creek.'

I'm surprised to hear that he was from Jarrett Creek. I never heard his name, but at the time he was a kid, I wasn't a cop. I was working as a land man for an oil company and I was out of town a lot. If he had played football, I might have heard the name, though.

'Did he play any sports in school?'

'Baseball. He didn't say much about it. You know how that is. The football players get all the glory. He said he was a pretty good pitcher, but they had a terrible team.' She smiles at the memory.

'Did he have siblings?'

'Yes, he has a brother who lives in Houston, and a sister in North Carolina. I had to call all of them this morning. It was awful. His parents are devastated. And his sister Shelly felt especially bad because she hadn't seen Paddy in a couple of years. The pandemic.'

I nod. A lot of people didn't travel the last couple of years.

'He did see his brother and his folks, though. We went down to Houston in June to see them. Had a week with them. I'm grateful he was with them.'

'Was there a particular reason why he didn't go back to visit friends in Jarrett Creek, or go to a reunion or just to visit?'

'I don't know. He told me he didn't like it much, but he didn't say why. We have a lot of friends here in town and he seemed happy to be with them.' She fingers her pearls again. 'I haven't had the heart to call anyone yet and tell them what happened.' Her breath catches. 'I called the children, of course, and they'll be here soon. But I know that when I tell my friends, it will make it real. For now I can pretend . . .'

'I understand. How long were you married?'

'Twenty-six years. We met in college. Our son is twenty-three and our daughter is twenty-one.' Her eyes fill with tears. 'They adore Paddy.'

'Let's go back to that phone call that sent him to Jarrett Creek. What time of day was it?'

'It was around six last night. I remember because we were ready to sit down to supper and I was a little upset because he said he had to go before we even sat down. I told him he at least ought to eat something first, but he said it was urgent and he'd eat after he got back.'

'When he didn't come home last night, weren't you worried?'
Her eyes flare. 'Of course I was.'

'I presume it was unusual. So what did you think?'

'My first thought was what any woman thinks. That he'd
gone to see another woman. I even wondered if he might be
leaving me. So stupid. He'd given me no reason to doubt that
he was happy.'

'You didn't hear from him after he left?'

'Yes, I did. I called him at nine. I didn't reach him, but he
phoned me right back and said he might be late coming home
and for me to go on to bed. I can tell you, I wasn't happy, but
there wasn't anything I could do.' She smiles sadly. 'I planned
to give him heck when he got home. But of course . . .'

Nine? That doesn't fit with the timing. I have a bad feeling
about this. Somebody was pretending to be her husband.

'When he called you back, how did he sound?'

She hesitates. 'I don't know. I did most of the talking. I was
sharp with him. I so regret that.'

'Did he sound nervous or upset?'

'He apologized.'

His body was discovered just after eight o'clock. So who
called Connie back?

'I want you to think carefully. Are you sure it was your
husband who returned your call? Did he sound different?'

She makes a little cry in the back of her throat. 'You think he
was already dead by then and it was somebody else I spoke to?'

'I'm afraid that's likely.'

'I hope it wasn't him I talked to.' Her voice is thick with
tears. 'I don't like the thought that my last words to him were
angry.'

'Connie, the highway patrolman who came to notify you
of your husband's death said that you told him you warned
your husband not to go to Jarrett Creek. Can you tell me why
that is?'

For the first time she looks flustered. 'Did I say that? I don't
think I did.'

I wait. Silence is on my side. People who aren't telling the
truth don't like silence.

'Well, maybe I did. I think it was something about the way

he looked. Like he was upset. I guess I asked him if everything was all right, and he said . . .' She looks scared now. 'He said he thought he could work things out. I asked him what things, but he did that thing that men do. That kind of, oh don't worry, it'll be fine.' Now, the tears start. She dabs at them with a tissue. 'That's when I told him not to go. It's almost like I knew something terrible was going to happen. I wish I had made a fuss and insisted that he stay home.'

'We all have times we wish we had done something different, but this is not your fault. Put that out of your head.'

'Thank you, you're very kind.'

'Connie, does your husband have a home office?'

'It's a desk in our guest room. He doesn't really bring work home.'

'I'd like to take a look at it, to see if there's something that might give me some idea of what might have led to his death.'

Her face closes up. 'Is that really necessary? Paddy was an honest man. I can't imagine that there's anything he was doing that would cause someone to kill him.'

I could bring out the big guns and tell her I can get a search warrant, but I'm afraid if I push her, she may go through his papers herself and get rid of anything that might spoil the image she has of her husband. 'No rush,' I say. 'We'll leave that for later.'

'Maybe later.'

'Before I leave, can you think of anyone in Jarrett Creek your husband might have kept in touch with. Best friend? Coach? Teacher? Next-door neighbor?'

She draws a deep breath. 'Chief Craddock, I never thought much about it, but it does seem odd that he didn't keep in touch with anyone. I guess I assumed that we were happy here and he didn't have a need to maintain old ties. Still . . .'

'If anyone comes to mind, would you call me?' I hand her my card.

'Of course I will.' We both stand.

'You said your kids are coming. Do you have a friend you can call to come and stay with you until then?'

'I'm not up to calling anybody yet, but June is here. She's

been with us a long time and she's a great comfort to me. I'll be all right.'

Driving back from Belleville, I think about Paddy Sullivan's lack of interest in his old home town. Did something happen to put him off the community? Or is it just, as his wife said, that he simply moved on and was happy and saw no reason to maintain ties? But if that was the case, what led him to go to Jarrett Creek so abruptly last night?

I need to locate his old high school buddies. Maybe I can find out if something happened to sour him on his hometown. Something that could explain why he was murdered. Or maybe Loretta can tell me something, now that I know he was called Paddy.

I go back to the bake sale where, true to what Loretta said, they are shutting down early. She and Ida Ruth are sitting at the registration table, totting up receipts and looking pleased with themselves. Ida Ruth and Loretta pretty much run the church ladies' organization, which means they also run the church.

'We exceeded our goal!' Ida Ruth crows. One side of her face is scarred and permanently damaged from burns when she was a child, but once you know her, you forget about it. She's a lively, sharp-witted woman with a warmth that makes her popular.

'Samuel, you won one of the raffle prizes,' Loretta says. She doesn't look as tired as she did earlier today. 'You won a set of baking pans.'

'That's nice,' I say. 'But I'd like you to draw another name. You know I don't need baking pans. I don't ever bake.'

Ida Ruth pipes up, 'You never know. You might decide to take it up as a hobby.' Both women erupt into gales of laughter.

'Have you two been drinking?' I say.

That makes them laugh harder. They're giddy. I finally convince them to draw another name.

'I need to talk to you for a minute,' I say to Loretta. 'And Ida Ruth, maybe you have something to add.'

'Is this about that man who got killed, Michael Sullivan?' Loretta asks.

'His wife said he went by the name Paddy Sullivan.'

'Paddy Sullivan!' Ida Ruth says. 'Isn't he from here?'

'That's right. His wife said he grew up here. He's fifty, so he would have graduated around 1990.'

Ida Ruth frowns. 'They moved away sometime in the Nineties, but I don't recall where they went.'

'The parents landed in Houston,' I say. 'You remember the son?'

'All I remember is his nickname,' Ida Ruth says. 'I always thought that was funny. You know calling somebody Irish "paddy" is an insult, at least back then.'

'I remember the name now,' Loretta says to me. 'He didn't play football, which is probably why you didn't know anything about him.' She knows I follow the Jarrett Creek Panther football team, but not so much the other sports. She blinks and looks off in the distance. 'There was something . . .' She shakes her head. 'Something to do with the family, but I don't recall exactly what it was. I think they moved because of some problem. But I don't think it was with the boy.'

'It was because the parents split up,' Ida Ruth says. 'The daddy was fooling around, and their divorce got ugly. Anyway, before that, the kids had all gone off to college, or wherever.'

'Any idea who Paddy hung around with? Any friends?'

'I would imagine his friends were boys on the baseball team,' Loretta says. 'You could look in the yearbook.'

EIGHT

I can't get Wendy's daughter's situation out of my mind, but since it's Sunday there's nothing I can do. Maria is gone until late tonight, but when she returns I'll ask if she can give me any insight about how to approach Mexican authorities. In the past she has complained that various members of her extended family in Mexico have been in trouble, so she may have some ideas.

I spend extra time checking on my cows, which I find soothing. The new bull seems to have made himself at home.

He's a fine-looking animal and the cows look at him with interest. Or maybe I'm reading that into the situation because I'm hoping that he takes to the job and the cows take to him.

I get into headquarters late, but I'm still the first one in. It must have been an unusually quiet Saturday night.

I call Bobtail PD and leave a message for Sheriff Hedge telling him that I didn't find out much from Connie Sullivan, but I can give him the details when he calls back.

Then I phone Gabe LoPresto.

'Question for you,' I say.

'I'm just getting home from church. Hold on a minute.' He tells his wife, Sandy, to go on in the house. 'I'll be there in a minute,' he says. 'Now, what can I do for you?'

'Do you know a building contractor by the name of Paddy Sullivan?'

'Works out of Belleville, that the same one?'

'He is. Or was. He was shot at the feed store Friday night.'

'Oh, for heaven's sake. I heard somebody had been killed, but I was over in Bryan all day yesterday and I hadn't heard who it was. What was he doing in Jarrett Creek?'

'That's what I'd like to know. Ever give you any competition?'

He's quiet for a few seconds. 'Not with anybody who cares whether they get good work. I don't want to speak ill of the dead, but he doesn't have the best reputation.'

'In what way?'

'Nothing big. Just cuts corners. Wins bids by buying inferior lumber. I've had a couple of people come to me to reinstall floors or walls when the wood was green and it warped.'

Maybe I can believe this, maybe not. I've never heard LoPresto say anything good about another building contractor.

'You know if anybody ever sued him?'

'I don't know. I wouldn't be surprised, but that's usually more trouble than it's worth unless you're talking big projects. If you're asking if that's what got him killed, I doubt it.'

'Have you ever met him?'

'I don't think so, and if I did, I don't remember him.'

LoPresto has been a builder around here for so long that people forget he isn't from here. He grew up in Bobtail, but his wife is from Jarrett Creek and they moved here after they married.

'By the way, I heard you helped Mark Granger get his permits.'

'Wasn't much to it. We're just doing some interior work. Not a big job.'

When I hang up, I ponder what LoPresto told me. Even knowing who the man was, knowing he was from here, finding his car in the lake, and now understanding that he did shoddy work, I still don't have a clue why he died, or who to question. I decide to swing by Melvin Granger's place to ask him if he knew Sullivan. Maybe this time Mrs Sholtz will grant me more access to him.

Granger's house is up on the hill near the road that parallels the east side of the lake. It's built from native rock, which you don't much see anymore. Granger's front yard is a lot like mine. A little grass and not much else except a couple of pecan trees and a scrawny post oak. The house is in good repair, though. It's hard to do much damage to rock, but the trim is also painted.

Mark answers the door and leads me inside, where it has that smell of a person in bad health, a combination of urine, ammonia, and alcohol. Like the yard, the house is well-kept, the curtains open, no dust on the furniture, and all looking reasonably tidy. Even if the kids are arguing, they respect their daddy's house.

We go down the hallway to Melvin's bedroom. On the threshold I see that Melvin is propped up on a hospital bed, with Chelsea sitting with him holding his hand. There's no caregiver in sight, but I hear dishes rattling somewhere in the house. Melvin's eyes are closed and Chelsea puts a finger to her lips. But his eyes open, and he looks straight at me.

I'm disconcerted by his stare. It's as if he's pleading with me, and I don't like the implication that he wishes he could find someone to put him out of his misery. None of us likes to think we'll ever be in that situation.

'Hey, Melvin, how you holding up?' I find myself speaking quietly, as if a normal tone of voice will disturb him.

'Purdy good.' His speech is slow and the words roll around on his tongue as if he can't quite tame them. But at least I understand him.

I don't want to plunge right into the business. 'Nice quilt you've got there.' It is a fine piece of work. 'Was your wife a quilter?'

He shakes his head. 'Friend.'

'Pretty good friend.'

He snorts, as if he knows I'm stalling.

'Melvin, I need to ask you some questions. Did Chelsea tell you what happened at the store?'

Mark clears his throat urgently and Chelsea shakes her head vigorously. Her eyes are wide. She's trying to communicate that this is a taboo subject, but I'm going to have to override her on this.

'No.' He glances at his daughter and frowns. 'Is the store OK?' He looks alarmed.

'The store is fine,' I say. 'Something unusual happened and I'd like to get your opinion.'

He mumbles something, but his eyes have brightened. I expect the prospect of being of use is good for him.

I look around for a chair, so I can sit at his eye level. Chelsea gets up and indicates the one she was sitting in, a straight-backed chrome and padded kitchen chair. I thank her and sit down close to Granger.

'Someone tried to set fire to the place, and—'

'Oh, oh.' Melvin's eyes go wide and he moves an arm, as if to fling aside his covers.

'Don't get excited,' Mark says. 'The store is fine.'

'Your neighbor in the back, Carlton Jones, saw the flames before much damage was done,' I tell him.

'Carlton. Good man.' His voice is more garbled.

'There's more to tell. When the fire department got there, they found something. It's not good.'

Melvin is breathing hard.

'We found a man dead. He'd been shot.'

He makes a distressed sound. 'Who?'

'Man by the name of Michael Sullivan. Goes by Paddy Sullivan. You know him?'

He blinks. 'Paddy.' He tosses his head and moves restlessly. 'Paddy,' he repeats.

Chelsea makes a noise in her throat and whispers, 'Please. Don't agitate him.'

Melvin groans. 'Don't know,' he says. 'Paddy.'

'Listen, don't worry. I just thought if you knew who he was, it might help figure out what happened. But if you don't know, it's not a problem.'

He sighs and closes his eyes.

The nurse comes in and when she sees him, she says, 'That's enough now. You've tired him out.'

'Melvin, you take it easy,' I say. 'We've got this.'

He mutters something.

I leave the room, but Chelsea stays put.

I feel bad about Melvin's situation. I hope I didn't make it worse.

Late in the evening, I get a call from Maria that she's back in town and has heard about the murder and fire. She wants to know every detail about what happened and what I've been doing. I tell her to come over, and she's there in ten minutes, to Dusty's utter delight.

I bring her up to date on the murder and fire. 'I still don't have a clue who attacked Mark Granger, and now we have a body.'

'Could the two be connected?' She takes a sip of the beer I opened for her. She isn't much of a drinker, but she says her family made her crazy this time and she can use a little something to ease her tension.

'Anything's possible,' I say.

'Mark was attacked by two men. Maybe they had a falling-out and one of them shot the other.'

'But why would they be at the store?'

'Good question.'

'They warned Mark not to continue with the renovation. Maybe something is hidden there and they went to collect it.'

'And had an argument,' she adds. 'Any sign of anything being tampered with?'

'Not that I could see. And the forensics team didn't find anything.'

She grimaces. 'Could Mark or his sister have met somebody there and killed them?'

I shrug. 'The sister said they were at dinner when they got the call about the fire. I suppose she could be lying, but I'm a little short on motive here. Mark already told me there were threats. So if there were more threats, why not just turn it over to me?'

'You're right.' She yawns. 'Maybe I'll be more alert in the morning.'

When she's gone, I remember I meant to tell her what's going on with Wendy's daughter. I'll do that in the morning. Maybe she has some ideas. As I'm climbing into bed, something about our conversation tugs at me, but I can't think what it was.

NINE

When I arrive at headquarters Monday morning at nine, there's a Department of Public Safety Dodge Charger in the gravel parking lot. I go in with Dusty and he rushes over to Maria, who has a funny look on her face. She usually makes a fuss over Dusty, but today she pets him a couple of times and tucks him under her desk. He's so surprised that he stays there.

Sitting across from her is a DPS officer, and there's another one, older, sitting in my chair. I don't recognize either of them. I don't like to be petty, but I feel a territorial clutch that someone has commandeered my desk. Plus, Maria has that look she gets when she's so mad she can hardly keep her mouth shut. My newest deputy, Brick Freeman, is slouched behind his desk in the corner. He looks like he's sulking, which contorts his usually handsome features.

Brick is outstandingly good-looking, or so women tell me every chance they get. Tall, muscular, and slim-hipped, he's got jet-black hair, twinkly blue eyes and a dimple in his chin. He's from Bobtail, and hopes that when there's an opening on the police force there, the sheriff will consider him. But for now, he's working for me, and as eager a recruit as I've ever had. I'm glad to have him, even if I know he won't be sticking around long. Except for Maria, most every deputy I get heads for greener pastures as soon as they get a little experience, if for no other reason than the fact that we can't pay a lot. Because of his job application, I happen to know Brick's real name is Brixton. But when I called him that, he said, 'Forget you know that's my name. If you ever tell anybody, you're a dead man.' I think he was kidding, but maybe not.

'How you folks doing?' I ask.

The man at Maria's desk stands up, but the one sitting in my chair remains seated, which I take as some kind of show of disrespect.

'You Craddock?' the standing officer asks.

'That's me. And you are?'

'Trooper Jimmy Ellison. And this is Sergeant Leland Reagan. He's the new head of the district.' Ellison is so respectful that it looks like he would have bowed if he thought it was necessary.

I shake hands with Ellison, but Reagan hasn't bothered to stand up, so I nod to him. 'Looks like they're sending the big guns for our homicide,' I say.

Reagan gives me a thin smile. 'I run a tight ship,' he says. 'I want you to turn over whatever information you have on this body that was found.'

'I don't believe we've met before,' I say, flummoxed by his aggressive manner. 'The last district head was Lloyd Matthews. He get promoted?'

Reagan finally stirs himself to stand up. 'Transferred,' he says. 'Now about your information?'

'I'll be glad to turn over whatever I've got,' I say. 'It isn't much as yet.'

'Your girl here tells me you went and questioned the widow. I told her in the future you all need to leave questioning the suspects to the DPS. Now I'm telling you the same thing.'

'*Deputy Trevino* would certainly have passed that message on to me,' I say. I understand now why Maria is so angry. His attitude is off the charts. Not to mention that he called her 'my girl.' The Texas Highway Patrol, which makes up a good chunk of the DPS, is ninety-five percent men, which Maria has pointed out to me more than once. 'And I don't see why there's a problem with me finding out whatever I can about a murder that happened in my town.'

'As you well know, homicide in a small town like this one is not your jurisdiction,' he says. 'It's mine.'

'Understood,' I say. I'm seething, but arguing with him would get me nowhere.

'Your . . . deputy also told me you questioned the man who owns the building where the crime occurred. That's also not in your purview.'

'I'll remember that in the future.'

'So let's start with you telling me what you got from those two interviews.'

'I got some information from the widow, but Melvin Granger, who owns the building, has had a debilitating stroke and wasn't able to offer much.'

'We'll see about that,' he says. He strokes his belly, as if content with what he finds there.

'Have you had a chance to take a look at the crime scene?' I ask. I'm trying to hold my temper, but this man's attitude is getting on my nerves. I glance over at Officer Ellison and see that he's staring at his shoes. His cheeks are pink. I wouldn't want to be paired with Reagan myself.

'I haven't. I want you to go over there with me to take me through the details. And while we're at it, you can tell me what might be pertinent to the case, and what the man's widow told you.'

'I can do that.' I turn to Maria. 'I'm going to accompany Sergeant Reagan here to the location where the body was found. If any more bodies turn up, you can call me.'

She looks down, but not before I see the smirk on her face. She doesn't need to be asked to keep Dusty with her. The last thing I need is Dusty making a fool of himself with Sergeant Reagan.

I tell Reagan he can follow me, but he orders me to get in the patrol car with him and Ellison and direct them to the scene. His attitude would be laughable if it wasn't so ridiculously arrogant.

I'd forgotten that the construction crew was arriving today to start demolition work. They are hauling their tools upstairs and into the back room and haven't actually done anything yet.

'Why are these people here in the crime scene?' Reagan says, when we get upstairs.

'County forensics team gave the OK,' I say. 'But the area where the body was found is still cordoned off. It's not where they'll be working.' It's across the room, but it's a big room.

Reagan orders the workmen to stay out until he okays them to come back.

I'm glad now that we put up yellow tape across the area. I take down the tape and usher Ellison and Reagan in. Reagan peruses the scene, and sniffs, as if by sniffing the air he can get all the clues he needs to find out who murdered Paddy Sullivan.

He struts around the area and finally has to admit that there isn't much to see. 'What do you think happened?' he says to me.

'We'll know more after the autopsy,' I say. 'Which should be done sometime today. All I can say is that somebody didn't want him found, and set the fire to cover it up. We're lucky the man who lives in back saw the flames before they could get anywhere.'

'And I presume you took it on yourself to interview him.'

'I did.'

Reagan's expression has hardened. 'Craddock, let's get this straight. There's no "we" here between you and me. This is my jurisdiction and we'll do things my way. I want the autopsy report sent to me, and I'll be sending a trooper to interview the relevant witnesses. You're to provide their names and how I can contact them. And that's the extent of your involvement. I don't need a small-town chief of police interfering with the investigation. Are we clear?'

'Perfectly. To tell you the truth, I'm happy for you to take it off my hands. I'm short-staffed at the moment.' The latter is true. It's always true. But the first part is not.

'Now, let's go over the information you got from the widow.'

I think we would be better off sitting in my office, but if he wants to stand here at the crime scene and gab, it's all right with me.

I tell him what I got from Sullivan's wife – that he was a building contractor and had grown up in Jarrett Creek. I describe the phone call he got that brought him to town.

He stops me there. 'Did you know the man personally?'

'I didn't. And according to his wife, he never came back here.'

'What else?'

'The patrol officer who first talked to the wife said she told him that when her husband got the phone call to come to Jarrett Creek, she warned him that it was a bad idea.'

He grunts. 'Wonder why?'

'I wondered the same thing, but the officer said she wouldn't say. And she told me she didn't want to admit saying that. Another interesting thing. When I asked the wife if I could look through his home office, she balked.'

'Did you tell her the DPS could get a court order?'

'I didn't push it. I figured she might settle down and be more open to it when she's had a chance to process her husband's death.'

'Well, I'm not as likely to coddle her as you are. We'll get into that office pronto.'

'One last point. The wife said she got a call from her husband at nine o'clock saying he'd be late.'

'And?' He's impatient.

'Sullivan was dead long before nine.'

He blinks. 'Which means somebody else made the call.' He nods to himself. 'I want you to write all this up and send it to me by tomorrow morning. We'll take it from here.' He shoves his card at me.

He takes me back to my office, and I'm relieved when he drives away. Even though theoretically he's right, he has jurisdiction, I don't like being bullied any more than anyone else does.

I'm trying to be philosophical. I've generally had free rein with solving the few serious crimes we've had in Jarrett Creek, but there has always been the possibility that the DPS would muscle in.

When I walk back into the office later in the morning, Maria leaps up from her chair. As I might have expected, she has worked herself into a fair old state. Hands on her hips, she snarls, 'Who does he think he is?'

'Now, Maria, calm down. He's new at his job and my guess is he's feeling a little insecure.'

'Insecure! Oh, you always try to see the good side. He's a . . . a . . . pompous ass.'

'Well, there's that, too.' I grin at her, but she isn't appeased.

'I don't understand why you let him push you around. You know this town, and he'll be starting from scratch.'

'True. And I know people will talk to me when they might not talk to a stranger.'

'So are we going to work on the case?' I notice she includes herself, which is fine with me.

'Let's just say we're going to pursue a parallel track. I have a suspicion that once Reagan tries to question some of the locals and gets stonewalled, he'll be glad to have my help.'

I'm not proud of being a little defensive, but I do know something about reality. People in town are comfortable talking to me, but may not be so forthcoming with a lawman they've never met before, and whose arrogant attitude will most likely be on full display when he's questioning them.

Besides, he won't have the first clue where to start. To be fair, neither do I at the moment. But at least I've got history on my side, and he doesn't. When I turn over to him the names of people I think need to be questioned, he won't know who's who in the cast of characters. Even when I tell him who they are, which I will, he won't know the underpinnings, the nuances of the town. He won't know who has moved away, who has died, who is secretive, who will tell him idle gossip that may or may not be true. He won't know who is easily offended, or who has a hide like a steer. I know all those things.

Most significantly, he won't have someone like Loretta Singletary, who has her ear to the pulse of town.

'Where's Brick?' I ask.

'Fender bender north of town. He went over to check it out.'

I realize I haven't talked to Maria about Wendy's daughter, and now is as good a time as any.

'Maria, there's something I need to discuss with you. It's something serious.'

She gets up from her desk and comes to sit down in the chair next to mine.

'Wendy's daughter is in big trouble. She got in an automobile accident in Monterrey, and is in prison.'

She groans. 'That's really bad. The same thing happened to a friend of mine and he said it was a nightmare. And he was Mexican-American. I can't imagine what will happen to a pretty young girl. What's her status?'

'Wendy has hired a lawyer in Bryan, Chuck Hernandez, and Allison was also assigned a lawyer in Mexico. Hernandez says we should try to get Allison another lawyer. The one she was assigned is young, and possibly connected to the case on the prosecution side.'

'I wouldn't be surprised.'

'I'd like to get Allison out of Mexico, but it sounds like Wendy may have to get the US Consulate involved.' I tell her that I called the DPS at the border and the officer there suggested that Wendy contact them.

'That's going to take time, and she needs to get out of jail now. Prison is no place to be in Mexico.'

'That may not be as big a problem as usual. Hernandez said that apparently she's in a better facility, whatever that means. She has a cell to herself, anyway.'

'That's odd. But they do tend to treat women better in Mexican jails. Has Wendy talked to her?'

'Not yet.' I don't tell her that Allison apparently doesn't want to talk to Wendy. That gets tangled up with family drama.

'Does Allison speak Spanish?'

I shake my head. 'No idea.'

Maria is thinking hard. 'You know, with you being chief of police, maybe the Mexican authorities would consider releasing her to your custody.'

'It's a thought. That would probably mean I have to go down there.'

'Or I could go as your deputy. Since I'm Hispanic, it might make a difference. At least I speak the language. And if Allison doesn't speak Spanish, she needs somebody on her side.'

'I appreciate it. Let me talk to the lawyer, Hernandez, about it.'

'I'll help any way I can. She's got to get out of there. Even if it means being jailed here. Do you know what happened in the accident? No one was killed, were they?' At the best of times, Maria has a stoic expression on her face, and now she's looking worried.

'I don't know, and I don't think Wendy has all the facts.'

'I'd like to talk to the Mexican lawyer.'

'I'll call Hernandez and get his name.' I fish his card out and make the call. His assistant says he's in court today, and she'll have him call me back later.

'Maybe Wendy knows,' Maria says.

I call Wendy and she's not answering her phone either.

Maria is tense. 'If we don't hear from her soon, I'll make a call to the authorities in Monterrey. At least I can try to find out where they're keeping her.'

'Here's the thing, Maria. I'm sure Hernandez has done all this. If he couldn't find out, I don't know that you would have any more luck.'

'Well, then I may have to go down there.'

TEN

I n the afternoon I make out the list of people Reagan needs to interview in his investigation of Sullivan's death, and write up my notes on my interview with his widow. She's one of the few people that Reagan may have more luck with, since he's got some clout, and she may bend to his status. I list Billy Crewes from the fire department, first on the scene when the body was found, and Carlton Jones, who called in the fire. And Melvin Granger. I hate to set Reagan on Melvin, but I'm not sure how Reagan will get past Mrs Sholtz anyway.

I email the information to him and then head out to do what I intended to do first thing this morning, before Reagan showed up.

It's August, but school started a week ago, and there's still an air of congenial chaos in the air. All the students look fresh-faced and excited.

I go straight to the administrative office, and the harried receptionist tells me that what I need can be found in the library.

Even the library is bustling. The librarian, Jaconda Washburn, is a stern, heavy-set Black woman, the kind of teacher whose eyes seem to be everywhere at once. I imagine when she hushes a student, they stay hushed. I tell her what I want and she goes with me to find the proper yearbooks.

In no time, I'm poring over the yearbooks. I find Paddy Sullivan in his senior year in pictures of the baseball team. There are a few candid shots, with Sullivan clowning around with a couple of other boys. I jot down their names. Maybe they kept up with him. But the other two boys are not in the senior class. I find out they were two years younger than Sullivan.

To my surprise, I see that Sullivan was a candidate for Homecoming King his senior year.

It seems odd that a boy popular enough to be a Homecoming candidate would dislike his hometown so much that he only came back to get himself murdered. I copy down the names of the candidates for King and Queen. Sullivan lost to a kid named Jarrel Washington, a Black kid with an infectious grin. I wonder how well the two boys knew each other. Maybe one of them remembers something about Sullivan; maybe he can even give me a clue as to why he didn't want to come back here.

When I return to headquarters, I've got a message that the medical examiner's office in Bobtail called with the autopsy results on Paddy Sullivan. I call the coroner, Tommy Larson. I don't know Larson well. He's a slow-talking guy, and serious. T.J. Sutter had been the ME as long as I've been the chief of police here in Jarrett Creek, but he retired last year and Larson took his place.

Larson tells me the murder is straightforward. 'Two gunshot wounds to the chest. .45 caliber. We dug one of the bullets out of the wall. It's not going to do you much good. It was flattened. No telling what kind of gun was used.'

I thank Larson for notifying me and mention that I'm surprised Reagan didn't tell him not to give me the information.

Larson gives a short bark of laughter. 'Yeah, I was told not to pass it on to you, which is why I did.'

'Reagan?'

'Yes, sir. He told me how the cow ate the cabbage.'

I laugh. I haven't heard that expression in thirty years.

'I don't necessarily appreciate his attitude,' he says.

'He's new on the job. I expect he'll figure out how things ought to be done.' I'm feeling magnanimous since having the ME on my side is a win.

Looking to gather information about Sullivan's high school buddies, I start with the Homecoming candidates and I strike gold when I talk to Homecoming Queen Reanna Barstow's mamma, Janine. She doesn't live far from me and is home when I call on her. Her house has bright, white siding with green trim, with a tidy gravel walkway leading up to the house.

A brisk woman, she's happy to talk to me, as if she's starved for company. She's the kind of woman who appears to live through her kids and keeps up with every one of their friends. She has already heard that Paddy Sullivan was killed and she exclaims over the state of the world, 'with people getting shot right and left.'

'Do you know who did it?' she demands.

'That's what I'm working on,' I say. 'I saw that your daughter and Paddy were both up for Homecoming King and Queen. Did your daughter know Paddy well?'

'Oh, yes, of course.' She tells me that Reanna and Paddy dated for a short time. 'It didn't work out. No reason. They didn't have any sparks. She got sparks when she met her husband Greg in college. They live in Austin. He's got some kind of government job. They have two of the darlingest kids you ever saw.'

I'll be here all afternoon if I don't take control of the conversation. 'Can you tell me who Paddy Sullivan's friends were?'

She cocks her head. 'He hung out with a couple of younger guys, Eddie Polasek and Jonas Miller.'

I wonder why he hung out with kids younger than him. Seems unusual. But then Janine adds, 'They all played baseball. You know, that's a small group.'

'Can you think of any reason why Paddy would have moved away and never visited Jarrett Creek?'

She crosses her arms across her stomach and stares into the past. After a minute she shakes her head. 'I don't recall anything about him after he stopped seeing Reanna in the spring of their senior year. Tell you the truth, I don't remember him well at all. He wasn't the kind of boy who makes a big impression, if you know what I mean. Not like that boy who got to be Homecoming King that year, Jarrel Washington. He was something else. Funny? He could make a dog laugh. Good-looking kid. He opened a restaurant down in Houston, and I think Reanna said it's won some awards. I'm not surprised.'

Steering her back on track, I ask, 'Do you know if Paddy dated anybody in particular after he and Reanna broke up?'

'I could call Reanna and ask her. I need to tell her what happened anyway. She'll want to know.' She tells me she'll do it now. 'My cell phone is in the kitchen. I'll be right back.'

I hear her talking for several minutes. When she comes back, she's shaking her head. 'Reanna doesn't remember, but she said to ask Missy Lockwood. Missy went out with Jonas for a while and she might remember. Missy still lives here in town. Reanna gave me her phone number.'

After some more chatter, I extricate myself and go back to headquarters to call Missy Lockwood. She isn't in and I leave my number and ask her to call me.

It's after five when I reach Chuck Hernandez. He sounds distracted and I have to remind him who I am.

'Oh, yes. Look, Craddock, today got away from me. I'll make some calls first thing tomorrow to see if I can hire Allison another lawyer.'

I tell him Maria's suggested that it may be helpful for her to go down there.

'It's a thought. You say she's smart?'

'And determined. If anybody can get information, she can.'

He's quiet for a minute. 'Tell you what, I'll make those calls in the morning and I'll get back to you. No sense in sending her on a goose chase.'

I call Maria and tell her what he said.

'Listen,' she says, 'you know as well as I do that lawyers procrastinate. Meanwhile, that poor girl is sitting in jail.'

'I'll keep after him.'

ELEVEN

Tuesday morning, I've just checked on the cattle and the new bull and am headed back into the house when my phone rings. It's Maria.

'What's up?'

'Big trouble. At the feed store.'

'Now what?'

'You wouldn't believe it if I told you. But I can handle it if you don't want to be in on the action. That's up to you. Suit yourself.' She's taunting me.

She knows there's no way I'll let that slide. Can she possibly be talking about another murder?

Back at the house, I grab a container of coffee and a muffin out of the refrigerator. I whistle up Dusty and jump into my truck and head out.

Besides the squad car that Maria drove over, there are a couple of pickups parked outside Granger's Feed Store, plus a car I recognize as Mark Granger's.

I presume the pickups belong to the men doing demolition work. I mount the steps and find Maria standing in the front room with Chelsea, Mark, and two young men in grimy coveralls. They must be the guys Gabe LoPresto sent to start work on the renovations. Everybody looks stunned, even Maria, who generally takes things in her stride.

Dusty rushes over to her, wagging his whole body. He hasn't read the somber room well. Maria tells him firmly to sit, which he does; something he won't do for me.

'What's going on?' I ask.

'There's a body in the floor,' Chelsea blurts. Her eyes are wild and she sounds hysterical.

I look from one to the next, but nobody seems ready to enlighten me. 'What do you mean "in the floor?"'

The siblings turn to me, glaring as if it's all my fault.

Maria steps forward. 'Come on back, you'll see.'

We all file into what now feels like familiar territory, the back room of the feed store. To the right is the area where Michael Sullivan's body was found.

'Over here,' Maria says, walking to the left. She leads me to a ripped-out section of boards in the floor at the far left back corner of the room. There's a long, trussed-up package lying next to the ripped-out area. The package is shiny, as if it's been washed in plastic and polished. As I get closer, I smell a peculiar odor, like varnish.

'Careful,' she says.

I step toward the 'package,' which I see now is an old-style canvas tarp, covered in a thick, hard substance.

'You found this?' I ask the workmen standing near Maria. They both nod.

Skinny young men, with ropy muscles, they're looking a little pale. Their clothes are covered with sawdust. They introduce themselves as Mike and Doug Green, brothers. They're from Bobtail and are regulars on Gabe LoPresto's demolition crew.

'How did it happen?'

'We were pulling up some old boards that needed to be replaced, and it was right there,' Mike Green says. He shudders.

'What is that shiny shell on the tarp?' I ask.

'We think it's shellac,' Green says. 'The floor has been shellacked, too.' That accounts for the shiny floor.

'Probably to mask the odor of the body,' Maria says.

The tarp has been slit open, revealing what looks to be a desiccated skeleton wrapped in another tarp. The inner one is rotting, but the outer one is stiff with shellac.

Although it's mid-morning, the windows are dirty and fly-specked, so the bright sunlight outside doesn't penetrate into the room. You can barely see the skull and bones peeking out of the dark tarp. I crouch down next to it for a closer look.

'Here,' Maria says. She hands me a flashlight.

Even with the direct light, I still can't see much, but clearly, the body has been here a good, long while. The clothes the man was wearing are in tatters and most of the skin has rotted away. It's a hideous sight, the surrounding canvas somehow making it more lurid.

I hear sirens and stand back up. 'You called the sheriff in Bobtail?' I ask Maria.

'Yes. I guess this early in the morning they didn't have a prior commitment.' She says it wryly. She's always annoyed because she thinks the sheriff's office in Bobtail takes their sweet time when anything happens here in Jarrett Creek, fifteen miles away.

'Medical examiner?' I ask Maria.

'They'll be along, too.'

Like everyone else, I'm shaken, and need a minute to process what I've seen. It looks like somebody killed the man and hid him here, under the floor, to keep the deed from being discovered. A long time ago. Why was he hidden here in the feed store, though? Is this Melvin's doing?

Two murders in a few days – even if one happened a long time ago – is a lot to take in.

Meanings begin to tumble into place. Is this why Mark Granger was warned not to continue with the renovations, and then attacked? Because whoever put this man here didn't want the body discovered? And does this have to do with why Paddy Sullivan was killed? What if he was one of the men who attacked Mark? What if he knew the body was here? I have no proof of that idea, but it's unusual that he was killed here, right where this body was buried. Although I believe coincidences can happen, this is a big one.

'Point out to me exactly how the bundle was positioned, if you would,' I ask the workmen.

Mike walks over and points down between two floorboards that look too narrow to have held the corpse. 'It was jammed in on its side.' He shakes his head, as if to clear it of the image of the moment. 'I wish to hell we'd left it where it was.'

'So you took it out and laid it down here?'

'Yes, sir. We didn't have any idea what it was.' He sighs and glances over at his brother, who is looking a little green. 'And then my brother, Mr Nosy, decided he needed to see what was inside the tarp.' He makes a growling noise. 'It smelled pretty ripe when we opened it. And when we saw what it was, I almost lost my breakfast. We called down to the station and your deputy came.' He nods toward Maria.

Mark and Chelsea have followed us and are standing at the threshold of the room. 'And when did you get here?' I ask them.

'We came in right after they found the body,' Mark says. 'We had gotten here early to help set up for the demolition.' He glances toward the mummified body and shudders. 'God, that's creepy!'

'No need for us to hang around here. Let's go back to the front room.'

We gather at the front counter, and I say, 'I don't suppose your daddy ever mentioned anything about this?'

'Eew, no,' Chelsea says, wrinkling her nose. 'Why would he know about a body buried in the floor?'

The medical examiner, Tommy Larson, arrives, and within a half-hour we've got a half-dozen people standing around watching him crouched over the body. We've rigged up a light to shine directly onto it.

I'm surprised Larson came out himself; he usually sends an assistant. In the county, the medical examiner does double duty as the Justice of the Peace, so he's busy. A laconic guy, big and rangy, in his forties, he reminds me of a big old bloodhound.

He stands up, arching his back to ease it after he's been stooped over the skeleton. 'I'll have to get a closer look to estimate how long this guy's been dead.'

'With the location of the body, I suspect it was put here at the time the room was built,' I say. Which I'll have to ask Melvin about.

Larson eyes me. 'Just because it was put here, that doesn't mean that's when he was killed. Somebody could have kept him on ice for a while.'

'Are we sure it's a man?' I ask.

'Not necessarily,' he says. He's a slow talker, as if he weighs everything he says. 'Could be a woman who was dressed up in trousers and a shirt.' He pauses and inclines his head to one side. 'But I'd bet it is a man – length of the body, the length of the femur, the large hands – what I can see of it, anyway.' He looks down at the body.

'Any idea of the age?' I ask.

'Not a clue. Once I get him up on a slab, I'll be able to find out more.'

'Any way you can speculate how he died?'

'I'm afraid not.'

'You mind if I attend the autopsy?'

'Not at all. I'll call you when I get to it.'

The EMT guys get to the task of moving the body onto a stretcher. They're young, but properly solemn for the occasion, if a little shaken, like everyone else.

Once the body is moved, I shine a light around the joists in case whoever left him here also left the weapon or any other clues, but I don't see anything right off.

Mark and Chelsea have stayed out of the way all this time, but now Mark approaches me. 'I don't want to be disrespectful,' he says, 'but we had planned to get moving on the renovations. How long do you think it will be before the workmen can get back in here?'

He may not intend to be disrespectful, but his impatience doesn't suit the moment. 'I wouldn't be in any hurry,' I say. 'These things take time.'

'Well, can we at least open the store? We have customers that need their feed.'

The same patrolmen who came by a couple of days ago when we found Paddy Sullivan's body, Mosier and Bowles, are standing by, hats in hand. 'Son,' Mosier says to Mark, 'you're going to have to cool your jets. I expect you know this is a strange piece of business here and somebody's going to have to go over it carefully before we can turn it back to you.'

I smile at his calling Mark, 'son.' He's maybe ten years older than Mark.

'Officer Mosier is right. You have to be patient, Mark. Once the forensics team goes over the site, they'll tell you when you can open back up.'

'That's your second body this week,' Mosier says, giving me an appraising look. He's got his hat tipped back. 'Things are getting out of hand here.' He says it with humor in his voice.

'Except one of the bodies has been there for a long time,' I say.

To get out of everyone's way, I ask Mark and Chelsea to come back to headquarters with me to discuss the situation. Chelsea says she'd like to get back to her daddy. 'I want to make sure nobody calls and tells him what happened. This could kill him. We have to find a way to tell him without upsetting him too much.'

If he doesn't already know. But even if he does, finding out that the body has been discovered might upset him.

Brick is at the station when we arrive and he says there's been a call. 'Something about goats in a garden.'

It's a weekly occurrence for Dell White's goats to get out. I've told him repeatedly that he needs to mend the hole and he swears he's done it, but then they get out again and run through Maylene York's flower garden.

Maria says she'll go sort it out. Maybe she'll have better luck setting Dell straight. She's stricter than I am.

'By the time you get back, the forensics team should be at the feed store. You can go over and observe. And take Brick with you.'

'Forensics for what?' Brick asks eagerly, when she's gone.

I introduce Brick to Mark and explain about the body in the floorboards. 'Looks to have been there a long time,' I say. 'Maybe twenty, thirty years.'

He looks stunned. 'Thirty years! That's, like, before I was born.'

As if he can't quite believe anything happened before he came into existence.

Before I can ask a question, Mark says, 'Surely you know that if we'd had any idea that man was buried in the floorboards, I wouldn't have had the floor torn up.'

'True, but I wonder if your daddy knew anything about it. You hadn't told him you were going to do renovations. He might have stopped you. How long has he owned the feed store?' It seems to me a long time.

'I never thought much about that. I know he had it when I was a kid, because Mamma used to set up a playpen in the store when I was little if she needed Daddy to watch me.'

'So you're what, thirty-five, thirty-six?'

'Thirty-two. Chelsea's two years older. Daddy was in his late thirties when we were born.'

'How is your daddy feeling this morning? Do you think he'd be up to answering some questions?'

'Mornings are always better.'

'Good, I'll come over now.' I want to go quickly. Reagan will no doubt hear about this second body and make an appearance to take over, or call and tell me to stay off the case.

On the way to the Grangers' house, I call Hernandez, but he says he hasn't been able to reach anyone in Monterrey. 'It's some kind of damn holiday. I told them it was urgent, but . . .' He sighs.

TWELVE

Mark lets me into the house and says, 'Mrs Sholtz is making Daddy some lunch, so this is a good time to get in to see him.'

He takes me back to Melvin's room, where Chelsea is sitting in the corner flipping through a magazine, snapping the pages as if she's mad at them.

Melvin looks the same as he did a couple of days ago, which is to say not good. The room is too warm, but that's Mrs Sholtz's territory, and I don't comment on it.

I ask Melvin how he's getting along and he mutters that he's OK.

'Melvin, I think your son told you he's doing a little work on the store.' I'm going to minimize my description of the work Mark was planning, to try to keep Melvin from getting upset.

'Yes?'

'Your storeroom in the back needed some repairs,' Mark says.

Chelsea makes a quiet sound of derision.

'OK.' Melvin eyes his son with suspicion.

'Turns out there was a little problem,' I say. 'They had to tear up some of the floor, and they found something unusual.'

'Why the floor?' His words are hard to understand, but I think that's what he said.

'Some dry rot,' Mark says.

Chelsea gets up abruptly and leaves the room, as if she can't bear to sit and listen to her brother prevaricate.

'All right,' Melvin says. He doesn't seem to have noticed Chelsea's departure.

'As I said,' I continue, 'the workmen found something odd. They found a body under the floorboards. It looks like it's been there for a long time.'

Melvin's eyes get round and he gasps. And then he starts to make distressed noises that could be words. His lips become slick with bubbles.

As if she's got superhuman hearing, the caregiver comes bustling in, with Chelsea hot on her heels. 'Everyone out,' she says, quietly, but with no question that she will be obeyed.

'I should stay with him,' Chelsea says. She's clasping and unclasping her hands in distress.

'No, you go, too. I'll call you right back in,' the woman says. 'He just needs a minute to calm down.'

Now Melvin is thrashing around, moaning and huffing. We leave hastily. Outside, Chelsea buries her face in her hands and moans. 'You shouldn't have told him. I knew it would upset him.'

Her brother puts his arm around her shoulders. 'Chels, he'll be OK.'

She shrugs him off and glares at me. 'He didn't need to know what happened. That damn store is everything to him.'

I feel at a loss. 'I'm sorry, Chelsea, but he had to be told sooner or later. And I need to find out if he knows how the body got there.'

'How would he know?' She's practically spitting. 'You don't actually think he could have had a hand in it, do you? And even if you did, what good will it do to accuse him now?'

'I'm not accusing him of anything.'

'Well, you could have left it to me to tell him the body was found.'

Left to her own choice, I doubt she would have gotten around to it. I've always known Granger to be a forthright man, and can't imagine he would like to be coddled. But of course he's frail physically now, and maybe emotionally, too.

'Look,' I tell Chelsea, 'all I'm interested in is what went on

when your daddy first had the store renovated, which I suspect
is the time the mummified body was put there. I want to know
who was working on it, the timeframe, that kind of thing. Does
your daddy have an office here at home?'

'Yes, he does,' she says, her expression wary.

'Maybe he keeps records from back then.'

'I'll show you,' Mark says eagerly, as if he's glad to have
a mission.

'I'm staying right here in case Daddy needs me,' Chelsea
says.

I follow Mark to the end of the hallway where there's a
crowded home office with a big old roll-top desk, a three-drawer
wooden file cabinet, and a bookcase. I glance at the books and
am not surprised to see most of them have to do with the feeding
and care of animals.

Mark sits down and starts rummaging through the desk
drawers. He pulls out a few folders. His actions seem aimless,
and I suspect he's just trying to keep busy.

'Why don't you let me look through that?' I say. 'Your mind
is on your daddy and I can do it.'

He gets up and takes the chair next to the desk. I sit down
and open each drawer, but find mostly office supplies, pens,
boxes of paperclips, a stapler and old electronic gear. In the
bottom drawer is an old Beretta handgun, the kind a lot of
people keep supposedly for self-defense, although they're
usually stuck in a drawer, like this one. 'Your daddy know how
to use this?' I ask.

'I don't know. I didn't even know he kept a gun.'

I walk over to one of the wooden file cabinets. 'You mind?'
I ask.

'Be my guest,' he says. 'I don't have a clue where Daddy
might have kept papers from so far back.'

Opening the drawers, I see that Melvin appears never to have
thrown away anything. But at least it's all labeled. In the middle
drawer I find a hefty file labeled, 'Store Purchase.' The papers
inside are yellowed with age.

'Here we go,' I say. I pull it out and open it on the desk. It
appears to contain every receipt he ever got from work he had
done in and around the building. I thumb through them with

Mark looking over my shoulder. 'Look here,' I say. 'It's the original specs for the building.'

We look at the details. 'It was built in 1945. And it was originally an icehouse.'

'An icehouse? I didn't know that. Daddy never told me.' He looks at me. 'What exactly is that?'

I smile. 'You know, people didn't always have refrigerators. They used iceboxes to keep things cold. In the winter, railroad cars came down from the north with huge slabs of ice from northern lakes. Every small town had an icehouse where the ice would be stored through summer. People would go there to buy a chunk of ice to keep in their iceboxes.'

'Seems like it would melt in the Texas heat.'

'The big slabs didn't melt as fast. And the icehouses were heavily insulated.' I look at the bill of sale. 'Says here your daddy bought it in April of 1975. By then people had refrigerators and the icehouses went out of business.'

He points at the spec sheet. 'Why was the store built so high up, on concrete blocks and stilts?'

'That was for loading the ice. There was a platform on the side where people could drive their wagons up and the ice could be loaded straight down into the bed of the wagon. I remember that when I was a little kid.' I also remember that they used to give away a free beer when you bought ice. My daddy would hang around the icehouse, and if a teetotaler bought ice and refused the beer, my daddy would ask if he could have it.

'Interesting,' he says. 'That platform is gone. I almost think it would have been better if he'd torn down the building and built a new one on the ground floor.'

'The building was probably sturdy and it would have been expensive to tear it down.' I take out a folded blueprint and smooth it on the desk. 'See, your daddy bought the place in 1975, but he didn't do a major overhaul until the Nineties.'

'Makes sense. My grandparents died in 1988 in a car wreck. Mamma was an only child and everything went to her. So they had money for renovations. I think Daddy had done some work on it himself over the years, but he never cared for carpentry work.'

I'm looking at the blueprint again when Maria calls.

I step out of the room to talk to her. 'How did things go?'

'With the goats? I told him we'd run him in and he could spend a night in jail if we get another call like that. But more important, I made a couple of phone calls about Allison.'

'To who?'

'You know me, Boss. I have all these cousins. One of them knows somebody in Monterrey who might be able to get some information.'

'Good.' I tell her Hernandez said today was a holiday.

She scoffs. 'That's what they always say when they don't want to talk to you. Anyway, my cousin will get back to me before long.'

I get back to the blueprints. 'Looks like work started in spring of 1992,' I say. Originally the place was one big room, and the blueprint shows the plans for the room to be divided into its current configuration. 'That's when they would have built the back room. The body could have been deposited there at that time. We have to wait for the autopsy to find out if that's approximately the same timeline in which the man was killed.'

Then, all I have to figure out is who the man was, and who killed him.

I look through the receipts for work done on the renovations and I see three names I recognize: Paddy Sullivan, Eddie Polasek, and Jonas Miller. High school friends. Baseball players. They were each paid $200 a week for demolition work. In addition, Paddy and Jonas did carpentry and were each paid $500 a week for three weeks.

'Do you mind if I take this?'

He hesitates. 'I imagine Daddy will want . . .' He trails off.

'I'll copy things and give them back to you. Before your daddy needs them.' We both know Melvin is not likely to ever need these papers again, but it seems kinder to pretend that he might.

'That's all right then.'

'What is it you're taking?' Chelsea's voice startles us. She's standing in the doorway and looks suspicious. I'd like to find a way to break through that wall. She's mad at the way her life is going, and it's magnified by her daddy's condition.

I show her the folder. 'There's information here that will be pertinent to the investigation,' I tell her. 'Like I said, I'll copy what I need and get it right back to you.' Before she can think of some reason to protest, I ask if Melvin has settled down.

'He's asking for you.'

The caregiver has propped Melvin up and he's looking more alert. I wonder if they have drugs to make that happen.

'Melvin, you're looking livelier,' I say.

'Never mind that.' I think that's what he said. The left side of his face is drooping, and it pulls his lips off-kilter so he slurs. 'Tell me again.'

I pull up a chair. Chelsea and Mark have come in behind me, but they stand near the door.

As I go over the information again, I can see that he's concentrating, but his gaze wanders away and then back and he starts plucking at his covers.

'Who?'

'We haven't identified him. I thought maybe you might have some idea.'

'Don't know,' he says. He frowns. 'Contractor.'

'I found the name of the contractor. I didn't recognize the name, so either the contractor died or moved away.'

He stops me with a wave of his hand. 'Passed away. Sometime around 2000.' It's hard work trying to figure out what he's saying.

'You still have a good memory.'

He grunts.

'Maybe one of the people who worked for him knows what happened.'

His eyes widen. 'Couple of boys. Don't know.'

'You mean Paddy Sullivan, Jonas Miller, and Eddie Polasek?'

'Yeah.' He nods, but his eyes are drooping and I can tell he's getting tired.

I get up. 'Listen, Melvin, I don't want you to worry about this. We'll figure it out.'

Mrs Sholtz steps up in her brisk way. 'I think that's enough right now. Mr Granger needs to rest.'

Chelsea pushes past me and stands next to the bed, taking her daddy's hand. 'I love you, Daddy. Don't worry, it'll be fine.'

The three of us go into the living room. I feel exhausted by the few minutes I spent with Melvin.

'What happens next?' Mark asks. He's asking about more than the investigation. He wants to know how his renovation plans are impacted.

'The forensics team ought to be over at the store by now. I'll drop by and get some idea of how long they think all this will take. I'd say not more than a couple of days. Somebody from the Highway Patrol will make the call, though.'

He frowns. 'Why not you?'

'The Department of Public Safety handles murder investigations in small towns. Although they may turn it over to me, depending on how busy they are.'

I'd pushed Sergeant Reagan to the back of my mind, and he comes roaring back. He's not going to like that I've talked to Melvin and gone through his office files. I haven't heard from him, though, although I'm sure he knows by now that we have another body. If he intends to push me aside and do the investigation himself, he'd better get to it fast. I have no intention of sitting back and letting the matter languish because he's too busy to make it a priority. I'm frustrated enough as it is, knowing he thinks I'm irrelevant.

THIRTEEN

When I arrive at the feed store just after noon, Maria is waiting for me, antsy because the forensics team still hasn't arrived. Between that and waiting for her cousin to call from Mexico, she's like a caged cat. 'Bobtail PD said the team will be another hour. I complained that they're taking their sweet time and they said the body has been there for a long time and a few hours isn't going to make any difference.'

I have to laugh. They're right. But I know it doesn't help Maria's mood.

'I've got something for you,' I say. 'Come take a look.'

I set the folder of receipts I got from Melvin Granger's house on the counter and flip it open.

'What is this?'

'It's the records from when Granger did the renovations on the store.'

She breathes out a long 'Oh. And that will have information on who was working on it.' Her tight shoulders relax a notch.

I tell her about the three high-school friends who worked on the renovation. 'One of them was Paddy Sullivan.'

'So there's a connection between the body and the murdered man?'

'Certainly looks possible. I have to turn these receipts over to Reagan, but when you get back to the station I'd like you to copy them all, so we have a record.'

My cell phone rings. Tommy Larson, the medical examiner, says he'll be starting the autopsy at two p.m. if I want to be there.

'You're not wasting any time.'

'This one has me curious,' he says. 'I'm putting a couple of things off to get to it right away.'

I tell him I'll be there. That gives me time to go see Loretta and try to jog her memory of the past. But before I leave, Gabe LoPresto phones.

'You heard about the body we found?' I ask.

'Yep. The boys that were working demolition on the Granger place told me they found it boarded up in the floor.' He laughs. 'They weren't too happy.'

'I imagine they weren't. It was pretty nasty.'

'Any idea who it is?'

'Not yet. The body appears to have been put in there around the time Granger had the store modified in 1992. I may come to you to find out some particulars about how things were done back then. You know, how floors were laid. Somebody took a chance putting him under the floor, and I'd like to know what would have made them think it was safe.'

'And the smell,' he says. 'Seems like it would have been godawful.'

I tell him about the shellac.

He snickers. 'A real cover-up then. I'll have to remember that trick next time I need to dispose of a body.'

I leave Maria looking through Melvin's receipts until the forensics team arrive, and head for Loretta's. I catch her working in the garden. This time of year, the flowers are starting to droop and she tells me that she can tell the flowers think fall is coming.

'Have you been out here all day?' I ask.

'No, this morning I had a meeting until ten, so I just got to it an hour ago.'

I ask her if we can take a break. 'I have questions.'

'I'll be glad to. It's hot out here.' Her cheeks are flushed from working in the heat.

We go in the house and she makes me a cup of drip coffee and gets herself a glass of water. We sit at her breakfast table.

Before I can begin, she says, 'They say the body those boys found had been there a long time. How long?'

'Probably since Melvin renovated the store in 1992. Thirty years ago. I can't remember hearing about anybody disappearing back then, do you?'

Loretta cocks her head. 'That would have been right after you took the job as chief the first time, isn't it?'

'That's right. I had my hands full between the family that got killed out on the outskirts of town, and the drug problems at the high school. Do you remember talk of anybody disappearing?'

She's frowning. 'No, I don't. But my boys were young and I probably wasn't as tuned to what went on as I am these days. You know that's a long time ago. Whoever killed the man may not even be around any longer. May be dead or moved away.'

'That's possible. But I at least want to know who it is. You know anybody who might have kept up with things back then?'

She hesitates. 'Samuel, have you considered that whatever happened, it might be best to leave it alone?'

'I'm surprised at you. Surely you don't think it's a good idea for somebody to get away with murder. Even after all this time.'

'You don't even know if it was murder. Might have been somebody got killed accidentally and whoever did it didn't want anybody to know.'

'Why would somebody hide an accidental death?'

She swats her hand as if shooing a fly. 'Oh, I don't know. Samuel, you need to be careful, though. Somebody told me Mark Granger was warned not to do those renovations, and he was roughed up. Maybe Paddy Sullivan was killed because he knew something bad. I'm worried that you're going to find out things nobody wants to know.'

What things, I wonder. 'Like I said, I at least want to know who the dead man was.'

'How will you find that out?'

'Talk to the guys who worked on the original renovation. At least the ones who are left. One of them was Paddy Sullivan.'

She looks alarmed. 'And the other two?'

'Two of his high-school buddies, Eddie Polasek and Jonas Miller.'

'I hate to tell you, but Jonas died of Covid early on in. His widow lives with their daughter in Burton.'

That narrows it down. 'You know anything about Eddie Polasek?'

'His mamma is Hazel Moore. You know her?'

'I've met her. Hazel must be in her seventies.' Hazel is an outspoken woman who works as a volunteer at the little railroad museum a few hours a week. I don't know her son.

'That's right, but in good shape. If you've seen her using a walker, it's because she fell and broke her hip. But she's mending well and she said she'll be back in high gear in no time.'

'Her name is different from her son's,' I say.

'She remarried after her husband died in an accident. He worked in Bobtail. As I recall, it was an industrial accident. Anyway, she remarried Dutch Moore. And then he passed a few years ago.'

'Is Eddie around?'

'He moved a while back to . . . where was it? Dallas, wasn't it?' She's talking to herself. 'Yes. Dallas. Long time ago.'

I grab a sandwich, make it to Bobtail by one thirty, and am ready when Tommy calls me in to observe the autopsy.

The body is laid out on the slab, and the smell isn't too bad. Still, I'm glad to be wearing a mask.

Larson indicates various points on the body while he makes his preliminary observations. The corpse was a male, five feet ten inches tall. 'I've revised the first estimate down a bit. He was somewhere in his late thirties. Hard to tell exactly with the state of the body.' Larson says he was in good physical health, according to the condition of the hair, teeth and nails. 'Brown hair,' he remarks. 'It's mostly gone, but there's still a patch here and there and you can see that the man's hair was dark brown.'

'Cause of death?' I ask.

He chuckles. 'I don't think that's going to be too hard.' With his gloved hand, he moves the skull sideways and points to the back of it. 'Cause of death was a blow to the back of the head.'

'I see.' The back of the skull has a big crack in it. Whoever this was, somebody hit him hard. 'Strong enough to kill him?' I ask.

'Yes, but from where the blow hit, I think it's possible he was hit and fell backwards.'

The clothes have been cut away and they're laid out on a nearby table. He was wearing jeans and a blue work shirt. Both are in tatters, rotted from exposure to the corpse's decomposition gases. 'Was there any identification on him?'

'Nothing. No wallet. I'll examine the clothing more closely when I get a chance. I don't know that it will tell us anything, but I'll give it go.'

'Fingerprints?' I ask.

Larson picks up one of the skeletal hands and points to the fingers. 'Not enough skin left on his fingers to take fingerprints. We can do DNA testing, but I don't know what good that will do. We'd have to have something for comparison.'

Unless the man had run-ins with the police and had DNA on file, there's likely no information to get a match on a database.

Larson drones on, describing decomposition. Then he says, 'I estimate time of death approximately thirty years ago. But the important thing is that he wasn't buried under the floor right away.'

'Oh?'

'When we cut away the tarp he was wrapped in, we found red clay soil on it. So he was buried in the ground first. Then apparently somebody dug him up, covered the tarp with shellac, and hid him under the floor.'

'What do you make of that?'

He shakes his head. 'That's your department. I'm just telling you what I found; not why.'

The timing fits with the time Melvin had the icehouse remodeled. But why bury him first and then dig him up? There are plenty of acres of barren land where a body could have been buried and never discovered. What prompted the decision to move the body?

'Any possibility of fingerprints on the wrappings?'

'Not likely. I've turned them over to forensics, but the tarp is too porous.'

The tarp was old. I don't know how long tarps have been made out of plastic, but I don't remember seeing one of those old canvas tarps since the Seventies. Somebody had that old tarp stored.

I go back to the station, intending to give Hazel Moore a call. Instead, I'm surprised to find Carl White sitting next to my desk. He was the best friend of Rodell Sim, the man who used to be chief of police before me. Rodell was a heavy drinker, and he and White spent most of their time out at White's fishing shack, drinking beer. Rodell died a few years back and I haven't seen much of White since then, although I do see him tearing around town in his big white Ford pickup from time to time. He heaves himself to his feet when I walk in. Time and heavy drinking have not been kind to him. He's got a substantial beer gut that hangs over his belt, and his nose is streaked with broken capillaries.

'Carl, what brings you here? You having some trouble?'

'Not so much. Life is actually pretty good these days. My son's boys are ten and twelve and they keep me busy. You never saw anything like the way they love to fish. I believe if their mama and daddy would let them, they'd quit school and fish full-time.' His laugh is raspy.

'Good to hear. So what's up?'

'Well, sir, I heard about the body they found this morning and I suspect I might know who it was. Not who put him there, mind you, but at least who it was.'

I pour us both a cup of coffee and we sit down. 'Let's hear it.'

'When I was a teenager, we had a field hand out at my folks' place. You know they had that big spread a few miles south of here.'

I nod. His daddy was a good farmer and had enough land to make it pay. As far as I know, Carl never worked the farm. He went to college and came back and became a local soft drink distributor working out of Bryan/College Station.

'His name was Lefty Ames. Left-handed, you know. The man was a little strange. He didn't say a word most of the time. Made my mamma nervous, but Daddy said he was a good worker. And I got on well with him because he treated me like I was smart. 'Course I was young and didn't have the sense of a goose.' He chuckles, looking off into the distance as if he's recalling some piece of nonsense that pleased him.

'Anyway, one day he didn't show up to work. Daddy didn't have a phone number for him, but he had an address for him in Bobtail, so he went looking for him. But the people at the address said they had never heard of him. Daddy dropped it. But when I heard about that body yesterday, it occurred to me that maybe Lefty got in trouble with somebody and ended up under those floorboards.'

'You know what year that was?'

'Let me see. I was maybe twenty-seven, and I'm fifty-seven now, so that's thirty years ago.'

I'm surprised that White is only fifty-seven. He looks ten years older. That's what hard drinking does to you.

'Do you have any particular reason to think something happened to him?'

'Just seems strange he didn't come to work one day and we never saw him again.'

'You know his real name?'

'I didn't remember, but I called my mamma – she's in a retirement community in Bobtail, but she's still sharp. She said his name was Duvall. Duvall Ames. She said she always wondered if it was a made-up name cause it sounded like a movie star. She said if you want to talk to her, she'd be happy to help.'

Suddenly, talking to Ed Polasek doesn't seem quite so urgent. If the body belonged to Duvall Ames, that would make things easier. I'd have two murders to investigate, but at least I'd know who the victims were. I call Carl's mamma and she says it'll be OK if I come over tomorrow morning. 'You need to get here before ten. I've got a bridge game at eleven.'

I also need to talk to her before Reagan gets wind of it. With any luck, I'll have this wrapped up before he gets a chance to ride herd on me.

Maria has been on the phone, and when she gets off, she looks bereft. 'I heard from my cousin's friend. He said it really is a holiday, but he promises he'll get back to me tomorrow.'

It's a little after five when my phone rings. A sweet voice says, 'Hi, is this Chief Craddock?'

'It is.'

'I'm Missy Lockwood.' She says it with an implied 'ta da!' as if I should be extremely honored that she called me. 'You left a message for me to call?'

In all the chaos of the last couple of days, I'd almost forgotten I phoned her. 'Yes, I got your name from Reanna Barstow's mamma, Janine. She said you might remember some things from back in high school.'

'Oh, Lordy, that seems like a hundred years ago.'

'You remember one of your classmates, Paddy Sullivan?'

'Sure I do. I heard he was killed. That's just awful.' She says it with a certain amount of relish. Some people love a good murder.

'Janine said you may remember who Paddy dated in high school.'

'Now why would she say that? Her daughter is the one who dated him.'

'How about after he dated her?'

'I went out with him a couple of times, not exactly a steady date. Stop that!' she yells. 'Excuse me. I have to . . . Emily, give her back her toy. It's not yours.'

An indistinct toddler's voice in the background.

'I'm going to put you both down for a nap if you don't cut it out.'

A wail starts up, then another one.

'Oh, hold on.' The phone clatters down. 'Come on, let's have cookies.' The wails cease abruptly. In a minute she comes back. 'My grandkids. I love them to pieces, but they'll drive me crazy. They're at that age, two and three. Oh, my Lord.'

'Sounds like a handful.'

'Now, where were we? Oh, right. I'd have to look in my yearbook to jog my memory. I swear those two kids have robbed me of my last brain cell. Let me call you back after their momma picks them up.'

I don't expect Missy to remember her intention to call me, but I'm just sitting down for dinner when she calls back. 'OK, I looked it up. Paddy went out for a while with Marsha Berry right after high school. But I don't know how you're going to contact her. She moved out to California after she graduated from college.'

As if she's moved to the moon. 'Would you have a phone number for her?'

'No, but her mamma still lives here after her divorce. Let me look up her phone number.'

She gives it to me and then I say, 'Missy, do you remember anything that might have happened during Paddy's senior year that would make him not want to come back here?'

She thinks about it. 'He was two years older, and I didn't know him that well. You'd be better off talking to Marsha.'

'If you talk to any of your high school friends, would you ask them?'

'I sure will. You think it will help you figure out who killed him?'

'Can't hurt.'

When I'm finished eating, I call Wendy. I had hoped to see her tonight, but her niece, Tammy, is staying with her again. Tammy doesn't get along with her folks, and spends a lot of time with Wendy. We talk a little bit, but she has to be guarded in what she says. She doesn't want Tammy to know what is going on with Allison. Tammy tends to be easily influenced, and Wendy doesn't want her to get any ideas. She's capable of deciding to go down to Mexico to break Allison out of jail.

FOURTEEN

The next morning my cell phone rings early, before I'm at work. I see it's from Reagan. I send it to voicemail. That way I can claim I didn't know he was trying to reach me.

I go into headquarters to tell Maria I'll be out for a while this morning.

'What are you up to?' She's suspicious. She doesn't like to be left out.

'I'm trying to get some information about the identity of the body before Reagan sticks his nose in.'

'And you're not telling me where you're getting information? If Reagan comes in, what should I say?'

'That you don't have a clue where I am. That's why I'm not telling you.'

Maria shows me that she has organized the receipts from Granger's office into piles and has a yellow pad covered with notes. She's big on taking notes.

'That's perfect,' I say. 'I'd like you to make two copies of all these receipts and any notes connected with the renovation, so I can give the originals back to the Grangers and turn over a copy to Reagan.'

'His Royal Highness,' she mutters.

I ignore it. Don't feed the bear.

I imagined the retirement community in Bobtail would be a tired one-story building with small units that looked like the last stop on a railway line. The only thing I got right is that it's a one-story building. But it's a sparkling new, modern octagonal building with wings jutting out in a kind of spiral.

Kay White greets me at the front door, a slim, bright-eyed woman, with a peppy demeanor. She escorts me into a large living room that's unusual because it has several conversation areas, as she calls them. 'There are eight of us who decided to have a place built and all live together. We didn't want to get on each other's nerves, so we had the place designed so that we each have our wing with a small kitchen and a sitting area and two bedrooms. But we share the big room here, and there's a big kitchen if a few people want to cook and have a meal together. We've been here three years, and it's wonderful.'

She says hello to a couple of women working on a jigsaw puzzle at a round table, and tells me we'll go to her wing to have our talk.

'Would you like some coffee?' she asks.

'I'm always up for coffee,' I say.

She shows me her kitchen area. It's small but she says it's just the right size. 'Not too big, so I don't always have to be cleaning up. I never was much of a cook, so I keep things in the freezer and heat them up.' She shoos me out into her sitting room to wait for the coffee. Like the kitchen, the sitting room is small but functional. There's a TV, three small armchairs, a coffee table and some shelves full of knick-knacks. It's warm and friendly, and for some reason it makes me think of Wendy's place, though hers is a lot bigger, with furniture sprawled out in it, and it's a riot of color.

Kay comes back with coffee and settles in one of the armchairs, tucking her legs up beside her. 'My son told me about that body that was found. Goodness! That must have been a shock.'

'I'm pretty sure the boys who were pulling up floorboards didn't quite expect to find something like that,' I say.

She laughs. 'Well, for some reason Carl seems to think it might be our field hand that disappeared on us.'

'I hope your man just took off for greener pastures,' I say, 'but I have to admit it would make things a lot easier if it turned out the body was his. What can you tell me about him?'

She hops up and goes over to a side table that has a pile of papers on it, which she hands to me. 'It's all right there. I kept a lot of our files when I moved here after my husband, Clifford, died. Clifford was always one for keeping things straight. I think it's all there.' She shakes her head.

'I appreciate you going to the trouble,' I say, brandishing the papers. 'What kind of person was Lefty?'

She cocks her head. 'Very quiet. I had a feeling he had something in his past that had hurt him, but we didn't have that kind of relationship where I could have asked him. I'm not sure he and my husband said more than two sentences to each other from week to week. But he worked hard and he got along with Carl.' She chuckles. 'Carl was a lippy teenager, anxious to get away from the farm, and my husband was unhappy about that. Lefty seemed to understand Carl.'

'Did Lefty ever get into any trouble with anybody?'

She shakes her head. 'I couldn't tell you what he did when he had time off. I know he went to town sometimes and I don't think he was above having a drink at that bar, you know, the Two Dog. But he never bothered us with that. The man we hired before him used to drink too much and he'd come back to the house rowdy and loud. We had to ask him to leave.'

'Lefty lived in the house with you?'

'Not with us. We had a little apartment built on the back of the house for my mamma to live in. But after she passed, we had our hired men live there.'

'Did he ever bring women home?'

'Oh, I don't think so.' She winces. 'At least if he did, he was quiet. I wouldn't have liked knowing he had a woman there. Not that I'm so much a prude, but I wouldn't have wanted all and sundry to be in the apartment. No, Lefty was quiet in his habits, and that's why I was so surprised when he disappeared without a word.'

'No notice?'

'Not a word. He left us in the lurch. It was harvest time, and Clifford had to hire a couple of boys from town. Carl wasn't all that much help. You know, teenaged boy.'

'So you don't know if Lefty ever had an argument with somebody, or maybe was sneaking around with somebody's wife.'

She chuckles. 'Well, that's one thing. Lefty wasn't a particularly attractive man. I'm not sure he would have been the man of somebody's dreams.'

'How old was he?'

'Not that old, maybe in his twenties.' She gestures toward

the papers. 'It's all in there. My husband paid his social security, although he didn't really have to.'

I should have predicted that Reagan would be in my office when I got back, but I'm still ruffled to see his patrol car in the parking lot. In the past it has been my experience that the officers from the Department of Public Safety assigned to small-town crimes usually don't make them a priority, which means I have free rein. Reagan either doesn't have enough to do, or he's establishing his position as boss of the territory. He might also be really curious about the mummified body. Can't blame him for that.

When I walk in, I see that my deputy Connor Loving's face is bright red. He blushes easily, but this looks more like anger than embarrassment. Connor has an even temper, so it's unusual for him to be angry. I don't know where Maria is and hope she doesn't come back while Reagan is here.

'Hey, Connor, what's going on?' I ask, ignoring Reagan, who is standing behind my desk. He really is playing the alpha gorilla.

Connor nods to Reagan. 'Sergeant Reagan was asking where you were.'

'Hello, Reagan.' I stick out my hand to shake his, knowing he'll be put off by my friendly gesture. Sure enough, he glares at my hand before reluctantly shaking it.

'You've got another body on your hands,' he says, stating the obvious.

'Coffee?' I ask.

He wars with himself over whether he should dismiss my show of friendliness or bow to his need for a cup. The coffee wins.

I pour him a cup of coffee and gesture to the chair next to my desk, which would mean he'd have to give up his position behind my desk. But to his credit, he steps away and sits down in the guest chair.

'We've got our hands full,' I say.

Reagan's expression hardens. 'There's that "we" again. How many times do I have to tell you that you're not involved in this investigation?'

'Look, Reagan.' I glance at Connor, and lower my voice. 'I

understand that you'll head up the investigation, but I'd like you to consider that I could be an asset. I know this town and these people and they're a damn sight more likely to talk to me than they are to a stranger.'

To his credit, I see him calculating. 'I can appreciate that, but I can't have you going off like a vigilante and thinking you've got jurisdiction, when you don't.'

I show my hands. 'It's yours. I just want to do whatever I can to help.'

He studies me. 'It's only a little more than a day since the second body was discovered and my guess is you've been busy. For one thing, I know you attended the autopsy.'

'You've read the preliminary report?'

He nods. 'Homicide for sure.'

'I'm going on the assumption that the two bodies are connected.'

He's intrigued in spite of himself. 'How do you figure that?'

'Couple of things. Last week Mark Granger, the son of the man who owns the feed store, was assaulted, and the men who attacked him warned him not to continue the renovation. I think they knew that body was there and didn't want it discovered. And I bet one of them was Sullivan.'

'Sounds like a leap to me.'

I lean forward. 'Not so much. Turns out Sullivan worked on the original renovation of the property back in the early Nineties. That means he had the opportunity to hide that body.'

'How did you find out he worked on the renovations?'

He's not going to like this, but I plow ahead. 'After the body was found yesterday morning, I went and talked to Melvin Granger to find out if he knew anything about it. He said he didn't.'

'Goddammit!' He bangs his fist on the desk. 'You know that was the wrong thing to do. He probably gave you the good old boy routine and he could have told you anything.'

I ignore the outburst. 'After we talked, I searched his office and found receipts and blueprints related to the renovation that was done in 1992. At that time the whole place was torn up and redone, so that would have been the time for somebody to hide that body there.

'And that's where I found Sullivan's name as one of the workmen. I told you Paddy Sullivan was from Jarrett Creek, but his wife said he had something against coming back here. I bet his reluctance had something to do with the body.'

Reagan's face is bright red. 'And these receipts. What did you do with them?'

I take a folder from my desk drawer. 'They're all here,' I say. 'Deputy Trevino made copies.'

Reagan is angry, but he can't think of anything to complain about with me handing him the file. He opens it and riffles through a few of the receipts and closes it back up. 'Who else worked on the renovations?'

'Two guys named Eddie Polasek and Jonas Miller. They were in high school, and this was a summer job. I figured maybe Polasek or Miller could tell me what was going on back then. But one of them, Jonas Miller, died of Covid early on in the pandemic. So I'm down to Eddie Polasek.'

'Have you contacted him?'

'Not yet. He lives in Dallas.'

'Any chance he came down here and killed Sullivan?'

'I suppose anything's possible.'

'Good. I'll have somebody from that district grill him.'

Grill him? I have to work to keep a straight face.

'I've been trying to find out who else Sullivan hung out with back when he was in high school here. Maybe somebody who can tell me if he was mixed up in something shady.'

'Give me the names. I'll take care of it.'

'I'll do that. But the thing is, we may not need it. I've got another lead. And if it pans out, it may not have anything to do with Sullivan.' I tell him about Carl White visiting me with the theory that the body might be that of the field hand. 'I went out and talked to White's mother this morning.' While I've talked, his expression has gone from outrage to something like resignation.

'You should have waited and let us interview the woman.'

'I thought I'd save you some time,' I say. 'In case she didn't really have anything to say.'

'Did she?'

'She confirmed that the man disappeared around the same

time as our corpse. She didn't know whether he'd had any trouble in town.'

'I don't suppose you have a name for the man.'

'He was called Lefty Ames, but his given name was Duvall. A man in his twenties. Kay White said he disappeared one day and they never knew what happened to him.'

He stands up abruptly. 'So where we stand now is that you've meddled in every aspect of this investigation, and no telling what kind of mess you've made of it.'

I stand, too. 'Reagan, like I said, I'm happy for you to take this on, but I won't have my methods or my experience called into question. I'm turning over clean information to you and I'll be the first to apologize if you find I've botched it.'

He raises his eyebrows. Something tells me he isn't used to people talking back. 'Time will tell,' he says. 'I'll have somebody look into this Duvall fellow, and I'll also question Granger again. We'll find out soon enough if he's holding out on us.'

'As I mentioned, Melvin has had a bad stroke. It left him unable to say more than a few sentences.'

'Maybe I can put a little pressure on him,' he says.

I get a mental image of Reagan berating poor Melvin, but I suspect once he sees the man, Reagan will back off. He may be pompous, but I doubt he's cruel or stupid.

'I have a question,' I say. 'You were going to get somebody to go back to Paddy Sullivan's house and search his home office. Has that happened?'

'Not yet. I've had other things to attend to. But I'll get to it.'

I could tell him that he's given me the same line that every district manager has given me before they wander away and lose interest. I don't think he'll lose interest, but I do think he'll figure out soon enough that he has a big job, maybe bigger than he envisioned. It's a wide territory with a lot of small towns and a few bigger ones. If he intends to micro-manage, he's going to fail.

'Why don't you let me go back to Sullivan's,' I say. 'I've talked to the widow once, and it might help smooth things out to see the same face.'

'Let me think about it.'

At least it isn't a no, but I'd like to have gotten to it right away. I'll have to decide if I want to cross him and go anyway.

When he leaves, all the air seems to come back into the room.

'I don't care for him,' Connor says. His voice is tight.

'Unfortunately, he's the new honcho and he's entitled to investigate. You gotta admit investigating two murders would strain our resources.'

'He acts like he thinks he's on TV.'

I laugh. That's a more astute assessment than Connor usually gives me. 'Well, I'll give him whatever he needs to clear up the cases.'

'I wouldn't,' he says in a sulky tone.

'Connor, between you and me, I suspect he's going to find he has more to do than try to figure out crimes in a small town like ours. I imagine, before long, he'll be kicking it back to us.'

FIFTEEN

After Reagan leaves in the afternoon, I go out to the car to bring in the box that Kay White gave me when I was leaving her place. I left it out there when I saw Reagan's car in the parking lot. I didn't want him taking it away before I had a chance to go through it.

As I'm getting it out of the car, Maria wheels in. She jumps out of her car and I can see she's upset.

'What's up?'

'Talked to my cousin's friend. He said he doesn't really have any connections. I don't know whether he was telling the truth or not. My cousin said he's a good guy, but he seemed a little shifty to me. Boss, I really think I ought to go down there.'

'I'm inclined to agree with you. I'm still waiting to hear if Hernandez has managed to get another lawyer for Allison.'

'Oh. About that. The guy did tell me that he couldn't locate the lawyer Hernandez said was on the case. Makes me really nervous.'

Maria follows me into the station. I set the box down and immediately call Hernandez. 'My deputy says her contact in Monterrey can't find the lawyer who was supposedly assigned to Allison.'

'I was going to call you. He's been reassigned. He told me they would be choosing another defense lawyer. I think they're stalling, so I'll get onto finding someone else as quick as I can.'

'How soon do you think that will be?'

'I've got the names of a couple of lawyers and they're supposed to get back to me to tell me if they can take her case.'

'I'm thinking it's time to get my deputy to go on down there,' I say.

He's quiet for a minute. 'Can you get her to wait until there's a new lawyer? Then she'll at least have someone she can contact directly.'

I give it a few seconds' thought. 'Until tomorrow. That's it. Every single day Allison spends in jail in Mexico is pure torture for her mother. And maybe for her, too.'

'I hear you. But I've been assured she's comfortable. I'll get back to you as soon as I know more.'

It isn't that I don't trust Hernandez. He seems like a straight-up guy. But I don't necessarily trust whoever has told him that Allison is 'comfortable.' And I trust Maria more than any of them.

Maria has been listening and when I hang up, she says, 'OK, tomorrow then. I'll book an airline ticket.'

While she gets on the internet to make her reservation, I look into the box I took from Kay White. I had hoped for a box full of information, like what I found in Melvin Granger's possession, but it holds very little. There's a small black notebook filled with tiny writing, noting weekly expenses for the farm. Each week there's an entry for Duvall Ames's salary. It's almost always the same amount, with an occasional variation of an hour or two's wages. It stops abruptly in August of 1992. That makes sense. Thirty years. There's no note that says Ames was fired or that there was trouble between employer and employee, or any curiosity about why he left. Nothing. A week later there's a new name fulfilling the job. White paid the new man a little less.

There is a 3 x 5-inch card in that same cramped lettering, with Duvall Ames's name and address, date of birth, social security number, and driver's license number. He was thirty-two. Kay White said they had tried to find Duvall Ames to no avail.

They certainly had plenty of information about him. But that was thirty years ago, and the ability to find people has changed. I open up my computer and enter Ames's name and social security number. I'm only slightly surprised when his name crops up in San Antonio. I expand my search and find that someone named Duvall Ames retired from a position as a high school teacher in San Antonio last year. Taught history. There was a small article about him in the San Antonio newspaper, saying he was a very popular teacher who won Teacher of the Year award, twice. I wonder what he was doing working as a hired man on a farm, and what led to him becoming a schoolteacher. If the social security number didn't match, I'd wonder if this is the same man.

There's a grainy photograph of him, and I can see what Kay White meant when she said he wasn't attractive. He's got a heavy brow and squinty eyes, and droopy jowls. But his eyes are lively and he's smiling.

I find a phone number for him readily enough, which again seems odd considering the Whites couldn't find him. Maybe they didn't try very hard.

The man who answers when I call has a hearty voice. I can imagine him being a teacher who commanded a classroom. I tell him why I'm looking for him.

He laughs. 'No, I'm not dead. I'm alive and well.'

'Kay White said you disappeared one day.'

'Huh.' He pauses. 'That's not exactly the way it happened, but I'm not surprised she failed to tell you the whole story.'

'What story?' Not that it matters, since he's not the dead man.

'While I was working for them, I had been looking for a job as a schoolteacher. I told them that. Right before school started that fall, a history teacher in San Antonio who was supposed to be coming back to his job had an automobile accident and couldn't teach that semester. They called me to fill in for the semester, and I figured that would give me a toehold. I gave

Clifford White two weeks' notice, but he fired me on the spot.
He seemed to think I was getting above myself.' He snorts. 'I
guess he thought being a hired man on a farm was my dream
job.'

'Well, I'm glad you're still with us,' I say. 'But that doesn't
help me much.'

He laughs that hearty laugh again. 'My wife will appreciate
the humor of that,' he says. And we ring off.

I call Wendy and she picks up right away. I can imagine her
sitting with the phone in her hand, willing it to ring with any
good news. I tell her that Hernandez is trying to find another
lawyer for Allison. 'And I haven't talked to you about this, but
Maria wants to go down to Monterrey personally and see what
she can find out.'

'You mean she'd be willing to do that?' Her voice contains
the first glimmer of hope I've heard.

'It was her idea. And I think it's a good one.' I don't tell her
that Maria will try to get Allison released to my custody since
I'm a lawman. I don't want to get Wendy's hopes up.

'I'll pay her way. I'll put her up in a nice hotel. I'll do
anything. I'm losing my mind here.'

'I know you're upset. But things are moving forward.'

'Can you come over for dinner tonight? If I make lasagna?'
She knows it's my favorite dish.

'I'll come over even if you don't make lasagna.'

She gasps. 'Oh, wait. I'm supposed to go to my sister's house
tonight. We're trying to figure out how to handle Tammy. She's
still giving her folks problems. Can you make it tomorrow night?'

'I'll make it happen.' By then Maria should be on her way
to Monterrey.

The autopsy report on the mummified body comes in in the
late afternoon, copied to both me and Reagan. I appreciate that
from Tommy Larson. I asked him for a copy, but I hadn't
known him long enough to know if he was a stickler for
protocol, and would send it only to Reagan, or if he'd take a
more expansive view of who needed to see it. I look it over
and see that the forensics team reported that no fingerprints

were found on the wrappings. But there will be an addendum to the report once they've had a chance to examine his clothing.

Now that I've located Lefty Ames, the identification of the body is again in question. I decide to ignore Reagan's orders and talk to Hazel Moore to find out what I can about her son, Eddie Polasek. I call and Hazel says she's home and it will be OK for me to come now.

Hazel lives in the old part of town, in a wooden house painted white with green trim. It has the usual pecan trees in the front yard. The tree is covered with pecans ready to burst and litter the ground. I wonder if Hazel has anyone who can come and help her gather them.

It takes her some time to get to the door and when she opens it, leaning on a cane, she's frowning. She's a gaunt woman, who reminds me of photos I've seen of women during the depression years, with hard mouths and stubborn chins, and a haunted look in their eyes.

'Hello, Samuel, come on in.' She sounds annoyed. Maybe her hip is still paining her.

We go into her living room, which is small but comfortable, with flowered armchairs and a love-seat sofa grouped around a TV. Within reach of one of the chairs is a swing-table for eating and reading, which I suspect is where she usually sits, except that a black and white cat has taken up residence in it.

'Get down from there,' she scolds the cat. 'I swear, the second I walk out of the room, he takes over my chair.' She pokes him with the cane and he glares at her before jumping to the sofa.

'How did you tear up your hip?' I ask.

'I'd like to say I was out dancing,' she says wryly. 'But it wasn't nearly as much fun as that. I stepped off the curb wrong at church, and fell down. I'm lucky I was with a bunch of people who could help me. I don't know how long I would have had to wait for help if I'd been home.'

'You don't have any kids around here?'

'Besides Eddie, I have a son in Bobtail, but I don't see him that often. Every couple of months. Anyway, I'm curious to know why you called. You said you have some questions.'

I tell her the details about the body found under the floorboard and she listens, but her expression never changes. When I'm done, she nods. 'I heard about the body, but I had forgotten that Eddie worked on that renovation for Melvin. Him and Paddy Sullivan and Jonas Miller.'

'Somebody said he lives in Dallas, is that right?'

She nods.

'Still in the building trade?' Paddy Sullivan was.

She snorts. 'Goodness, no. He never liked it. He just needed to make some money for college. It was a summer job.'

'Tell me, do you remember anything unusual happening while he was working that summer? Something he and his crew came across that surprised him?'

'Samuel, he wasn't that kind of a boy, to come home and tell me about his day.'

'The other boys, Paddy Sullivan and Jonas Miller – did you know them?'

'Not well. Eddie had them over for a beer after work a couple of times. Seemed like regular boys. As I recall, one of them didn't say much, but I can't remember which one it was. More than thirty years ago.'

'Maybe Eddie knows something about them. I'd like to get a phone number for him.'

She ponders that for a few seconds. 'That would be fine.'

She hauls herself to her feet. 'I'll get it for you.' I'm surprised she doesn't know it from memory.

Even with a little prodding, she doesn't remember anything else. But I got what I came for, her son Eddie's phone number.

Back at headquarters, before I leave for the day, I put in a call to Eddie Polasek in Dallas, but get another request to leave a message. Why doesn't anybody answer their phone anymore?

SIXTEEN

At home, I'm just walking in the door when Mark Granger calls.

'I was wondering if I could treat you to some barbecue?'

'You don't have to treat, but I'll be glad to go out and get barbecue.' We arrange to meet at Smoker's on the road out to Bryan/College Station. When I get there he's waiting for me and we find a picnic table outside because it's too hot inside. He insists on treating me and I order a brisket platter and a beer.

I've brought Dusty with me and he looks expectant, so when Mark comes back outside with the beer, I go in and order a small hamburger patty for Dusty.

Mark sits down across from me. He looks tense. I can imagine what he's going through right now with his daddy so sick, the renovation held up, and his sister giving him grief. But he starts off on a different subject. 'There are some good barbecue places in Houston, but there's nothing like country barbecue.'

I mention a place over in Spicewood that I think is one of the best and we kick the subject around a little bit. I'm in no hurry. He called for a reason, and he'll get to it eventually.

Our order number gets called out and he goes in and brings out our food. We're quiet while we dig in. Dusty is done with his hamburger before we've had a chance to eat two bites, and sits looking at me in case I have a notion to share with him.

After a minute Mark puts his fork down. 'I'm wondering how long this investigation is going to take,' he says.

'I wish I could tell you, but it's not up to me.' I remind him the DPS is in charge. 'You'll be better off if you call the area headquarters in Bryan and ask him.'

'That guy Reagan called me. I didn't care for his attitude. He told me he was coming over soon to question Daddy. He seemed to think Daddy's holding out on giving information.'

'When he sees the situation, he'll understand that your daddy is sick.'

He huffs. 'He's going to have to get past Chelsea and Mrs Sholtz first.'

That makes me laugh. 'I'd like to be there for that.'

'Any idea yet who that mummy is?' he asks.

'Not yet.' I describe the dead end I found with the 'missing' Lefty Ames.

He chuckles. 'That's a good story.'

'Has your daddy said anything more about the matter?'

'He's been pretty upset. Kind of obsessed, but not making a lot of sense. But he did tell me one thing that you might make something of.'

'I'm ready to hear anything you've got.'

'He said the boys working on the renovation got mad at each other, but he never knew what about.'

'Mad at each other? Did he hear them arguing? Or did it get physical?'

'Arguing. He said he came in one day . . .' He pauses. 'Now you understand I'm putting this together from phrases and parts of words that he said. He's not communicating well.'

I nod. 'I know. I had a hard time understanding him.'

'He said he came in and heard one of them say something like, you better keep your mouth shut. He said he asked them what was going on, but they clammed up. He figured one of them had made a mistake and the other one was making fun of him.'

Maybe it was more than that. 'Anything else?'

'That's all.'

'Did he ever notice a smell? You know the body would have given off some odor, even though it was masked pretty well.'

He shakes his head. 'Never mentioned the smell. But it bothers him that the body was there all that time.'

I can imagine. 'I hate to ask this, but is there any chance your daddy might know more than he's saying about the body?'

He looks startled. 'I hadn't thought of that.' He cocks his head, thinking. 'But it's hard for me to imagine. I never saw Daddy be violent. Not that he didn't raise his voice with us from time to time, but he was always fair and kept his temper.'

Interesting that he interpreted my question to mean I suspect Melvin killed the man found under his floorboards. 'I'm not suggesting he was responsible, but I wonder if he knew the body was there.'

'If he did know, he's not talking.'

'I know you have big plans for the place. Are you worried that having the body found there will put off customers?'

He ponders the question. 'I don't think so. Whatever happened was a long time ago.' He gives a wry chuckle. 'If anything, it might be good for business. You know a sign pointing to the back room, saying, "This is where the body was found." People can be pretty cold blooded.'

'And curious,' I say. 'I was surprised when I heard you had decided to stick around and renovate the place. What gave you the idea of adding a gift shop?'

He shifts uncomfortably. 'Nothing big. Seeing how Bobtail has kind of exploded in the last several years. And Jarrett Creek has that art center. And you know how Sally Hayslip spruced up her antique shop and put up that new sign?'

I laugh. The so-called antique store used to look like a deserted junk shop, but she cleaned up the outside and put up a sign reading, 'Sal's Bygone Treasures,' and now you see cars parked out front all the time.

'She told me business is way up,' Mark says. 'People passing through on Highway 36 stop by because of the sign.'

He's right. And Loretta told me a few days ago that somebody bought the old Kestler place on the north side of town near the cemetery. Rumor is he's planning to open a bed and breakfast.

'How does your daddy feel about the idea for the store now that he knows?'

He shrugs. 'He doesn't seem bothered, but it's hard to tell what goes on in his mind. At least he didn't get upset, not the way he did about finding that body. It's my sister who's on my case about it. She's still not happy with the idea.'

'Why not?'

He finishes off his beer. Then he sighs. 'Remember I told you I had a business in Houston that went belly up because of Covid? It wasn't really because of the pandemic. It was already in trouble before that. My partner and I were limping along. My sister thinks I don't have a good head for business and that the idea to expand Daddy's store isn't going to work. She's worried I'll go bust and daddy will suffer.'

We decide to get another beer. It's still hot outside, even though it's getting on to eight o'clock.

When we have the beer, I say, 'If your sister is against renovating the store, can you go ahead without her OK? Is she in a position to stop you?'

'She would be. The store goes to both of us. But I don't think she'll stop me.'

'Is her objection a matter of money?'

He smiles. 'Bingo. That's a lot of it. I don't know why, but my sister has always been tight with a dollar. She holds onto a bill so hard it leaves ink stains on her fingers.'

I laugh. I never heard that expression.

'I told her that whatever money the store makes, she'll get half of it.' He looks embarrassed. 'I don't mean to push Daddy into the grave. I just mean at some point we're going to inherit the store.'

'Maybe you can get her involved in the renovation project. It'll give her something to do.'

'We'll see.' He drinks the last of the beer. 'I'd probably better head on back. I told Chelsea I'd bring her some barbecue.'

We both get up. I'm stiff from sitting at a picnic table. The annoyance of getting old. Dusty dances around and runs back and forth between me and my truck.

'By the way,' Mark says, 'I don't know if you got everything you needed from Daddy's office the other day, but there are also some papers at the store. Not many, but he kept a couple of boxes under the counter.'

I tell him I'll come by tomorrow and look at them.

SEVENTEEN

The next morning I take Dusty down to the pasture to check on my cows, which I do every morning. But today I stay longer because I need time to think. My mind is torn between concern for Allison, and the desire to find a break in one of the two murder cases. Dusty doesn't seem bothered that I'm distracted. He spies an early morning rabbit and takes off after it. Not that he'll catch it. I've noticed that he likes the chase but veers off before he gets too close to his prey. Fine with me. I'd rather not have to pry a creature from his jaws.

I decide I have to keep my mind off Allison. It's no use dwelling on it until there's something I can do. And the two murder cases need to have my full attention.

I wonder if Reagan has actually assigned anyone to investigate them. If he has, they've been awfully quiet.

When I get back to the house, Loretta has left coffee cake on my kitchen table.

At eight o'clock I'm in the office. On Mark's behalf, I'm going to call Reagan this morning and try to persuade him to release the crime scene. By now they should have gotten all the forensic information they need.

Reagan is clearly a go-getter, so I'm not surprised that he's in the office early.

'What can I do for you?' His tone is barely civil.

'First of all, I'd like to know if you'd be willing to release the crime scene in the feed store. Mark Granger would like to get on with his renovation project, and I expect your people have been thorough enough.' Buttering him up.

He makes an impatient sound. 'I don't know what the rush is. He's not likely to get people to work on the weekend.'

'He says they'll be willing to come in anytime. You know, this is a small town, and people need the work. They're flexible. Did you get the witness list I sent?'

'I did. I'll have somebody on that Monday.'

As usual, the DPS takes its time on small town investigations. But it hardly matters. By now the list is more or less useless, but if he wants to send somebody out to go over old territory, that's on him.

'Now about this crime scene,' Reagan says, 'I tried to get in to talk to Granger the other day and there's a woman there, a health-care worker, who turned me away.'

'The dragon lady,' I say. 'Yeah, I had the same experience with her. Mark told me his daddy is pretty agitated about the body being found.'

'Agitated? Maybe feeling guilty?'

'Anything's possible.'

'Well, before I can release the crime scene, I have to have a conversation with Mr Granger.'

'I'm not horning in, but I wonder if maybe having me there, somebody familiar, might be useful.'

'Could be. You available this morning?'

'I'm ready anytime.'

'I'll be over. Call the son and tell him we'll be there in an hour.'

I don't like the way Reagan orders me around, but I'll swallow my pride to get the outcome I want.

'Chelsea won't be happy,' Mark Granger says when I tell him I'll be coming over with Reagan as soon as he gets here.

'If it's too early, I can stall Reagan,' I say.

'It isn't that. Daddy isn't doing so well. He's in his own world sometimes, and this morning he's not making much sense.'

'We'll do the best we can.' I think it might not be a bad idea for Reagan to get a dose of reality.

While I wait for Reagan, I do a computer search of the three men who worked on the original building addition: Paddy Sullivan, Jonas Miller, and Eddie Polasek. I also include Hazel Moore, Eddie's mamma.

I find that Eddie Polasek has done well for himself. He's vice president at a Texas state bank. No arrest records, nothing questionable.

I don't find anything shady about Paddy Sullivan. His business is front and center, but he's also listed as deacon of his church. Apparently he played a good game of golf, even winning a few local awards.

As Loretta said, Jonas Miller died of Covid. He left a wife and two kids. His wife might be worth visiting to find out if he ever talked to her about his early days.

Hazel Moore likewise doesn't have a shady past; not that I would have expected it.

When I was questioning Kay White yesterday about her missing handyman, she mentioned the Two Dog bar. It occurs to me that Oscar Grant might also be a resource worth mining. He owned the Two Dog, our local bar, until a couple of years ago. It was a notorious place for guys getting into scraps that Oscar had to break up, and for passing on a surprising amount of gossip.

When he retired, he moved to Galveston to be near his daughter – a daughter he didn't even know existed until he moved. He said he'd been married when he was really young and divorced soon after, and lost contact with his first wife. He only found out he had a daughter when she hunted him down.

I'd like to catch up with Oscar anyway, see how he's liking Galveston. I call him, but he doesn't answer his phone. So what's new? I leave him a message to call me back, telling him I have an intriguing question for him. If I don't spark his interest, he's likely to ignore my call.

While I'm leaving the message, Maria comes in. She always wears her uniform, although I told her it isn't necessary, and it's always as crisp as if she just ironed it.

After Dusty has done his leaping, yelping dance in greeting, she firmly sends him to lie down on the bed I keep next to my desk. She's the only one who can make him behave and is always on me because I'm too lenient with him.

'I've got a flight at nine tonight from San Antonio that gets there a little after ten,' she says. 'So I have the day. I'll leave around four.' She sounds excited. Looking at it as kind of an adventure. I hope it isn't a bigger challenge than she anticipates.

'Good. You can be ready to tackle the Monterrey bureaucracy tomorrow morning. Did you book a hotel?'

'Not yet. I thought I'd call my cousin and ask him to book one.'

I call Wendy and tell her.

'No, let me get her a hotel. I want her to stay somewhere nice, and I'll pay for it. She deserves the best for doing this.'

I'd like to argue that JC police department will pay for it, but helping Wendy's daughter isn't exactly in our budget.

When I hang up, I have a text from Hernandez giving me the information Maria needs. I hand it to her and she grins. It seems like everything has fallen into place. Almost too easily. I hope it isn't giving us false hope.

'OK, so what's on for today?' she asks.

'Couple of things. I haven't had time to listen to the messages. Why don't you do that?'

She pours herself a cup of coffee – or a half-cup, to which she adds water, because I make the coffee too strong for her. She also gets a piece of coffee cake, which I brought from home. One less piece for Connor to gobble down. Then she listens to the messages. It's the usual – someone complaining about cars racing on the dam road; a woman certain that someone has stolen her car; and a complaint from a weekender with a house at the lake who came in to find the house had been burgled.

'You better go see about that one,' I say. 'You're not going to want to be here anyway. Sergeant Reagan is coming in.'

'Say no more.' She calls the homeowner and says she'll be right over.

Before she leaves, she asks why Reagan is coming. I tell her we're going to call on Melvin Granger.

'Poor man. As if he didn't have enough trouble.'

She's barely gone before Reagan comes striding in. 'You ready?'

'I am.'

'Let's go have that conversation with Granger. I've got to get back to Bryan as soon as we're done.'

Music to my ears.

EIGHTEEN

C helsea Granger answers the door, and doesn't look at all happy to see us. I introduce Reagan. 'He's head of the DPS in the area and he's taken an interest in the case.'

Reagan takes off his hat. First time I've seen him without it, and somehow he looks more human. He's got a fine head of dark hair shot with gray.

She glares at us. 'I don't understand why you have to badger my daddy. My brother told you he's not up to being questioned.'

To my surprise, Reagan seems to soften before my eyes, holding his hat in front of his body as if he's protecting his manhood. 'Ma'am, I apologize. I'm going to be as gentle as I can with your daddy. But you must see that he's our best chance of finding out what happened all those years ago.'

'I suppose. Just . . .' She appeals to me. 'Keep it short, can you?'

'We'll do our best,' I say.

She leads us back to Melvin's bedroom. Mrs Sholtz is not in evidence, which is a relief. But I can see right away that Melvin has deteriorated. His body seems to have shrunk since I was here two days ago. His face is wizened and his mouth slack.

'Mr Granger, I am so sorry to trouble you,' Reagan says. In his soft voice, I hear the man who's hiding behind all that pomp.

Granger mumbles something and looks at his daughter, who has come in with us and is standing in a protective way next to the head of his bed.

'Daddy, it's OK. They're just trying to find out what happened.'

He thrashes his head back and forth, and I think what he means is that he doesn't know what happened, but then he says, 'Poor woman.' His voice is very clear in that moment.

Chelsea looks startled. 'What woman?' she asks.

Granger scrabbles at his sheet with one hand. I know the other hand is useless. 'Poor woman,' he mutters again.

I can't help wondering if he even knows why we're here. He's talking about a woman, but the body we found was that of a man.

'Mr Granger,' Reagan says, 'can you tell us the name of the woman you're talking about?'

Granger's mouth twists and drool seeps out of one side, which Chelsea immediately wipes away. I can see he's trying to form words, and his eyes are desperate. But then he closes his eyes and moans.

'Daddy, you rest a minute,' Chelsea says. 'There's no hurry.'

I see the rise and fall of the sheet, so I know that Granger is breathing, but otherwise he's still.

Behind me, I hear footsteps, and Mark Granger comes into the room. He walks around to the other side of the bed and nods to us. 'This is pretty much the way he's been since yesterday,' he says quietly.

It seems obscene to intrude on the death watch of the two young people, because surely that's what it is, but Reagan is right, Granger is our best hope of finding something out. I wonder who he meant when he said, 'poor woman,' and if the woman in question even has anything to do with the case. And then I have an idea.

'Has your daddy had any other visitors?' I ask. It's possible somebody came by who mentioned a woman that Granger fixated on.

'A few have come by, but they don't stay long.'

'What about his close friends?'

Mark nods. 'He's friends with Zeke Dibble and Dale Waller. He and Zeke go fishing together.' He grimaces. 'Went fishing together. Zeke has come by a few times. And Daddy and Dale have known each other their whole lives. They went duck hunting together. He's come by, too.'

I know both those men. Zeke was my deputy for a few years. And Dale is a local realtor with more energy than any one person should have. I find it hard to imagine him sitting in a duck blind waiting for ducks to show up.

Melvin has opened his eyes again, but they are unfocused. Reagan glances at me and shrugs. We aren't getting any more out of Melvin today. Or, I suspect, maybe ever. He looks like he's sinking right before our eyes.

'Melvin, I appreciate you talking to us,' I say, looking him in his unfocused eyes. 'Don't dwell on it. We'll clear it up.'

He mutters something unintelligible and his legs thrash around. He's trapped in a body that is failing, and I wonder if he's aware of it. I hope not.

In the car on the way back to headquarters, Reagan seems subdued.

'I know those old boys that are friends of Melvin's,' I say. 'If you'd like I could have a chat with them and report to you. Then you could follow up.'

He doesn't say anything for a minute, then he sighs. I look over and meet his eyes and for the first time I see a glint of humor in them. 'You don't need to butter me up. I'm starting to get the picture here. And I talked to my predecessor about you and he set me straight.'

'In what way?'

'You know in what way. That you're competent. He told me you've got more sense than some of these small-town chiefs who got appointed because they were the only person who volunteered.'

I can't help smiling. In small towns the choice of law enforcement officials is sometimes limited. You get your eager beavers, who think they're going to take the policing world by storm. Or people who think the job is easier than it turns out to be. Or those who are pressed into service because, like Reagan said, there's no one else, and they aren't really that interested.

'I've had some luck,' I say. 'And I also have my secret weapons: Loretta, who knows pretty much everything and everyone in town; and in the last couple of years, Maria, who never lets details escape her.

'Craddock, it turns out my job is more pressing than I thought it might be, so if you've a mind to put in a hand, I'd appreciate it.'

'I'll do that.'

'And if you need backup, you'll let me know, right?'

'Of course.'

Maria has returned, so I'm glad Reagan doesn't come in with me. He says he needs to be on his way back to Bryan.

'Did our *sergeant* have any success?' she asks, when I walk in.

I tell her that he's changed his tune, and she gives a smug smile. 'Figures.'

She tells me that the people out at the lake who reported the theft this morning remembered when she got there that they had taken the supposedly missing items back to Houston with them.

I tell her we need to have a talk with Dale Waller and Zeke Dibble. 'They were Melvin's friends, fishing and duck hunting buddies. Fishing and duck hunting takes a lot of sitting around, and maybe Melvin dropped information about something from back in the day.'

While Maria phones Dale and Zeke to set up a meeting, I make a call I've been meaning to make to Marsha Berry's mamma to get Marsha's cell phone number. According to Missy Lockwood, Marsha dated Paddy Sullivan for a while toward the end of his senior year.

She gives me the number without a lot of chat, which I'm grateful for.

Of course Marsha doesn't answer her phone, but I leave a message.

NINETEEN

D ale Waller has always been a ball of fire. He's a local realtor whose signs are seemingly on every piece of property for sale. He has asked Maria and me to come to his place this afternoon to question him. He lives in a large house out at the lake with a trim, modest yard. There's a boat on a trailer sitting outside the garage.

'Dale, thanks for seeing us on such short notice.'

'I've decided to take a day off every week,' he says. 'I'm not as young as I used to be, and I need a day of rest. But I can't sit around and do nothing. Come with me and I'll show you my latest project.' He leads us into the kitchen. 'I'm afraid you're going to be guinea pigs. I'm trying to learn how to cook. Since Bonnie died I've been at the mercy of ladies bringing me casseroles. I decided it was time I learned to fend for myself, so I've made muffins.' Dale's wife has been gone at least a year. I remember those days when I finally decided I either had to cook, eat all my meals out, or starve.

'They look good,' Maria says.

We watch while he pours coffee. I notice his hands are shaking, but he manages to get the cups to us without spilling any. 'I made it!' he says. He sits down. 'Doctor tells me the tremor in my hands doesn't mean much, that it's just old age, but I can tell you I don't like it.'

'You're doing better than a lot of us,' I say. I bite into a muffin, and it's not half-bad, although I could do without the raisins. 'These are good,' I tell him.

'Getting there. Now, what's on your mind?'

'I suppose you've heard we found a mummified body in Granger's Feed Store.'

His smile disappears. 'I did. Do you know who it was?'

'We haven't identified the body, but it seems to have been

stashed in the floor of the building back in 1992, and he looks to be about your age.'

'And you want to know if I think Melvin killed somebody?' He's not making a joke.

'That would make it nice and easy, but I doubt it's going to be that simple. You've known Melvin a long time. Did he ever indicate to you that he might have been involved in anything leading to someone's death? Or to hiding a body?'

'Never. And I'd be surprised if I found out he killed anybody. He's awfully mild-mannered. But whether he conspired to hide a body, I guess that would depend on who it is and why they died.'

Good point.

'While you guys were holed in a duck blind, did he ever tell you that he had anything on his mind? Something from the past? Nothing?'

He chuckles. 'You know as well as I do that men don't talk much about things like that. He mostly dithered about getting a bird dog, which he never did. We always used my dogs.'

At the word dog, Dusty leaps to his feet.

'Now there's a dog that looks like he could be trained to hunt.'

'Hunt for his next meal,' I say.

He laughs.

'Let me ask you something else, Dale. You've always had a good idea of what's going on in town because of the real-estate business. Do you remember any drama about anyone missing here in Jarrett Creek back thirty years ago? Anything come to mind?'

'I have to think.' He chews on a muffin and takes a sip of coffee before he continues. 'That's the time that family was killed outside town. You were the new chief of police then.'

'That's right.'

'Makes sense that you might not have paid attention if someone went missing. And to tell you the truth, that murder was on everybody's mind. I don't imagine people in town would have focused on somebody going missing.'

Maria speaks up. 'Except the man's friends or relatives would have been concerned, wouldn't they?'

'You'd think so,' he says. 'But I don't remember any gossip about a missing man.'

We're all quiet for a minute, and finally Maria says, 'Unless the family was glad he was gone.'

Which suddenly makes Melvin's mutterings make sense when he said, 'Poor woman.' Maybe he was referring to a woman who was relieved to be rid of her husband.

Dale looks uncomfortable. 'I suppose that's one possibility. I assume you've asked Melvin about the body.'

'Tried to. You know he's in bad shape and not making a lot of sense. He did say one thing that I couldn't quite figure out. He kept saying, "Poor woman." Any idea who he meant?'

He shakes his head. 'I don't have a clue. But I'm not sure Melvin knows what he's saying. Last time I was there, he asked me if I'd sold my house yet. I have no intention of selling this house, so I was surprised. I think he was remembering that I deal in real estate and he was trying to put it together in his mind that I sold houses.' His expression is bleak. 'I hate to see him like that. He's been my friend for a long time.'

Zeke Dibble doesn't look a day older than when I first met him -- when I hired him as a twenty-five-year veteran of the Houston PD.

'Hey, Dusty.' Dusty is leaping and yelping, having recognized Zeke from the couple of times he's dropped by headquarters to say hello.

'You want coffee, right?' he says to me. 'And how about you, Maria – what can I get you? My wife has some sun tea made if that suits you. I'm sorry she's not here. She's always got some kind of activity going on.' He says it with equanimity. When they first moved here, his wife drove him crazy with jobs she needed done.

'Sounds like she's settled in,' I say.

'Happily.'

Maria accepts the tea, and Zeke brings a dish of water for Dusty.

He invites Maria and me into the backyard, where we sit at a picnic table in the shade.

'I heard you found a mummy,' Zeke says. 'But what that has to do with me, I can't imagine.'

'You're friends with Melvin Granger.'

'Oh, yes. You think he put that body there?' He grins.

Maria rolls her eyes at me. She doesn't find Zeke all that funny.

'I'd be surprised, but it wouldn't be the first time I'd been fooled. I know you two go fishing together and there's plenty of time for gabbing while you fish. I wondered if he'd ever said anything that might make you think he knew that body was there.'

'I don't remember anything like that.'

We kick the idea around for a few minutes, but in the end Zeke says he can't recall ever hearing anything from Melvin that might make him suspicious. Then we mull over Melvin's son's big plans for the feed store.

'I kind of like the idea,' he says. He holds his hands out wide. 'I can see it now, the sign that says "Granger's Feed and Sophisticated Gifts Store."'

Even Maria laughs at that.

I tell Zeke to keep his ears tuned in case he hears any gossip that might have a bearing on the case.

'Will do,' he says, snickering. 'You know me, the town gossip.' Which is the opposite. He's as close-mouthed a man as I've ever known.

Once we're back in the car, Maria says, 'Now what?'

'I'm not sure. Short of going house to house and asking if the residents missed someone thirty years ago, I'm short on ideas. I have a call to Oscar Grant. Maybe he has some ideas for me.'

'I remember him vaguely. Where did he go?'

'He retired to Galveston.' I tell her he discovered a new family he never knew he had.

At the office, I've had a message from Wendy, giving me the name of the hotel she has arranged for Maria to stay in. Maria looks it up on the internet and gives it a firm no. 'Boss, this is too grand.'

'You'll be fine. Wendy is grateful for what you're doing, and she wants to treat you.'

'Oh, don't get me wrong, I'd love to stay there. But if authorities in Monterrey look into it and find out I'm staying at some fancy place, they'll be suspicious. They'll think I'm there to bribe somebody, or that I'm lying about being a cop. Better that I stay at some regular hotel.' She calls Wendy and tells her the same thing.

By four o'clock I send Maria on her way to San Antonio. 'The traffic is going to be bad, and you don't want to be late.' I tell her I expect to hear from her tomorrow. 'I don't know what kind of situation you're going to find down there, so don't get into trouble.'

She scoffs. 'I can take care of myself.'

I'm glad to be having dinner with Wendy, even if we have to put up with her niece, Tammy. We're in the middle of eating lasagna, listening to Tammy gush over her latest boyfriend, when my cell phone rings. I see that it's Mark Granger and I tell them I need to take the call. Mark's voice is somber and I suspect I know right away what he's going to tell me.

'Daddy died an hour ago,' he says.

'I'm sorry to hear that. Were you and your sister with him?'

'Yes, thank goodness. Mrs Sholtz told us she thought he was sinking, so we stayed by his side. Chelsea's a basket case. I finally gave her a valium and she went to sleep.'

'Is there anything I can do?'

'Not really. I just thought you should know, since that means Daddy won't be giving you any more information about that body.'

And with him dies the question of who he meant when he said, 'Poor woman.'

'I won't bother you tomorrow, but before long I need to get back into your daddy's office. The first time I was there, I did a quick search. I'd like to be a little more in-depth.'

He hesitates. 'Will that man Reagan be with you? I don't mind saying I found him hard to take.'

'This time I'll be on my own. Meanwhile, you and Chelsea call if you need anything. And Mark, do you know Loretta Singletary?'

He chuckles. 'I've heard of her. They say she knows everything that happens in Jarrett Creek.'

'That she does. If you don't mind, I'll call her and tell her that your daddy passed. She'll want to organize some help for you, whatever you need. Meals and that sort of thing.'

'I don't know if Chelsea will appreciate it, but I sure will. I hate to say it, but Chels isn't much of a cook. Not that I'm much better, but at least I admit it.' He's trying to make light of his situation, but his tone is gloomy.

'Leave it to Loretta.' I don't bother telling him that he'll get tired of tuna casserole soon enough. Maybe that's just me.

When I hang up, I call Loretta. It's late, but she answers at once. It took a long time for her to get a cell phone, but now, the way she uses it, you'd think she invented it. I tell her the situation and she says she'll have food to them first thing in the morning. 'And for as long as they need it. Poor things.' She speaks of them as if they were children.

I feel like there's more I ought to do, but I don't know what it would be. I'll call Reagan tomorrow and let him know.

After dinner Wendy asks Tammy if she'd rather wash dishes or go to her room. She scoots out of the kitchen. 'Smart move,' I say.

'She'll be back as soon as she knows the dishes are done,' she says.

Wendy's so nervous that I'm afraid she's going to break dishes, so I take over washing and tell her to sit down with a glass of wine. I try a couple of starts of conversation, but her replies are so desultory that I'm at a loss what to say. But she perks up when I tell her that Maria called me from the airport to say her plane was on time and she'd be in her hotel before midnight.

'Oh, that's wonderful. I hope she has success.'

'If anyone can, she can,' I say.

'It's the first time I've been excited since all this happened.'

'What's so exciting?' Tammy asks. She has an uncanny ability to come in at the wrong time.

'Something Samuel has planned,' Wendy says.

'Really? What? A trip?'

'No, Miss Nosy, and I'm not going to talk about it right now.'

TWENTY

With Maria gone, I'm going to be shorthanded, so when I get to headquarters Friday morning, I'm glad to see that Connor Loving has come in. I'm surprised to see him. He was supposed to be off today. 'I just came in to see what was going on,' he says. 'I'm not going to stay.' He has cut himself a hefty slice of the cake I brought in from last weekend's bake sale. I meant to throw it out yesterday. It doesn't look that appealing, but he's devouring it with gusto, so at least it must be edible.

I tell him about the mummified body. And then I tell him that Maria has gone off to Monterrey, Mexico, to help with a personal matter for Wendy.

He looks alarmed. 'Mexico. Will she be OK?' He and Maria don't get along, so I'm glad to hear him express concern for her well-being, but I have to smile at his caution. He's not the world's most adventurous person.

'I expect so. She can take care of herself.'

When he leaves, I tell him to take the rest of the cake with him. He eyes it and grimaces. 'That's OK, I'll leave it here. It's not very good.'

After he leaves, I dispose of it in the outside garbage can. If Connor can't eat it, nobody can.

I have to contact Ed Polasek in Dallas, hoping he'll remember something from when he was working on Melvin Granger's expansion of his store.

I would prefer to question him in person, but it hardly seems worth a trip to Dallas to question him about an incident from thirty years ago.

'Sorry to bother you at work,' I say when he finally comes on the line.

'I have a few minutes. Mamma told me about the body you found. She said you'd probably give me a call.'

'I hope you can remember something from that time.'

'I wish I could help, but that was a long time ago. Seems like I've always lived here in Dallas – my memory of days as a teenager are vague.'

I've been considering how the body could have gotten there without the young men knowing. 'Let me refresh your memory. Here's a scenario. You would have come in to work one day and part of the floor would have been done overnight. Maybe you and the boys you worked with would have said something to one another about how odd that was.'

He's silent for several seconds. 'It does seem like that would have been unusual, but I don't remember anything like that happening. Like I said, my memory of those days is hazy.'

'Consider this. There would have been a strong smell of shellac.'

'Oh, my. Now *that* I remember.' He lets out a long breath. 'You know, that was a big job. I worked demolition in the spring, and as soon as they started on the carpentry in the summer, I went onto a different site. Those two liked the carpentry work better than I did. Hammering. Sawing. I'm fit for banking, not for building.' He snorts. 'Anyway, I stopped by to say goodbye because I was leaving for college in a couple of days. I remember complaining about the pungent odor. It made my eyes water.'

'Did you ask them what it was?'

'I don't remember, but I assume it was some kind of varnish or something like that.'

'What can you tell me about the other two boys that worked with you?'

'They were OK. We'd known each other all the way through school. Mamma told me Paddy Sullivan was murdered just before the old body was found.' He gives a half-laugh. 'What the heck is going on in that town? I don't remember it being so dangerous.'

'It's not the way I would want it. So tell me what you remember of Paddy.'

'Well, sir, he was a little wild. He'd come to work hungover half the time. He was a couple years older than Jonas and me.' He pauses, and I wait. 'Funny the things you recall. He always said he wasn't going to stay in Texas. He wanted to see the world.' He laughs. 'Although I expect, like a lot of guys, what he meant was he wanted to go to Hawaii and lie on the beach and watch the girls in their bathing suits. Whether he got out of Texas, I don't know. Probably met some girl and settled down like I did.'

'Would it surprise you to find out he was in the construction business in Belleville?'

'Not really. He was into the work.'

'I don't know if you heard, but Jonas Miller died of Covid.'

'Really? That's a damn shame. Jonas was a character. He made us laugh.'

'And neither of them mentioned anything funny going on while you were working?'

He's quiet again. 'Now that you mention it, Jonas seemed to get a little quiet at some point. Not clowning around so much. Maybe he had something on his mind.'

It strikes me that Eddie Polasek grabbed at the opportunity to turn my attention to a man who is dead and can't defend himself, and can't point a finger at anyone else.

'One more question. You said Paddy Sullivan was older. Why did he hang around with a couple of guys younger than him?'

He clears his throat. 'Paddy was friends with my older brother Dylan, and we all hung out in high school. We all played baseball. When this job came up, Dylan didn't want to take it, so he recommended me to Paddy, and I brought in Jonas.'

As soon as I hang up from Eddie Polasek, Oscar Grant calls me.

'Oscar, how's retirement treating you?'

'If I'd known how good it would be, I'd have retired a long time ago,' he says. He can't have gotten too much money from the bar when he sold it, but my guess is he'd been socking money away for years. He was known to be frugal.

He tells me he's getting to know his daughter. 'And that grandson is the finest boy you'd hope to know.' He says the boy is ten and they spend every minute they can together. 'My daughter tells me she's jealous, because all he wants to do is hang out with Granddaddy.'

I've never heard Oscar have so much cheer in his voice. He was always a little morose. 'That sounds like a good retirement.'

'It's the best. But you didn't call to check up on my welfare. What can I help you with?'

I tell him we found a mummified body in Granger's store. 'We're talking approximately thirty years ago, which I know is asking you to go back a ways, but I wonder if you remember anybody disappearing from that time? Or can you recall any altercations that anybody gossiped about?' The Two Dog bar is only a block from the feed store.

'Let me think,' he says. He's quiet for at least a minute. 'That was around the time that Black family got killed and their house burned, am I remembering the right year?'

'You are. And I think that's why, if somebody disappeared around that time, people wouldn't have paid as much attention.'

He clears his throat. 'Well, I do remember an argument at the Two Dog one night around that time, but I don't know that it's relevant. A couple of men came in with an underage boy and wanted to buy him a beer. One of the men was the boy's daddy. I told 'em I couldn't serve him and they got a little fussy with me, said the boy was well out of high school and old enough to have a beer. But of course that didn't fly. I said they could abide by the rules or be on their way.' He pauses.

'That can't be the only time that ever happened. So what made you remember that time in particular?'

'You're right. It wasn't so unusual. But that particular night, that wasn't the end of it. The boy said he was fine having a coke, or whatever, I don't remember exactly what. But then they went outside to the patio and took their beer with them. I went out to check to make sure they weren't slipping the boy some beer. You know, I could lose my license if I was serving underage kids.'

'That's when I was chief the first time. You think I would have pulled your license?'

'Naw, I wasn't so worried about you. You were green back then and had your hands full. But if you recall, Jarrett Creek was thick with highway patrol officers due to that family that was killed outside town, and I wouldn't have put it past one of them to shut me down.'

'So you went out to check on the boy,' I prod him.

'And the two men were having an argument. They'd had a few beers by then, and their voices were raised. But when they saw me they clammed up. Again, that wasn't unusual. But the thing that makes me remember it, is the boy was trying to calm them down, and he looked really upset. I mean like, he was about to cry. He wasn't a little kid, he was out of high school. It just stuck with me that he was that upset.'

'Who were these men? Do I know them?'

'One of them was Gil Webb. You know Gil. He had that well-drilling operation. I imagine he's long retired. The other man was . . .' He pauses. 'I can't remember right off. Let me think.'

'What do you remember of Webb? I didn't know him well.'

'Funny kind of a guy. He was a gossip. Loved to gossip. You know, tending bar all those years I got to understand that although women have the reputation for gossiping, men love it just as much. It's just a different kind of subject.'

'Different how?' I'm enjoying this talk with Oscar. I've known him a long time and didn't realize until now that I miss him.

'I'd say darker. They like to know the little underbelly of things. Women like to gossip about relationships, and men like to talk about mayhem.' He laughs. 'Listen to me, the old philosopher.'

'Well, if Gil Webb is still alive, maybe he remembers something of that argument.'

'Wait a minute. I remember now who was out there. It was Tim Polasek and his son Dylan. Tim was aggravated with me because I wouldn't serve Dylan. Dylan was twenty, a year shy of legal for drinking. Tim thought I ought to fudge it, but I wasn't of a mind to do that because Dylan was a little skittish. Antsy. I had a feeling he wouldn't take alcohol well.'

'Speaking of gossip,' I say.

He laughs.

'Well, that's what I remember anyway.'

'Did Dylan join in the argument?'

'That I don't remember.'

'One more thing. Can you think if there was anyone else outside who might have witnessed the argument?'

He's quiet again. 'Nothing comes to mind. But I'll think on it some more and I'll let you know.'

'I appreciate your help on this,' I say.

'I don't know that I gave you much help, but I can give you a thought.'

'What's that?'

'Maybe you ought to consider letting this lie. It's been thirty years. People have moved on. Since nobody reported the man missing at the time, maybe whoever killed him had a good reason.'

'That's a thought,' I say. I don't agree with him. Whatever the reason, murder is murder and somebody needs to account for it. But no need to argue the matter. The strange thing is that Loretta said the same thing. It makes me uneasy. I don't know if they both remember more than they say, but it sure gives me pause.

TWENTY-ONE

I go over to Town Café for lunch, and while I eat I think about Connie Sullivan's reluctance for me to search her husband's office. Did her hesitation mean anything, or was it a general protection because news of her husband's death was fresh? Either way, it's past time for that search. If there's a link between the mummy and Paddy's murder, I need to find it.

Something in the phone call Sullivan got that night alarmed him enough that he left his dinner uneaten. One thing I can think of that might have alarmed him was if the caller threatened to reveal knowledge of the thirty-year-old death. Maybe even blackmail was involved. So what did Paddy Sullivan do, or know, back then that made him vulnerable?

While I'm walking back, I get a call from Wendy.

'I had a call from Chuck Hernandez this morning. He said he has arranged for a new lawyer in Monterrey. I'm worried that it doesn't make any difference who the lawyer is, that the authorities are stonewalling.' I've never heard Wendy so anxious.

'Wendy, if anybody can cut through stonewalling, it's Maria. Try to be patient. She's barely had time to get there.'

When I hang up, I phone Connie Sullivan. 'Connie, I'd like you to reconsider whether we can take a look at your husband's home office for any indication of why he was targeted.' I hope she'll see reason and allow me to search her husband's home and work office. Otherwise, I'll have to call a judge and I don't know if I can get a warrant this late on Friday afternoon.

She sighs. 'I talked to my son and he said I had to let you do it. I know he's right. I just hate to have someone rummaging through Paddy's things.'

I tell her I understand and that we will be respectful.

I want to get right to it in case she changes her mind, and I ask her if tomorrow morning will work. She says it will be fine. I tell her I'll be there at ten.

Then I put in a call to the medical examiner in Bobtail to ask if forensics got anything useful from the mummy's clothing.

'His clothes were pretty standard: blue jeans, a T-shirt and tennis shoes. Nothing to identify him.'

So still no idea who the man is. I have to dredge up ideas for other avenues to pursue. Tax records? Did someone pay taxes up until thirty years ago in town, and abruptly stop? I know one person who might have that kind of information.

I leave a note on the door to call me if anybody needs me, and head over to city hall. Martha Olderman has worked at city hall for fifty years. It's high time she retired, but she clings to the job like it's a lifeline. She shows me into her tiny office, pleased when I tell her she might be able to help me. She's a tall, big-boned woman, carefully groomed, with her gray hair short and trim, and wearing tan slacks and a white blouse with simple gold jewelry. She's most likely past seventy, but moves briskly, like a younger woman.

'What can I do for you?'

'It's your memory I'm after.'

'Oh, I'll bet this is about that man whose body was found.'

'It is. I wonder if you can look back at records from 1992

to find out if somebody who had been paying taxes or water or electric bills suddenly stopped paying.'

She gives a snort of laughter. 'You don't want much, do you?'

'Well, I figured if anybody could get that information, you could.'

She taps her lips with a forefinger. 'Can you give me a little time? I have to get out those old files.'

'You have records from back then?'

'In the basement. We're on computer now,' she says proudly, 'but we don't have the manpower to key in all those old files.'

'Anything you can do to help,' I say.

'It seems strange that nobody reported anybody missing, doesn't it?'

'It does. But you know, that's around the time those people were found dead and their place burned up.'

'Oh, yes, that was a big story.' She laughs again. 'I guess if anybody wanted to get rid of somebody, that would have been a smart time to do it, when everybody's attention was on that tragedy.'

'That's what I'm thinking.'

'And then you have that man who got killed last week. Paddy Sullivan. I can't help wondering what's going on at Melvin's feed store. But I guess with him dying yesterday, you can't ask him.'

Her words remind me that I need to go back to Granger's house and look more closely at his office. The first time, I found the names of the boys who were working on his original renovations, and it seemed like enough. But is there more?

I thank her for her trouble, and ask her to call me if she finds anything in her search.

As I'm walking back to headquarters, I finally get a call from Maria.

'What's happening?'

'Not much,' she says. 'Authorities won't talk to me. They said it's an ongoing case and they can't comment. And won't let me see Allison. No surprise.'

'Have you met with the lawyer?'

'Not the new one, I did manage to talk to the old one. He

was annoyed at being taken off the case. He told me something strange is going on, but he didn't have any idea what it was.'

'You have a plan?' I know she does. That's the way she is.

'Sort of. I looked up news of the accident in the local newspaper. I found an article, but it was short and not very informative. It said that an American tourist ran the stop sign and hit the other car. The only name mentioned in the article was Allison.'

'Wait. The story I got was that Allison rear-ended someone. So somebody's got it wrong.'

'Not surprising. The article did give a location. I'm going to go over there and see if I can find anyone who might have seen the accident.'

'Good idea.' I doubt if either lawyer bothered to do that. 'I wonder what happened to the car she was driving?'

She's silent for a moment. 'I didn't think about that. I'll look into it. I'll see if any merchants on the street can tell me if they saw the car being towed. Tomorrow is Saturday and I'm not sure what facilities will be open. And Sunday I know nothing will happen.'

'Take a day of vacation.'

'With Wendy's daughter sitting in jail somewhere? No way.'

As soon as we hang up, I call Wendy. I don't have much to tell her, but at least Maria is on the job. I try to put her mind at rest. 'Have you brought Jessica up to date about what's going on?' After all, it's Jessica that Allison called to begin with.

'I called her this morning. She said she hasn't spoken to Allison again. She's going to come over tomorrow.'

Then I call Chuck Hernandez. For once, he's in the office. I ask him if he's had a chance to notify the US embassy of Allison's incarceration.

He sighs. 'I did call. They said they have been made aware by Mexican authorities of Allison's arrest, and that someone from the consular office is ready to visit her to make sure she's all right. But they also said it could take a few days before they send someone. You know how border issues are these days.'

'A few days? She's already been in prison a few days.'

'I'll keep after them. And I told Wendy to call them also. You know, the squeaky wheel and all that. The man I talked to did say something that caught my attention, though. He said the officer he spoke with said she wasn't in the local jail, that she was in a "different situation." He didn't know what to make of that, but he said the official assured him she was being well-treated.'

I wish Maria was here to help with the search of Paddy Sullivan's house tomorrow morning. She has a keen eye. But there's Brick. He's eager to prove himself. He isn't supposed to be at work tomorrow, but I'd bet he'll want to go with me, despite it being a Saturday.

He sounds eager when he says he'll come in at eight tomorrow morning.

I still haven't heard back from Marsha Berry LeBlanc, the woman who dated Paddy Sullivan towards the end of his senior year, so I call again and this time she picks up. She's been gone from Jarrett Creek long enough that her Texas accent has almost disappeared. 'Hi, Chief Craddock. Mamma told me what happened to Paddy Sullivan and said you might call. I intended to call you back, but we're here in New York and I've been busy every minute. Hold on. My husband is going off to a meeting.'

She says goodbye to her husband and I hear the door close. 'OK, I have a few minutes. What can I help you with?'

'Missy Lockwood told me you went out with Paddy in high school.'

Her laugh is delightful. 'Oh, that's funny. She would remember something like that. I'm not sure what you want to know, but I don't remember much about Paddy. Can barely remember what he looked like.'

'Well, Paddy became a builder in Belleville. But his wife said he never wanted to come back to Jarrett Creek. I wondered if you could think of any reason why. Did something happen that upset him, or did he ever tell you he was unhappy here?'

'Hmm, I can imagine somebody not wanting to go back if they weren't popular, but he was well-liked. A little wild, as I recall. But not like crude. Just kind of would take a dare or do something a little dangerous. Oh. I guess I shouldn't say that. He got himself killed.'

'Do you remember him working with two other boys, Eddie Polasek and Jonas Miller, on a building renovation the summer after he graduated?'

'I'm sorry, I don't. I left the minute I was out of school. Went on a wilderness expedition with a bunch of kids from my church and I was gone almost all summer. Best time of my life! It's where I met my husband.'

'Well, think about it a little bit and, if you remember anything else, I'd appreciate a call.'

'Absolutely. And Chief Craddock? Would you look in on my mamma from time to time? She's got some health problems and I worry about her.'

I tell her I'll be glad to do that.

Despite the fact that I didn't learn anything from Marsha LeBlanc, I'm glad I chatted with her. She sounded young and energetic and full of life, and it was good to get a dose of that.

TWENTY-TWO

It's after five, but I call Mark Granger anyway. I tell him I don't want to intrude on the mourning for his daddy, but I'd like to spend some time in Melvin's office. He says I should come over now. 'We have relatives arriving, and it's just going to get worse. No one needs to go into his office anyway. You can take your time.'

There are cars in the driveway and parked in front at Melvin's house, and several people in the living room. There are open bottles of wine and glasses on a side table, and the mood is almost festive. Mark introduces me as the chief of police, and points out Melvin's younger brother and his wife, and a few cousins. Chelsea's husband, Conrad, has come out from Lubbock.

People look at me curiously. I wonder whether they've been told that a mummified body was found in the store. And that another man was murdered there last week.

I ask to talk to Chelsea and Mark privately. 'Let's get some coffee and a piece of pie,' Mark says. 'People have brought so much food that I don't know how we're going to eat it all.'

We go into the kitchen, where the counters and table are crammed with food. A turkey lies in ruins, there's a ham, and at least thirty desserts. The kitchen is surprisingly modern in contrast with the rest of the house. 'Nice kitchen,' I say, as Chelsea cuts me a piece of coconut cream pie. Her husband is hovering at her elbow and she casts him an annoyed look.

'Mamma loved to cook and Daddy thought she ought to have a nice kitchen.' Carrying our desserts and coffee we head to Melvin's office. Chelsea's husband starts to follow us, but Chelsea takes him aside and I assume tells him she doesn't want him to come, because he turns around and goes back to the living room.

Melvin's office is more chaotic than it was when I was here last week. 'Sorry for the mess,' Mark says. 'We've been trying to figure out what needs to be done. Also, we haven't been able to find Daddy's will. He told me there was one.'

Chelsea sits down behind her daddy's desk and Mark directs me to the only other chair in the room. He ducks out and comes back carrying a folding chair for himself.

'First, let's clear up the business about the will,' I say. 'You do know it's not a problem, right? If your daddy had a lawyer draw it up, he'll have a copy of it.'

'Yeah, it's a guy in Bobtail. His office said he'd call us tomorrow. We're just impatient. Everything is so up in the air right now.'

'We actually know what's in it,' Chelsea says. 'Or at least we know what Daddy told us.'

Chelsea looks ravaged. 'Have you found anything more about the guy, the mummy?' she asks. 'I mean we can't even focus on putting poor Daddy in the ground. We've got to worry about the store being closed and no money coming in.'

'Chelsea, we'll be OK, I told you that,' Mark says.

'Oh, yeah, like you know anything about business,' she says bitterly.

Anger flares in his eyes, and he looks away from her, grimacing. 'I do know some things,' he says.

I ask when the funeral is going to be.

'Tomorrow at two,' Mark says.

'It can't come too soon,' Chelsea says. 'I mean, I love some of my family, but right now it's hard to make small talk with people. I want them gone.'

'Was Melvin close to his family?' I ask.

'Daddy was close to his brother.' Her shoulders slump and she looks at me helplessly, chewing on her lower lip. 'I shouldn't have said I wanted people gone. I love my uncle. I know I'm being a bitch. It's just . . . having my husband insist on coming and not bringing the boys has been hard.' She throws her hands up. 'The whole thing has been hard.' There are tears in her eyes.

'Chels, I don't think Conrad meant to hurt you,' Mark says. 'He told me he thinks the boys are too young to be at the funeral. And they're starting school next week. Plus, they didn't know Daddy that well.'

'I disagree. I think they should be here. I just . . . everything is awful right now. I mean someone gets killed in Daddy's store? And then there's that creepy body? I'm almost glad he isn't alive to have to deal with it.'

'Your daddy didn't say anything more about that body before he passed?'

'No after you left, he pretty much went into a coma.'

'Look, I would like your permission to go back through your daddy's files more thoroughly to see if I can dig up anything that pertains to that body.'

'Of course,' Mark says at once, but Chelsea holds back.

'What is it you're looking for exactly?'

I open my hands out. 'I don't know. I admit it's a fishing expedition.'

'You can't think Daddy had anything to do with this,' she says. She looks fearful.

'I don't think anything right now. The store was the site for two murders. Something happened there thirty years ago that was never resolved. Even if your daddy had nothing to do with the actual deaths, he might have some knowledge of it – maybe knowledge he didn't even know he had.'

Mark says, 'Chelsea, unless you know some secret that I don't know about Daddy, we have no reason to refuse Chief Craddock's request.'

Chelsea looks around the room, her expression distraught, as if her daddy is somewhere in the room but she can't see him. 'I suppose you're right. It's just . . .'

'I understand. You don't want your daddy's belongings violated.' I lean forward, elbows on my knees. 'Chelsea, I've known your daddy for a long time. I promise I will treat his papers with care. I don't have an agenda here. I'm only trying to do my job.'

I give her a moment to consider my words. Finally she nods. 'OK.'

'Why don't you two go back to your family and I'll get on with it. The sooner I tackle it, the sooner I'm out of here.' I smile. 'Maybe I'll find the will while I'm at it.'

When they leave, I admit to myself that looking through Melvin's papers is a long shot. It's a daunting task. When I was here before, the office was tidy, but by looking for the will, Mark and Chelsea have left a mess.

What am I looking for? A note from someone that he tucked away and forgot about? Something that proves Paddy Sullivan came back here, despite his wife claiming he hadn't? Whatever it is, it's something so obscure that I have to look through every piece of paper.

I'm methodical, starting with things in the folders and loose papers stacked on the floor. Apparently Melvin kept every order he ever made to buy feed, and he never met a receipt he didn't hold onto. I soon learn the names of his regular customers. And soon learn that most of the papers scattered around here are not connected with the two dead men. Nor do I find any trace of a will.

After an hour, I tackle the file cabinet and the desk drawers. I take the folders out of one drawer at a time. More orders and receipts – thirty years' worth.

But eventually I come across personal files. I clear a place on the desk for a folder of household expenses, another of auto, another of medical, and still another of personal documents, like birth certificates, social security cards and the like. There, I find expired passports for Melvin and his wife. Looks like they took a trip to Mexico early in their marriage. One trip.

I look more closely at the household expenses. And I ferret

out at least one interesting item. It's a bid for a deck to be built at the back of the house. A bid from Michael Sullivan, dated fifteen years ago. So Melvin knew Sullivan was a contractor in Belleville. Why did he act like he hadn't heard of him when I asked? Hard to tell. Maybe his memory was just gone.

I find cancelled checks made out to Sullivan's company, so yes, they did the work. I sit back and contemplate how this happened. Maybe it's a coincidence, but Gabe LoPresto pretty much has construction sewn up around here. Why did Melvin Granger reach out to a company situated thirty minutes from here, from a guy who worked on the original renovation, rather than having LoPresto do it?

I look through the cancelled checks again, and realize something else. The deck can't have been very elaborate. The checks total only $1,000. Even fifteen years ago, that wasn't much money. I need to take a look at it.

I assume Sullivan sent a crew to do the work. So who was on the crew? I'll try to find out when I go through Paddy Sullivan's office in the morning.

I tackle the files with renewed vigor, but nothing else of interest pops up. I turn to the desk, but it only has shallow drawers not the right size for files.

By now I've been at it a couple of hours. There's a knock on the door and Chelsea comes in. She's got a cup of coffee. She sets it on the desk. 'I thought you might need some.' Her tone is conciliatory.

'I appreciate it. This is heavy work.'

She glances over the piles of papers that I've organized while I was going through them. 'Have you found what you're looking for?'

'Nothing earth-shattering. I found one interesting thing. Looks like your daddy hired Paddy Sullivan's company to build your back deck fifteen years ago.'

She looks to the door as if she could see through it to the back of the house. 'I remember when that deck was put on. Paddy Sullivan is the man who was killed, right?'

'That's right.' I don't know what it has to do with anything, but before I leave I'll take a look at the deck that a thousand dollars bought. 'Is there anywhere else your daddy would have kept papers?'

She shakes her head. 'At work maybe?'

'I looked there. He only kept a few things. Maybe he didn't want to clutter up the feed store.'

She smiles tenderly. 'He used to carry a briefcase home every night. Mamma used to tease him about being a businessman with his papers and such. He'd bring them in here and file them. Every night as soon as he got home.'

'Well, I didn't run across the will, so maybe he kept some things elsewhere. Bedside stand? Kitchen?'

'We've looked everywhere.'

I get up and stretch. 'Before I leave, I'd like to take a look at your back deck.'

'Sure. It's our favorite spot. We always sat out there when Daddy cooked out on the barbecue.'

She takes me through the kitchen, out the back door. The deck is a fine piece of work, big enough for a table, four chairs and an umbrella, the charcoal barbecue and a couple of chaises. It's shaded by pecan trees. There's a railing around it with planters filled with all kinds of plants. I'll need LoPresto's assessment, but I think it's worth a lot more than $1,000.

'Chelsea, this is a nice deck. Your daddy said he didn't know Paddy Sullivan, but that's who did the work on this deck and it was only fifteen years ago. I can't help wondering why he didn't remember Sullivan.'

'What are you saying? That he lied?'

'Maybe.'

'You listen to me,' she says fiercely, 'Daddy had a stroke. His mind wasn't what it was and you know it. Don't go trying to pin that murder thirty years ago on him just because you can't figure out anybody else to blame.'

Mark must have heard her raised voice because he comes out onto the deck. 'What's going on?'

'Oh, nothing, Chief Craddock is trying to say Daddy killed that man thirty years ago.'

Mark looks startled.

'Wait a minute, Chelsea. That's putting words in my mouth that I didn't intend. All I'm saying is it's unusual that he hired

Paddy Sullivan thirty years ago, and then hired him again to build this deck fifteen years later, and yet he said he didn't remember him. Seems odd.'

'And I said his stroke left him impaired. There were a lot of things he didn't remember.'

'Chelsea's right, he did have memory problems,' Mark says. His tone is conciliatory.

Even if Melvin Granger was lying, there's no way to prove it now that he's gone, so there's no need to belabor the point. 'I understand. But I'll ask the two of you, if anyone mentions knowing anything about Paddy Sullivan, I'd appreciate your letting me know.'

'Of course,' Mark says. 'We want this cleared up, too. It's not a good thing to have hanging over our heads.'

Chelsea stays quiet, fuming.

At home, I put in a call to Gabe LoPresto to tell him I'd like to get together. I want to ask him if the price of the deck is as unlikely as I think it is. He says he has to run to Bobtail first thing in the morning, but he can meet me in the late afternoon, after Melvin's funeral.

Then I call Allison's sister, Jessica. Jessica has always struck me as being a calm person, and when I tell her I'd like to ask her some questions about Allison's situation, she says that would be fine. 'But I don't know what she was up to. I can't believe she got herself into this mess. Well, that's not true. I actually can believe it. Poor Mamma!'

'When was the last time you spoke with Allison before she got in trouble?'

'Oh, goodness, we don't talk often. Maybe a month ago?'

'Did she tell you she was planning a trip to Mexico?'

'No.'

'Where is she living now?'

She laughs, but there's no humor to it. 'That's a good question. She flits from place to place. I don't know if she crashes with friends, or what. But I do know, last I talked to her, she was at Padre Island. She said she was there with some friends.'

I prick up my ears. 'Any idea who any of these friends are?'

'No one in particular. She hangs out with a friend from

college a lot. Her name is Carina . . .' She hesitates. 'I have to think of her last name. Williams? Williamson? That's it. Carina Williamson. I may have Carina's phone number on my phone. Allison called me from there once.'

'That would be a help. Do you know if Allison has a boyfriend currently?'

She laughs, this time with more humor. 'I like the way you put that. Currently. She never stays with one man long, that's for sure. If anybody can tell you who Allison's current boyfriend is, Carina can.'

She says she'll try to find her number and will call me back.

An hour later, I'm finishing up eating some beef stew when Jessica calls back with Carina's phone number. 'Sorry it took so long. We were sitting down to dinner when you called, and I just got a chance to search for it.'

It's almost nine, which is not late for someone the age of Allison and her friends, so I call the number. The call goes straight to voicemail, and I don't leave a message. I'll phone her in the morning.

As I'm hanging up, the phone rings and the first words I hear are, 'Wayne Singletary.'

'Excuse me?'

'This is Oscar. I remembered somebody who was there the night of that argument. Loretta Singletary's husband, Wayne. I remember because he didn't come into the bar often, and when the two men started arguing, he tried to get them to calm down.'

TWENTY-THREE

I spent a restless night and Saturday morning I'm up by six, and grumpy. I don't have too many mornings like this, and I count on my cows to calm me. I stand at the fence and drink my coffee, while the cows come over to say their version of hello, which is to stare at me and chew their cuds.

I started raising a small herd thirty years ago, around the same time as the old murder I have on my hands. At that time, it wasn't enough that I was busy with the murder of the family on the outskirts of town, and the drug problems at the local high school, but I was also wrapped up in the logistics of getting my cows here. Thinking back on that, I smile, remembering that my wife Jeanne was almost as excited as I was that the cows were arriving.

This afternoon I have to carve out time to attend Melvin Granger's funeral. Maybe in the mix of people there I'll spot somebody I hadn't thought of who might remember a disappearance thirty years ago.

I get back to the house at seven, in time to intercept Loretta bringing a plate of cinnamon rolls. She sits out on the porch with me. 'I only have a few minutes. I've got to get to the church and help with the flowers for Melvin's funeral.'

Wendy said I could share Allison's situation with Loretta, so I bring her up to date on what happened and tell her that Maria has gone to Monterrey trying to find out more.

'Maria told me she was on her way to Mexico, but she didn't say why. Now I'm worried about her down there trying to pry information out of the police.'

'I talked to her last night and she's already gotten more information than we had before.'

'What was Wendy's daughter doing down there in the first place? She's putting Maria in danger, having to go down there and poke into things that the authorities may not want anybody to know. I don't understand young people these days, flitting around all over the place getting into trouble.'

'Allison has always been something of a free spirit. Maria will sort it out,' I say.

'If anybody can, she will,' she says.

'I need to ask you about somebody. Dylan Polasek. He's Hazel Moore's older son. You remember him?' I'm curious because he's Eddie Polasek's brother and neither Eddie nor his mother said much about him.

She nods. 'Let me think. Dylan was a few years older. I believe Eddie has been successful, but Dylan was one of those boys who never quite gets along in life. Why are you asking about him?'

'His name came up.' I'm actually asking as a way to ease

into questions about her husband in connection with the fight Oscar remembered. I still think it's unusual that Oscar remembered that argument from so long ago. It had to have made a big impression for Oscar to have recalled it after all those years. But the important thing is that the timeline of the argument fits with the death of the man whose body was found in the floorboards. 'But there's one other thing I need to bring up.'

'What?' She seems startled. My tone must have given away the fact that I'm going to ask her something personal.

'This is about your husband.'

'Wayne?'

'As far as I know, he was your only husband,' I say dryly. 'What about him?'

'Oscar Grant told me something that happened thirty years ago at the Two Dog that stuck in his mind. An argument.'

'Well, he's got a long memory. What does that have to do with Wayne?'

'He told me the argument got heated and that Wayne tried to intervene. You wouldn't happen to remember anything about that, would you?'

She's quiet for a minute. 'Was he sure it was Wayne? You know, he wasn't much of a drinker. I don't recall him spending much time at that sleazy bar.'

'That's why Oscar remembered him being there, because it was unusual. And that's why I think you would remember if he told you something.'

She sighs. 'Samuel, now that you mention it, I do remember that night because we had a fight about it. You know Wayne and I didn't fight. But I was mad because I said he was setting a bad example for the boys, going to a bar.'

'Did he say anything about the argument?'

'Only that a couple of men got upset with each other and he tried to intervene. But Oscar told him to stay out of it.'

'Did he say what the argument was about?'

'If he did tell me I don't remember. Why is it important?'

'I guess it bothers me that you told me I ought not to investigate this murder, and I wonder if there's something you're not telling me.'

'No, there isn't. But with Paddy Sullivan being killed, and

Mark Granger being attacked, and now they've dug up that body, the whole situation seems dangerous. Somebody doesn't want that murder solved. I'm afraid if you get too close to finding out who did it, they might go after you.'

'I hadn't thought of that, but you let me do the worrying. It's my job to figure out what happened. The day I decide to lay off an investigation because I'm afraid for my own safety, is the day I need to resign.'

'Don't say I didn't warn you.'

When Loretta leaves, I hurry to headquarters. Before Brick and I head off to Belleville at eight to search Paddy Sullivan's home office, I want to call Hazel Moore and ask her for her son Dylan's phone number. If Oscar remembered the incident at his bar all those years ago, maybe Dylan does, too.

'Good morning, Samuel. What can I do for you?'

'When I talked to you, you said you had a son who lives in Bobtail. Is that Dylan?'

'Yes, it is.'

'I'd like to get a phone number for him.'

She gives it to me, but then says, 'He's probably at work by now.'

'What kind of work does he do?'

'He works for Gordon's Farm Equipment Store in Bobtail. Why do you want to talk to him?' She sounds anxious.

'His name came up as a possible witness.'

'Witness to what?' Her voice is alarmed.

'Don't worry, Hazel. He's not in trouble. It's just routine.'

I hope I'm not lying when I say it's routine. Was the bar fight at the Two Dog relevant to the man killed thirty years ago? And, more to the point, is it relevant to Paddy Sullivan's murder?

Before I leave, I call Carina Williamson again and once more get sent to voicemail, but this time I identify myself and leave a message for her to call me. 'It's about your friend Allison Gleason.'

TWENTY-FOUR

B rick arrives as promised and we get to Belleville right on time. Despite Connie's consenting to the search, she's unhappy to see us. A young woman is standing next to her. Connie introduces her as her daughter, Melissa.

'I don't see why you couldn't have put this off,' Melissa says. 'Mamma needs time to grieve.'

'I'm sorry for your loss,' I say. 'I know it's a tough time, but your daddy was the victim of a homicide, and the sooner we investigate, the more likely we are to find out who was responsible.'

A young man has walked into the foyer behind Connie and her daughter. 'Melissa, you need to let law enforcement do what they need to do,' he says, his voice stern. He invites us in with a sort of odd bow and a flourish of his hand. We troop into the living room.

The young man introduces himself as Sean Sullivan, Connie's son. He says he's a sales rep for a 'big company' in Houston.

'I still don't see how rummaging through Daddy's office will help you,' his sister says with a stubborn pout, but she sneaks a glance at Brick and her expression softens.

'We'll be as quick as we can,' Brick says. 'We don't want to intrude any more than we have to.'

'Honey, Sean is right,' Connie says. 'We need to let them do a search.' To us, she says, 'Let's get this over with. Come with me.'

Connie leads us to a home office and I tell her that we need to take a look at other parts of the house as well. 'We don't know where we might find something useful for the investigation.'

To her credit, she nods and says, 'I understand. Do what you have to do.' She asks if we'd like coffee.

'I'd appreciate that,' I say. Brick asks for a glass of water instead.

I tell Brick that I'll take the home office and he can start in the kitchen and bedroom. 'Look for places where he might have tucked away notes or letters, that sort of thing.'

'Got it,' he says. And I believe him.

When Connie brings me a cup of coffee, I stop her when she starts to leave. 'Let's sit down for a minute.'

She's brought herself a cup of coffee, too, and we sit near the desk. 'I'd like you to think back to when you first met your husband. Did he ever talk about working on a building site in Jarrett Creek when he was a youngster, maybe twenty years old?'

'Do you mean the renovation of that icehouse?'

'I do.'

She smiles. 'He said working on that job made him realize he liked building, and that's why he decided to go into the construction business.'

'Did he ever say there was anything strange that happened on the job? Anything that bothered him?'

She frowns. 'Oh my, that's a long way back.' She takes a sip of coffee and stares off to one end of the room, where a window looks out into the backyard. 'Something strange? No, I don't recall anything like that. He just said it was a good way to learn on the job.'

'Did he ever talk about the men he worked with on that site?'

She takes another moment to think. 'He didn't, but you know . . .' She lifts a finger. 'I think I have a few photos from back then. I remember seeing a photo of him with two other boys. Let me see if I can find it.'

She isn't gone long, and comes back with a big photo album. She sets it down on the desk and flips it open near the front. 'Here it is.' She takes a photo from the album and hands it to me. There isn't much to it. Three young men grinning in to the camera with their arms slung around each other's shoulders.

Connie points out Paddy, in the middle, a cheerful-looking young man, lanky like the other two, all dressed in jeans and T-shirts. 'He was such a cut-up,' she says, wistfully.

I turn the photo over and sure enough the names 'Eddie and Jonas' are scribbled on the back. It was taken in front of the feed store, but there's nothing in the photo that suggests they were at odds. 'And he never mentioned the other two in the photo?'

'If he did, I don't remember. Why are you asking about this?'

'Something has come up that could be tied to Paddy.' I tell her about finding the body from thirty years ago.

'What do you mean when you say it may be tied to Paddy? Are you saying he killed that man? That's absurd. Paddy would never have done anything like that.' She's twisting her hands and looks distraught.

'There's no reason for me to think he killed anyone.' I'm soothing her, for now. 'Problem is we haven't been able to identify the man yet, and I was hoping he might have confided in you if he knew anything about it.'

'He certainly didn't. I would have remembered. Can't you ask one of the other men who worked with Paddy?'

'One of them is deceased. I talked to the other one, and he said he didn't know anything.'

'Well, then, it probably didn't have anything to do with those boys. They were awfully young. Why would they know anything about a body?'

She's right. They were young. And it's possible that the body was put there by somebody else who knew that work was being done and used it as a convenient burial place. But why put the body there?

I thank her and ask if she remembers anything, to let me know. She says she will, but her manner is stiff. She's angry at the implication that her husband was anything but an honorable man.

Paddy Sullivan wasn't as organized as Melvin Granger. His filing system seems to be to cram file folders in wherever they happen to land in the three-drawer cabinet. It takes me an hour to admit that there's nothing here but his business records, none of which pertain to Melvin Granger. There's no record of the work he did on Granger's deck. I'll have to check his business office.

Brick Freeman has likewise come up empty-handed. We go back to the living room.

'Connie, does this house have an attic or someplace you'd store old stuff?' I ask.

'There is an attic, but it's a little hard to get to.' She cocks her head. 'We don't use it much, but I think there are some boxes of old items up there. Paddy was a pack-rat, so I don't know what all is there.' In the hallway, she points to a cutout in the ceiling. 'There's a pull-down ladder, but you need a stepladder to reach the trap door.'

I send Brick out to the garage with her to fetch the stepladder and, since he has young knees, I send him into the attic to take a look at what's stored there. Sean Sullivan insists on going up with him, as if he thinks Brick might stuff his pockets full of valuables.

Brick calls back down and says that it's mostly old furniture, but that there are five boxes of goods. 'You want me to bring them down there?'

I look at the rickety ladder. 'Why don't you open them up and see if there's anything that might be of interest to us.'

I hear him talking to Sean while he rummages through the boxes. Sean even chuckles at something he says, which means Brick is doing a good job of putting Sean at ease.

He calls down, 'Four of them are only things from when the kids were in school. But one of them has some old things that belonged to Mr and Mrs Sullivan.'

He brings that box down and takes it into Sullivan's home office.

Connie watches us unpack the box. It contains clippings from when Sullivan was on the high school baseball team. He was a pitcher, and seemed pretty good at it. There are two high school yearbooks and framed photos of his high school classes. There are report cards (Sullivan was a middling student), and articles containing Sullivan's name, and photos of Sullivan with Reanna Barstow when they were running for Homecoming King and Queen.

'Oh, look at that,' Connie says fondly. 'Weren't they adorable?'

Brick agrees that they were. 'Looks like he was a good base ball player,' he says. 'Did he ever play in an amateur league?'

Connie smiles at him. 'No, but it's kind of you to ask. Paddy was a golfer.'

We're coming up empty-handed until we reach the bottom,

where there is a manila envelope marked 'Eastman' that
contains only a clipping of an article. It's from 2007 and is
about a man named Andrew Eastman who had just opened his
CPA office in Bobtail. Attached to it is an unsigned note that
says, 'We done good.'

Brick is reading over my shoulder. 'I think that's my daddy's
accountant, but I never met him.'

I show Connie the article. 'Did Paddy ever mention this guy
Eastman?' I ask.

She takes her time to read the article 'No. Where did you
find it?'

I show her the manila envelope. 'The note attached makes
me think someone must have sent it to him.' And I wonder why
Sullivan didn't keep it in the original envelope.

'Why would someone send it to Paddy? Oh, wait a minute.
The note says they did good. So maybe it was about the golf
tournament. Paddy played in a charity tournament every year
and the proceeds went for someone's education. Maybe that
was Andy Eastman.'

That will be easy enough to find out.

I put both the notes and clipping in an evidence bag, and I
ask her for the address of Paddy's business. 'Do I have your
consent to search his business files?'

She sighs. 'Of course.'

'Will there be someone there who can show us into the
office?'

'Let me call and see if his foreman is there.'

She makes the call, and no one answers the phone.

'Connie, I have your husband's keys. They were found with
him. I suppose one of them is a key to his office. So it's not
necessary for anyone to be there.' I turn to Sean. 'Unless you'd
like to come along.'

'Yes, Sean, please. I'd appreciate it,' Connie says. 'Not that
. . .' She trails off, looking distressed, realizing that it sounds
like she doesn't trust us.

'I'm happy to have him come with us. We may have questions,' I say, rescuing her from her discomfort.

Before I leave I ask if they've made funeral arrangements.
'The coroner says he'll release Paddy's body Monday, so we'll

have the funeral at the end of the week. That will give every-body a chance to get here. His sister's family has to come a long way.'

Sullivan's office is closed, but there's a note on the door announcing his death and giving a number where the foreman can be reached. I call him and tell him we're going into the office with Connie Sullivan's consent. I ask him if he can come to the office and he says he's at a job site and will be here as soon as he can get away.

There are lots of file cabinets. Thirty years' worth of construction work. It's daunting, but we get right to it. I don't think it's necessary to go through all the paperwork from the projects, but we need to be on the lookout for any personal file folders. Also, I'm particularly interested in any information related to what seems like a tiny amount Melvin paid for his little deck. 'And any other jobs in Jarrett Creek,' I tell Brick. Which means we have to look through every folder, at least for location.

Unless I've missed it, I don't find any information about the deck, which seems strange considering that he seems to have kept all his construction information. When the foreman arrives, I ask if he was around at the time the deck would have been done, but he says he's only worked for Sullivan for ten years. 'That was before my time. And a small job like that, he might have done it as a favor if the guy paid as little as you say. And then he wouldn't have kept records of it.'

As we're leaving, he says, 'Sullivan was a good boss. I hope you catch the son-of-a-gun who killed him.'

TWENTY-FIVE

Melvin Granger was a long-time fixture in the commu-nity, and everyone knew him for one reason or another, so between them and visiting relatives, the Methodist Church is full of people attending his funeral.

As soon as the service is over, I corral Gabe LoPresto and we head over to stand next to my truck so I can ask him about the price Granger paid for his deck.

'You're kidding. A thousand dollars? Something wrong with that. Maybe Melvin paid him some other way. Maybe cash? Or in kind. Did Sullivan have a farm? Could be that Melvin supplied him with feed in exchange.'

'I don't know of a farm.'

'It's not like it's a tax write-off, so maybe there was some other arrangement that would cut down on paperwork.'

It sounds legitimate, but it doesn't quite satisfy me. Do I think Granger could have been involved with putting the man in the floor? Of course. It was his property. But do I think he killed the man? There'll have to be a lot more evidence before I'm ready to believe that.

I pick up Dusty back at my place, change out of my funeral clothes and head back to the office. All the while, I'm thinking about what my next steps are, and I want to make some notes.

Two murders, and no substantial leads. Just the suggestion that the boys working on Granger's renovations back in 1992 had a falling-out and that's when the body was hidden. What was the falling-out about? And why did Paddy Sullivan pick up and leave town afterwards and never come back?

Maybe I can get answers from Jonas Miller's widow.

I also want to talk to Dylan Polasek. He didn't work on the renovation, but was a good friend of Sullivan's. Plus, I want to know what Dylan's daddy and Gil Webb were arguing about, an argument that distressed Dylan, and which was so heated that Oscar Grant remembered it. It likely had nothing to do with my thirty-year-old body, but it happened around the same time, so I want to check it out.

Dylan's daddy, Tim, was killed in an industrial accident, so he's out of the picture. But Gil Webb is still around. Maybe he can recall what the fight with Tim was about.

Another thread I want to pursue is the odd article we found in Paddy Sullivan's belongings about the accountant, Andrew Eastman. There has to be a reason Paddy kept it. I look up Andrew Eastman and he has a large accounting office in Bobtail.

I'll talk to him to find out what his connection was with Paddy Sullivan.

I'm getting ready to go home when my phone rings. It's Allison's friend Carina. 'I'm calling you back,' she says cautiously. 'Do I know you?'

I tell her who I am. 'I understand you're a friend of Allison Gleason.'

'That's right.' Still sounding suspicious. 'Did something happen to Allison?'

'I don't know if you've heard, but she's gotten herself into a little trouble in Mexico.'

'Mexico? What's she doing there?' There's rustling in the background. She's busy with something else.

'I was hoping you could tell me.'

'No clue. If you know Allison, you know you can't ever tell what she's going to do next.'

'When was the last time you saw her?'

She's quiet for a minute. 'I don't know, three weeks ago?'

'And she didn't say she was planning to go to Mexico?'

'Nope. I wish I could help you, but . . .' She's getting impatient.

'This is a little delicate. Do you know if Allison was involved in drugs at all?'

'What do you mean involved? She dabbled a little, like everybody does.'

'But she wouldn't have been in Mexico to buy drugs or sell them?'

'Oh, hell no. She's not that stupid. Did somebody say that's what she was doing?'

'No, she was in an auto accident and she's been arrested. There was some suggestion that her visit to Mexico was drug-related.'

'That's not true. So when you say arrested, you mean she's in jail? Yikes! Why? Wouldn't they just fine her? Was somebody hurt?'

'I don't know if anyone was hurt, but she had no auto insurance to be driving in Mexico.'

'That is so dumb! But it sounds like Allison.'

'Carina, do you know anyone who might know anything

about her trip? If she was traveling with someone? Or what her plans were?'

'I could ask around, but you know Allison is impulsive.' She sounds dubious. 'She might have decided on the spur of the moment to go down there.'

'I'd appreciate it if you'd ask her friends. And please call if you have any success.'

'Sure.'

TWENTY-SIX

I call Wendy Sunday morning to see if she'd like to go somewhere to take her mind off things, but she says she promised Tammy she'd take her to the movies. 'You want to come with us?'

I hear something in her voice that alerts me. 'What movie?'

She chuckles. It's a good sound that she hasn't made recently. 'It's called *Senior Year* and, trust me, as much as I'd like your company, you don't want to be roped into coming with us to see that.'

'I suddenly remember I have a lot of work to do,' I say.

'I'll bet. Anyway, come for dinner,' she says. 'I'm going to try to make Tammy spend the night at her house.'

'No, we'll go out.'

I wanted to spend the day with Wendy, but since she's busy, I have plenty to do.

I call Andy Eastman, who says his family is involved in a church garage sale all afternoon and it would be easier for him to see me tomorrow. We arrange to meet on his lunch hour.

Jonas Miller's widow doesn't answer her phone and neither does Dylan Polasek. I don't leave messages. My last possibility to get something done today does pan out. Gil Webb lived most of his working life in Bryan/College Station, which is where his business was, but he has since moved back here to Jarrett Creek. He's home and says he'll be glad to talk to me. 'Otherwise I have to make up a different excuse not to paint the garage.'

He lives in the older part of town, in a house that's been spruced up in the last few years. Like many of the older homes, it's made of native rock. The trim is painted a cream color that looks nice with the rock. Somebody in the family is a gardener. Alongside the house there are beds of mature vegetables – green beans and zucchini, and some melons. And the front is a riot of bright color – orange, deep blue, and yellow.

'Come in, come in,' Gil says when he answers the door. 'I've poured us some tea. We can sit in the shade in the back.' He's around seventy, with a hearty manner.

The backyard is as well-kept as the front. We sit at an iron table in the back in the shade of pecan trees. Gil says his wife is the gardener. 'She's at it all day, every day. We didn't have a big yard in our place in Bryan, so she really likes it here.'

'What brought you back?'

'We liked Bryan, but when my folks died they left us this place and since I was close to retirement, we decided to come back. We're both from here and we have friends, and my wife's brother lives a couple blocks away. Now, what brings you here?'

'I guess you heard about the body that was found in Granger's Feed Store.'

He holds his hands up. 'I swear, I didn't do it.'

'Well, that takes care of that.'

He laughs.

'Gil, we haven't identified the body, and I'm trying to get a handle on who it is. As you can imagine, the leads from that far back are scarce. But I talked to Oscar Grant and he remembered something from back then that you might know something about. There was an argument that you were involved in. With Tim Polasek.'

He chews his bottom lip, frowning. 'Doesn't come to mind.'

'From what I was told, it sounded like the squabble got pretty heated.'

'Huh. Was there alcohol involved, by any chance?'

'I believe there was. Anyway, Oscar said that Wayne Singletary intervened, and—'

'Oh, wait a minute. I do remember that because I was surprised to see Singletary there. He wasn't a drinking man.

And I was surprised when he butted into the argument. But the argument wasn't between me and Tim, it was between Tim and his son, Dylan. And when Singletary tried to calm them down, the son got even madder. Oscar told everybody to calm the hell down or go home.'

'OK, listen. This is important. Can you remember what the argument was about?'

Webb shifts in his seat and clicks his tongue. 'I really don't recall. That's a long time ago. Why is it important, anyway? How can that argument have anything to do with that man whose body was found?'

'I don't know, Gil, I'm pretty much fishing for information now. Tim Polasek's younger son, Eddie, was working on the renovation that was going on at the feed store then, and that's when the body was hidden. I'm looking for anybody who remembers anything that could help me identify the man. And of course anybody who could help me figure out who killed him.'

He's shaking his head. 'I don't believe Tim Polasek would have anything to do with killing a man.'

'You and Polasek were friends?'

'Yeah, we went way back. He was a good man.'

'I heard he was killed in an industrial accident.'

'Industrial? Not exactly. He worked for Gordon's Farm Equipment. The accident was one of those stupid freak things. A combine they rented out came back with a balky motor. Tim was tinkering with it and somehow the thing started up and he fell into the feeder.'

'How long ago was that?'

'I don't know. Fifteen years?'

Gordon's Farm Equipment. I heard that name recently. It takes me a few seconds but then I remember. 'His son Dylan works there, right?'

He nods. 'The owner, Jess Gordon, kept Dylan on after what happened to Tim, even though Dylan was struggling. He had some addiction problems. Gordon felt some responsibility to him with his daddy gone. I admired Gordon for that. Dylan can't be the best employee, sort of a shiftless kid who's grown into a shiftless man. Although, maybe he's come around. I haven't talked to Gordon in a while. I should give him a call. His wife had a bout of cancer. I think she's OK now.'

That tendency to gossip that Oscar mentioned . . .

I ask Webb to think more on the argument and, if he comes up with any better memory, to call me.

In the late afternoon, Maria calls. She sounds perky. 'I told you I got the location of the accident, so I went there to look around. It was a basic intersection, with stop signs.

'It's Sunday, and I figure I'll have more luck with witnesses during the week, but I wanted to get a head start. I did talk to a few people on the street and I found this old guy who kind of camps out on a bench there in a little pocket park. He told me something interesting. Allison's car didn't run a stop sign, the other car did.'

'Uh oh. So she's being set up.'

'Sounds like it. Anyway, there was a passenger in the back seat of the car that hit Allison. The guy saw the driver turn around and say something to his passenger. Because it was dark he couldn't see the passenger, but he thought it must be somebody important because, when the driver got out of the car, the guy saw he was wearing a uniform, like a chauffeur.'

'That's good to know. You did well. I'm surprised no one else saw the accident if it was a car involving someone important enough to be driven around town.'

'With it being Sunday, I knew shop owners and people who work around there wouldn't be around. But I wanted to get started and I hit it lucky. Tomorrow people will be back at work, and now that I've got one witness, I may be able to persuade somebody to corroborate his story.'

'Trouble is,' I say, 'if the passenger was somebody important, people who witnessed the accident may not want to get involved. But one witness may be enough.'

'Usually, yes. But in this case, I doubt it.'

'What do you mean?'

She sighs. 'When I talked to him he was drinking, and not very coherent. I had to really persist to get this information from him. And I have a feeling he's drunk most of the time. So not a great witness.'

'At least you've got some information we didn't have before. One thing. It seems odd that Allison would drive down to Mexico by herself. Seems like she'd want to be with a friend. Did your witness mention if anyone was with her?'

'No, but I didn't ask. I'll do that.'

That night, I take Wendy to one of our favorite restaurants near her place. She tells me the movie was as sappy as she thought it would be. 'But Tammy loved it, so I guess that's a win.'

I wanted to wait until we were in the restaurant before I told her what I heard from Maria.

'Oh, my God. So it wasn't Allison's fault?'

'That's what it sounds like. Maria is going to try to find other witnesses so she can build a case.' I don't tell her the witness she has might not be the best.

'I'm still aggravated with Allison. She won't talk to me, got herself into a pickle and I'm having to bail her out. I have half a mind to let her stew for a while.'

I know she doesn't really mean that.

'Look, the news from Maria is good. Sit with that for now.'

TWENTY-SEVEN

I talk to Hernandez first thing Monday and tell him what Maria found out.

'Interesting. I'm going to call my contact at the Embassy and tell her. It may light a fire under somebody.'

I call Jonas Miller's widow and this time she's home. 'I don't know that I can be of help, but come on over.' She gives me her address in Burton.

As I'm leaving, I get a call from Martha Olderman at city hall. 'I'm sorry, Chief, I've scoured the tax and utility records and couldn't find anybody who dropped off the rolls. I don't know what else I can do.'

'I appreciate your effort. It was a long shot anyway.'

'Could be it was somebody who didn't live here.'

'Maybe so.' And when I hang up I realize that, if that's true, I may never find out who he was. It would be ironic if I made such a fuss with Reagan and then couldn't solve the case.

The trip to Burton takes a half-hour, through usually green countryside, but at this time of year everything looks tinder-dry.

Jonas's widow lives in a double-wide trailer in a well-maintained trailer park, with grassy areas, trees, and flower beds. I knock on the door and she opens it right away. She's careworn and I wonder how she's making ends meet with her husband gone.

But the inside of the trailer is spotless and she has a little puff of a white dog who jumps all over me, then sniffs my pant legs for 'news' of Dusty, who I didn't bring.

'Fluffy, get down. Don't bother Chief Craddock,' she says.

'It's fine, I've got a dog of my own.'

I hear the sound of a machine in the other room and what sounds like a TV. I look toward the sound.

'That's my daughter Leona. She's a seamstress. I don't know how she does it. She sews twelve hours a day and never seems to get tired of it. But she keeps entertained because she watches all the soap operas and talk shows while she works.'

'How about you? Do you have a job?'

She gives me a wan smile. 'You want to know whether I'm OK with money with Jonas gone. That's kind. But we're fine. Jonas wasn't a ball of fire, but he had sense enough to leave me with a little life insurance policy. I work part-time at a dentist's office. Between Leona and me, we're better off than some.'

'I'm sorry to hear about your husband. Covid took too many, too young.'

'Jonas had diabetes and he didn't take good care of himself. I'm just sorry he had to suffer at the end.' Her eyes tear up and she swallows. 'He was a good husband and we had a lot of fun together.'

I tell her that I lost my wife a few years back, so I know it's hard. 'I hope you can help me with a case I'm working on. This goes back thirty years. And your husband may have known something about it.'

'I didn't know Jonas then. We met at junior college in Bobtail.'

'Well, maybe he told you something about what I'm asking.'

We sit down in the small, cozy living room and she seems interested.

'Back when Jonas was in high school, one summer he worked doing renovations on the feed store in town. Did he ever talk about that?'

'He mentioned it. Let me get my daughter in here. He was always telling stories and the kids paid more attention than I did.'

She gets up and goes to the back of the trailer and I hear her say something. She comes back followed by a skinny woman wearing glasses, and stooped slightly.

Her mamma introduces her and tells her what I've asked.

'Oh, yeah, Daddy told us about that. He always tried to make us laugh and he had a story about everything.' She has a nice voice, melodic.

'Anything in particular you remember?'

She blows out a breath in a whoosh. 'Let me think about it for a minute. I'm going to get myself a glass of tea. You want one? And what about you, Mamma?'

Neither of us takes her up on it. She walks into the little kitchen at the end of the living area, and takes her time, but I can tell she's pondering my question. When she comes back, she sits next to her mamma on the loveseat. 'Now this is going to sound odd, because it was,' she says. 'He told us that when they were working on that building, one morning the guys came in and somebody had put in some flooring overnight. Nobody would confess that they'd done it. He told us they decided it had been elves that came in and did the work. We were young when he told the story to us, so I remember thinking there really were such a thing as elves.' She laughs.

I ask more questions, but there's no more to be gleaned from Jonas Miller's family. Still, what Jonas's daughter remembered verified that somebody who hid that body had enough carpentry skills to lay some floor in afterwards.

On the way back to Jarrett Creek, I think about the man who was killed thirty years ago. No one seems to have missed whoever it was. It seems likely he was from somewhere else, but if so, what was he doing in Jarrett Creek? He must have had people there, someone who would have noticed that he was gone. Could be he was visiting friends or family and got caught up with someone on the way out of town, and ended up dead. He could have been walking along the highway and was the victim of a hit-and-run, or some other accident. But even if that happened, when he didn't show up back home, somebody would have missed him. Somebody would have tried to find out what happened to him.

Unless no one wanted to find him. Unless they were glad he didn't come home. What kind of man would that suggest?

At the highway, instead of going north toward Jarrett Creek, I head south to Bobtail. Maybe I'll find Dylan Polasek at work.

On the way, I call headquarters and talk to Connor, who's had some back issues and is trying to take it easy. He says it's quiet. Brick is supposed to come in this afternoon and he's going to take the squad car to be washed. I tell Connor to go home when Brick gets there.

Gordon's Farm Equipment is a big, sprawling place on the south side of Bobtail. There is a main store, flanked by a couple of warehouses. In the field at the back I see the larger farm equipment 'For Sale or Rent.' Tractors, big and small; combines; plows; and others not so easy to identify.

In the store, I'm greeted by a hearty man in jeans and a Harley Davidson T-shirt, with a red and green plaid vest, and a name tag that says, 'Hi, I'm Gary.'

'Gary, I'm looking for Dylan Polasek. Is he here today?'

His sunny smile clouds up. 'No, he isn't. Tell you the truth, he called in and quit this morning. Can I help you?'

'No, I need to ask him some questions.'

'You a lawman?'

'Samuel Craddock. Chief of Police over in Jarrett Creek.'

'Is Polasek in trouble?'

'Not that I know of. I just have some questions about a matter I'm investigating. Is there a manager?'

'That would be me.'

'You got an address and phone number for Polasek?'

'Yep. In the office.'

We walk to the back of the store, to a large office. Gary heads over to a tall file cabinet and opens one of the drawers. 'He just quit without notice?' I ask.

He pauses and turns to look at me. 'Yes, and I'm not really surprised. Not that anybody's going to miss him.'

'Why is that?'

'Oh, he's nice enough. But he never pulled his weight. He's been here some fifteen-odd years, and never seemed to take to it. My daddy is the owner of the company and he hired Dylan when his daddy was killed on the job. Kind of a favor.' He raises his brows. 'Between you and me, I don't know what kind of work would suit him.' He stops. 'I shouldn't bad-mouth him, I'm annoyed that he left us in the lurch. It's not so easy finding help these days.'

He pulls out a file folder, sits at his desk and opens it. 'Our newer employees are on the computer, but we haven't gotten around to entering the older employees' information.' He jots down Dylan's address. 'I hope everything is OK,' he says, when he hands me the printout. 'He's not a bad guy, just not a ball of fire. I don't think he was ever suited to being in a nine-to-five job.'

I call Dylan again from my car, but there's no answer. Even so, on a whim I drive to his place. I've arranged to talk to Andrew Eastman at his office at noon, so I have time.

Dylan lives on the east side of town, in an area not exactly run-down, but looking like it could use a few cans of paint and some power washing. Dylan's place is a duplex, no worse than the surrounding houses. The front yard is patchy grass, with dead areas, but not overgrown. He doesn't answer my knock, and neither does the neighbor.

I walk around the side and call out in case he's in back. It's a small yard with a straggly post oak. Behind the yard along the back is an alley with carports. The ones directly behind the house are empty. Maybe Dylan got another job, or is out looking for one.

TWENTY-EIGHT

A ndrew Eastman is a slender guy in his forties with close-set eyes behind thick glasses, and hair slicked over to one side to hide a balding spot. He's wearing tan slacks and a blue sport jacket over a white shirt, with a striped tie. Could be an accountant's uniform in my experience.

He has a ready smile and his handshake is firm. He says to call him Andy. 'You hungry? I thought we could go down the street and have some lunch while we talk.'

We walk to a café a block away, where Eastman is greeted cheerfully. The waitress, a girl aged about twenty, asks if he wants the usual and he says he does.

'What's good?' I ask.

'I get the chili, but I'm a big fan of chili. If you don't want that, their sandwiches are good. And their fried chicken.'

'Fried chicken is a lunch special today,' the waitress said. 'And it's really good.'

'Can't beat that salesmanship,' I say, so I order it.

'So what can I do for you?' Eastman asked. 'I must admit I was intrigued by your call. I don't have much cause to talk to the police.'

I describe the body found under the floor, and finish up by telling him that someone else was killed in the feed store. 'His name was Michael Sullivan, went by the name of Paddy. We still don't have an identification for the body from thirty years ago.'

'Wow, you've got your hands full.'

'I could be wrong, but I'm going on the assumption that the two deaths are linked. If I can identify the body we found under the floor, I suspect I'll have a better idea of who killed Sullivan.'

He gives a puzzled smile. 'I'm not sure how you think I can help with that.'

'I'm not either. The reason your name came up is that when I was investigating Sullivan's murder, I found this in his belongings.' I hand him the article we found in the box in Sullivan's attic, with the attached note that said, *We done good.*

Eastman scans the article. 'Yeah, that was a nice article.'

'I'm wondering why Sullivan would have kept this. And what this note meant.'

He looks baffled. 'I don't have a clue.'

'His name doesn't mean anything to you?'

He grimaces. 'I'm sorry, it doesn't.'

'His wife suggested that maybe he helped you by donating money for your education. Is that possible?'

'I got a full ride scholarship to Texas A & M. And my step-daddy took care of anything else I needed.'

Our food comes and we tuck in. I'm still trying to find anything that might tie him to the murders, however obliquely. 'Did you ever live in Jarrett Creek?'

'No, but I've visited there a lot. I have cousins there.'

I can't even hope. 'Who are your cousins?'

'Oh, they don't live there anymore. One of them lives here in Bobtail, and one in Dallas. Although my Aunt Hazel is still there.'

'Hazel Moore is your aunt?'

'Yes, sir. My mamma's sister-in-law.'

'So Tim Polasek was your mamma's brother?' My pulse speeds up. Something feels like it's going to fall into place.

'That's right.'

'Do you keep up with Dylan and Eddie?'

He takes a sip of ice tea. 'Eddie not at all. I mean, I see him at Christmas at his mamma's house most years, but we don't have much to say to each other. He was always a little aloof. But I see Dylan sometimes. Not often. Joan and I have three kids and they keep us busy. All of them doing sports. I was the least sporty person you ever met, so where they got that, I don't know.' He laughs, but I can see the pride in his eyes.

But then his mood changes and he looks rueful. 'I'm sorry I don't see more of Dylan. When we were kids he was really kind to me. I needed a friend, and he was good to me. He was eight years older and he was my hero.'

'What changed?'

'I don't know. After he got out of high school, we didn't see as much of him. My mom remarried and I've always gotten along with my stepdad, so it seemed like I didn't need Dylan's guidance quite as much.' He pauses, reflecting. 'Also, we were very different, and that became more apparent as we got older. Dylan never figured out what he wanted to do with his life. In college I found out I liked dealing with numbers and I gravitated toward being a CPA. After college, I set up the business here in Bobtail and made a go of it.'

'But Dylan not so much.'

'Right.' He sighs. 'I don't think Dylan resents me exactly, but it's like he's embarrassed that he didn't make more of himself. Plus, he was into drugs for a while. Got into a motorcycle accident that left him a little wonky.' He sits back and pushes his empty bowl away. 'I'm having pie. You want some? They make the best lemon meringue pie in the world.'

'Say no more.'

He orders the pie and then glances at his watch. 'I don't know whether I've been able to help you at all.'

He thinks we're almost done, but I have more questions, some real ones. 'You said your mom remarried. When did she and your daddy divorce?'

He shakes his head. 'I don't know the details. Daddy left us when I was twelve years old. Just took off. Never saw him again.'

'Must have been hard at your age for your daddy to skip out.' I'm going to proceed carefully. I don't want to jump to conclusions, but for Eastman's daddy to disappear thirty years ago seems to dovetail with that body.

His smile is grim. 'Not so much. He was not a great family man. Didn't treat us right.'

The waitress sets down the pie and coffee. I take a bite. 'You're right. It's pretty good pie.'

We eat a few bites and then I say, 'If your mamma remarried, your daddy must have agreed to a divorce.'

'Must have, I don't know, I never asked. All I know is that I was glad she married my stepdaddy.'

'You said your daddy took off. You know where he went?'

'Colorado. He called us from there sometimes, but Mamma didn't know why he'd decided to go there.'

'So you talked to him in Colorado?'

'I didn't, no. Mamma didn't want me to talk to him when he called.' He hunches over, leaning close as if he doesn't want to be overheard. 'That's not exactly true. Truth is, I didn't want to talk to him. I was afraid of him. He was mean. I don't think he was cut out to be a daddy. I try to make up for it with my kids.'

I found out both more and less than I wanted to from Eastman. Less, because he couldn't tell me why Paddy Sullivan would have kept that article. And more, because now I know that Eddie and Dylan Polasek were his cousins and that his daddy disappeared. I'm going to talk to Hazel again and see if I can tease out something more. And I need to question Andy Eastman's mother. I got her phone number from him.

I call Dylan again, but he's still not answering.

But Andy Eastman's mother is in and says she'll talk to me, although she sounds hesitant.

Cheryl Eastman is an attractive woman in her sixties. Andy looks a lot like her, the same friendly brown eyes and light brown hair. She suggests we go to the back deck. 'I like to be outside,' she says. 'I don't care how hot it is, I don't like to be cooped up.'

As we pass through the kitchen, I note that her refrigerator door is covered with children's art. 'My grandkids. They're pre-teens now and they're embarrassed that I keep those things up. But I like to remember when they were little.'

The back deck is shaded and looks over a well-tended lawn. We sit down in wooden chairs with colorful cushions. She sighs with contentment and smiles as she asks what I want to talk to her about.

'I spoke with your son Andy, and he told me his cousins are Eddie and Dylan Polasek. So that makes you Hazel Moore's sister-in-law.'

'That's right.' She looks puzzled.

'She was married to your brother, Tim. And he died in an accident.'

She nods. 'Horrible accident.'

'The reason I'm interested has to do with a man who was

shot and killed a couple of weeks ago in Jarrett Creek. His
name was Paddy Sullivan. When we searched his belongings,
I found an article about your son, from when he opened his
office here in town.'

'I'm awfully proud of him.'

'The thing is, I wondered why Sullivan would have kept that
article.'

She laughs. 'Lord, I hope nobody goes through my things
and wonders why I've kept clippings and photos. I don't
remember myself. He probably stuck it away and forgot
about it.'

'Could be. But there was a note attached to it that said, "We
done good."'

She winces. 'Grammar! Forgive me, but I taught fourth grade
for many years. I can't abide bad grammar.'

I chuckle. 'Bad grammar aside, the note implies that your
son's success was due to someone's intervention. At first I
thought maybe he had had financial help with school. That's
what Sullivan's wife suggested. But your son said he never
needed any financial help, that his schooling was paid for
between a scholarship and help from his stepdad.'

'That's right. My second husband was more than happy to
help with both our kids' education.'

'You have another child?'

'My husband had a daughter from his first marriage. His wife
died of cancer when the girl was ten, so she and my son were
the same age when Curt and I married.'

'Andy tells me his daddy took off and left the family.'

Her open expression shuts down, her mouth tightening. 'And
we were better off for it. My first husband was not a nice man.'

'In what way?'

She looks startled. 'Andy didn't tell you? He hit me. And
Andy, too. You'd think it was from drinking, but he was a
teetotaler. He just had a hair-trigger temper. Anything could set
him off. We walked around on alert all the time. Tell you the
truth, I'm surprised Andy came out of it so well-adjusted. I
credit my husband Curt for that. He sat Andy down and told
him we were starting over and he would never hit him for any
reason. He said he expected Andy to do his best to behave, but

if he got out of line, they'd talk about it and there'd be no physical violence involved.'

'Sounds like a good man.'

'A saint. He treats me so well.' She tilts her chin up as if challenging me to argue with her.

'Did you change your name when you remarried?'

'I couldn't wait to change my name. I wanted nothing of that man's name.'

'What was his name?'

'Tolleson. Lamar Tolleson.'

'How did you manage to divorce him? Did you send him papers?'

Her expression clouds up. For the first time she looks wary. 'Is that important?'

The only reason it's important is if she actually didn't know where he was, so he couldn't consent to a divorce. But I'm not going to pursue that line yet. 'Not really. But let me ask you. Did anything in particular happen that made Tolleson decide to leave when he did?'

She's knitting her hands together. 'This is hard for me to talk about. Andy seems to have come out OK, but I still have traumatic memories from it. Yes, something did happen. Apparently someone told my brother, Tim, that Lamar had hit me. And Tim said he visited Lamar at work and told him if he ever laid another finger on me again, he'd kill him.'

'When did you find this out? Before Lamar left? Or after?'

'It was a few weeks after. You have to understand, Lamar left us high and dry. I didn't work back then because Lamar wouldn't allow it. When he left, I had to go to my brother for financial help. That's when he told me he'd threatened Lamar. He said he hoped that's why Lamar had skipped town.'

'Do you know who told your brother about the abuse?'

'He said a friend of his told him. I don't know how the friend knew. It's embarrassing to think our business was the subject of gossip.'

I wonder if it was Gil Webb who told Tim Polasek that his sister was being beaten up by her husband. And why he didn't mention that when we talked.

'Where did Lamar work at the time?'

'He was an auto mechanic, worked at a garage downtown, so he made good money. But of course when he left us, there was no paycheck.'

'How long ago was this?'

'Well, let me see. Andy was twelve and now he's forty-two. So I guess thirty years ago.'

Coincidence? I doubt it.

'Did you hear from him after he left?' Andy said his daddy had called, but I want to be sure she had the same story.

'Once or twice. He said he'd gone to Colorado. Surprised me. I don't know why he decided to go there.'

'Did he have family there? Friends?'

'His folks lived on the east coast, South Carolina, and as far as I know he didn't have anybody in Colorado.'

'Do you remember how he sounded when he called?'

She cocks her head. 'I remember every word. I'll never get it out of my mind. I was terrified he'd want to come back. But he sounded like he was set on staying there. I thought maybe he'd been abusive because he didn't like having a family to take care of. Whatever the reason, I was glad he was gone.'

I hesitate with the next question. It's loaded. 'You sure it was him on the phone?'

She goes still, and then makes a sound like a half-laugh. 'Good question. Maybe it wasn't him. Maybe that's why he sounded happy for a change.' She frowns. 'But if it wasn't him, who was it?'

'Did you get a phone number for him?'

'I did. I told him I needed to be able to get in touch with him in case something happened to Andy.'

'Do you still have it?'

'Maybe. I can look.'

'If you would.'

It takes several minutes, but eventually she comes back with a little black book. 'This is an old book that I threw in the back of a drawer. The number's here.' She hands it to me and I jot it down.

I tuck it into my shirt pocket and get up. 'You still friendly with Hazel?'

She shrugs. 'We have a family get-together at Christmas, but that's about it. After Tim died, we didn't have much to talk about. Our kids. Grandkids.'

'You ever run into your nephew, Dylan?'

A shadow crosses her face. 'Well, Dylan. He's not an easy person to know. I love him, of course, and he was good to Andy in the days when Lamar was so cruel. He changed after his daddy died. Got moody. I think Andy keeps up with him, but I only see him with the family at Christmas.

'Mrs Eastman, do you remember Lamar's birth date?'

She reels it off. 'He'll be sixty-nine.'

If he's still alive.

TWENTY-NINE

Finally, a missing person. And one who seems to have deserved to disappear, which would account for why no one was looking for him. Supposedly gone to Colorado.

As soon as I get back to work, I call the number Cheryl Eastman gave me for him. I get the three-tone sound that tells me it's either a wrong number or disconnected. I'm not surprised, but it may not mean anything. He could have moved out of Colorado. Or died. If he was ever in Colorado to begin with.

I turn to Google. I find a surprising number of men named Lamar Tolleson, but no one who would fit his age. I enter the name into the database law officers use, and come up with a Lamar Tolleson who was in jail for a time for petty theft in Houston. But he's forty years old.

I enter the phone number into a national database for identification and it comes back that the number belonged to a now-defunct grocery store. It's possible he was working at the grocery store and used their number for personal calls. It takes me a while, but I manage to track down the son of the previous owner of the grocery store, who says he never heard of anyone named Lamar Tolleson. 'And the store was a mom-and-pop operation. My folks are both gone, but I can tell you they never hired anybody. Us kids worked in the store, but it was mostly Papa and Mamma.'

With growing certainty, I sit back and ponder what it means that whoever called Cheryl Eastman and said he was her husband gave her a fake phone number. Was it Tolleson and he didn't want her to track him down? Or was it someone pretending to be Tolleson? Does it make sense that she didn't recognize that the man she spoke to wasn't her husband? Did she know he was dead, and concocted the Colorado story?

And what about her second marriage? In Texas, you don't have to prove you're divorced in order to get a marriage license. Although if you remarry knowing your spouse is alive, you can be prosecuted for bigamy.

It's easy enough to track down the certificate of marriage. She and Curtis Eastman married two years after Tolleson disappeared. So either she's a bigamist, or she knew her husband was dead. Which is it?

At the heart of it is whether her former husband is dead or alive. I have to get a DNA sample from Andy Eastman so a comparison can be run on the mummified body. If there's no match, I'm at a dead end. But my bet is on the match.

I call Eastman, who sounds busy. 'Sorry to interrupt. I need to see you first thing tomorrow. What time do you get to work?'

'Eight. What's this about?'

I don't want to alarm him and keep him up all night, so I say, 'An idea I had. Let's talk about it tomorrow.'

He agrees to eight o'clock.

It's after five when Maria calls. 'I've had a little more success,' she says. I recognize that sound of satisfaction in her voice.

'Tell me.'

'I found another couple of people who witnessed the accident. It happened in front of a strip mall with little shops, in a nice residential area. The two people I found who would talk to me at all didn't want me to use their names because they know the car that was involved belongs to the wife of a city council member, and she's vindictive. They worry that if she found out who talked, she'd have their business licenses revoked.'

'Were they able to tell you the same information that the man you talked to earlier gave you?'

'Oh, yes. But there's more. I talked to a barber, who saw the accident clearly from his shop. I asked him why he was working after dark and he said he's open until eight most nights. Anyway, he happened to be standing outside with his last client when the accident happened. He told it exactly the same. Except for one thing.' Her voice is practically gleeful. 'You remember when you asked if Allison was alone? Well, you hit the jackpot. Not only was she not alone, but listen to this. Allison wasn't driving.'

'What?' I was about to take a sip of coffee, but I bang the cup down.

'That's right. The barber said that right after the accident, a man got out of the driver's seat of the car Allison was in, and took off running. It was evening, so although he saw the guy get out of the car, he didn't see him well. But as soon as the guy took off, Allison ran around and got in the driver's seat. I asked him how it was possible that no one noticed. He said he didn't know, that people probably didn't pay much attention because it wasn't much of an accident.'

'That changes things entirely.'

'Not just that. He said the police came maybe ten minutes after the accident, but then some guys in suits arrived in a big SUV and chased the cops away and took Allison away themselves.'

'Did he have any idea who was in the SUV?'

'He thinks it was the municipal police department, not the local. He explained to me that there are two police departments. The suburb where the accident happened is policed by a general police force. The city itself is under the jurisdiction of the Policia Regia. He thinks that's who came and picked up Allison.'

'Why would they do that?'

'He didn't know, but I talked to another woman who has a restaurant there. She also saw the guy with Allison get out of the car and the guys in the SUV pick her up. She said if the wife of the city council member called her husband, he probably wanted the city police to take charge. That way he could have control of the situation.'

'I wonder where the guy who was actually driving went? And why Allison tried to make them believe she was driving.'

'That's not hard to understand. The law treats women better than men in jail.'

'Hernandez said that the consulate officer he talked to said Allison was in a comfortable situation. With those men taking her away, I wonder if she's even in jail.'

'The lawyer I talked to said she might be somewhere under house arrest because the authorities want to keep her safe. In jail she'd be likely to be beaten up.'

'So have you talked to the police?'

'No, I wanted to get all my ammunition together before I approach them. I'm glad I waited, because now I know I need to talk to the city police, not the suburban police.'

'It sounds to me like you've got all the information you need.'

'Almost. Let me poke around a little more. Maybe go to the mayor's office. Maybe try to talk to the woman who was in the other car and tell her I have a witness who said her driver was at fault.'

'Maria, be careful. I don't need to have two people in jail in Mexico.'

'I'm not too worried. As it turns out, I got in touch with the guy who's friends with my cousin. His father is a judge. And he swears his daddy isn't corrupt.'

I start laughing. Maria seems to have connections everywhere.

She doesn't laugh, but her voice is pleased. 'Anyway, he said he'd make some phone calls tomorrow to make sure I won't get in trouble.'

'OK, play whatever angles you can, but remember, I want Allison home, but I also want you to stay safe.'

I call Chuck Hernandez to run Maria's information past him. I reach his secretary, who tells me he was in court today, and is probably having a drink at the local pub where lawyers go after hours. 'He'll want to talk to you. I'll call over to the bar and have him get back to you.'

When Chuck calls a few minutes later, I can hardly hear him for the noise in the background, but then he apparently steps outside because it's abruptly quiet.

'That's interesting news,' he says, when I tell him what Maria said. 'Your deputy did a good job to turn that up. Maybe I should hire her for my team,'

'Don't even think about it,' I say. 'She's my deputy and I'm not giving her up.'

He laughs. 'I'd like to know who the guy is who was driving Allison's car. I don't suppose Wendy or her other daughter would know.'

'I doubt it.' I tell him I have someone trying to find out that information. I haven't heard back from Carina, but she didn't seem all that excited to help me in the first place. She's supposed to be Allison's best friend, but she seemed pretty casual about Allison's situation. Maybe it's time for me to give her some particulars as to what Allison could be facing if I don't find out who the man was who was actually driving the car in the accident.

I call Carina and, as expected, she doesn't answer. I remember that my grand-niece Hailey told me recently that young people don't use the phone except with 'old people.' She said they text. So I text Carina that it's urgent that I talk to her. Ten minutes later, when I'm walking into my house, she phones.

'I don't have much time. I'm going to a party. What do you need?'

'First, have you found out anything about Allison's trip?'

'Um, I talked to a couple of people, but they said they didn't know anything.'

'Well, it turns out that witnesses say Allison wasn't actually driving. There was a guy driving and, when the accident happened, he fled the scene and left Allison to take the blame.'

'Oh, shit. That sounds like J.D.' For the first time, she sounds interested.

'Is that her boyfriend?'

'Not really. They hang out together sometimes. Somebody said they'd seen them together recently. He's not good for her. He's even more impulsive than she is. And not the smartest guy, either. I can see them deciding on the spur of the moment to go down to Mexico. No plans. No insurance. Nothing. And I can absolutely see him ditching her to face the cops.'

'You have a last name for him?'

'Nance.'

'Phone number?'

'I can get it.' She finally sounds like she's taking this seriously. 'I may not get right back to you, but I'll text you. OK?'

After I hang up, I'm restless, impatient for tomorrow to get here. I scare up some leftovers to heat up, and barely notice what I'm eating while I decide what to do next.

Afterwards I pace around with Dusty following me until I tell him to go to bed. He slinks off, looking worried, as only a dog can.

I think I'm getting somewhere on the mummy case, but there are still knotty questions. Did the same person who killed the man we found under the floorboards also kill Sullivan? If that corpse is Lamar Tolleson, I have a handle on why he was killed. He was abusive, which several people apparently knew about. And when he disappeared, nobody seems to have looked too closely at the explanation of where he went. Logically, someone close to Cheryl killed him. Or she might have done it herself, although how would she have gotten him to the feed store to stow him under the floorboards? And why?

I'm even more convinced that one of the boys working on the renovation was responsible for stashing his body. They may not have been directly responsible for killing him, but they may have known who did, and were willing to help disappear him. They knew that tucking him away under freshly laid flooring was a way to ensure he might never be found. And he wouldn't have been found if Mark Granger hadn't had the wild idea to do a new renovation. But why did they bury him first and then move the body?

THIRTY

I manage to sleep, but am up early Tuesday and on the road to Bobtail by seven thirty.

Andy ushers me into his office, looking a little nervous. The office is as tidy as I would have imagined. An inbox, an outbox and photos of his family on his desk. He doesn't go behind his desk, but sits down with me at a little conversation area.

'Something tells me this isn't going to be quite as innocuous as you made it sound last night.'

'Andy, have you ever considered that maybe your daddy didn't go to Colorado? That maybe he died?'

His smile is haunting. Tired and vulnerable. 'Only about a thousand times. I once asked Mamma, but she shut me down. So you think the guy whose body was found in that feed store might be him?'

I nod. I see no reason to hold back.

'But I don't understand why Mamma would tell me she was getting phone calls from him. Why not just tell me he left and she never heard from him?'

'Could be because she didn't want you to worry. But it also could be that someone called her and pretended to be your daddy.'

He looks stunned. 'Why?'

'Because whoever killed him – if it is him, remember we don't know for sure – might have wanted to make sure she didn't raise an alarm. Even if she was abused, she might have felt some loyalty to him. After all, she did marry him and he was your daddy.'

'Not much of a daddy. I don't mind telling you that if that man turns out to be him, I won't mourn.'

He might be surprised. No matter how much he thinks he's put his ordeal with his daddy behind him, there's always that little hope in the back of someone's mind that the abuser will change and come back to make amends.

'To know for sure, I need a DNA sample from you. Will you do that?'

He rubs a hand across his mouth. 'My wife said you'd probably want that.'

'You told her what we discussed yesterday?'

'Of course. I count on her opinion.'

'And what was her opinion?'

'To do it. She said it's best that I know the truth, no matter what.'

I'm relieved. Even the most reasonable people can sometimes

balk at the idea of having their DNA taken. Some kind of visceral taboo at work. I take out the DNA collection kit I brought 'in case,' and the deed is done within seconds.

'How long is it going to take to find out?' he asks. 'I heard it takes a long time.'

'It used to, but things have speeded up, and I'll try to get it expedited. Since I'm looking for a match, they'll only have to do a comparison test. What takes a long time is when they're casting a wide net.'

'I wonder if I ought to tell my mamma.'

I can imagine all kinds of problems if Cheryl finds out, especially if she had anything to do with the murder, or knew who did. 'Why don't you wait until we get the results? If it isn't a match, she won't have been bothered. If it is, there's plenty of time to tell her.'

He looks relieved. 'Good plan.'

I head straight for Bobtail PD, where I tell Sheriff Hedges exactly what's going on and why I need the DNA right away.

'You know, you'd be better off asking the DPS head. What's his name, Reagan?'

'That would mean I'd have to talk to him.'

He laughs.

'I could take it to him, but I have things to do here in Bobtail and it will take a while. I'm anxious to get it sent in.'

'OK, let me see what I can do. I may have to have it over-nighted to Austin or San Antonio.'

I leave it with him and go on a mission to hunt down Dylan Polasek. Before, looking for him just seemed like tidying up a loose thread. Now, it's important. He's Andy Eastman's cousin, and he was protective of Andy when they were kids. Could he have known that Tolleson was hitting Andy? Did he decide to take matters into his own hands and get rid of Andy's tormentor? Or does he know who did? I drive back to his place, not calling first because I don't want to alert him. Turns out to be a good move. There's a beat-up pickup truck in the driveway, and he answers the door on the third ring. He looks like he's been on a bender. His T-shirt is stained and his jeans hang off him as if he's lost weight.

'Dylan Polasek?'

'Yeah.'

I introduce myself and ask if I can come in. He looks furtively behind him, as if he is harboring a crime scene inside, but opens the door wider for me to step in. His place is a wreck, beer bottles and plates with crusted food on every surface, and a smell of unwashed body and clothing. There are stacks of books everywhere as well. 'Sorry about the mess,' he mutters. 'I had Covid couple of weeks ago and I still haven't got any energy. But I'm not contagious. I don't think.'

He waves to a saggy chair that doesn't have anything piled on it, and I sit down. He clears some books and clothing aside to sit on the sofa, but then hops back up. 'I was getting some coffee. You want some?'

I normally never turn down coffee, but I can imagine the state of the dishes in his kitchen, and I don't want to be handed a cup that might not have been washed for weeks. 'I'm good, thanks.'

He's gone longer than I think he should be to just get a cup of coffee, and at one point I hear a crash, and he swears.

I get up and go into the kitchen, where a cup has shattered. He's looking at it with disgust, and shaking his hand. 'Damn hand doesn't always work. Nerve damage.' I remember somebody telling me he had a motorcycle accident.

'Can I help?'

'No, I'll clean it up later.'

I go back into the living room and when he comes back, he's holding a steaming mug that bears an ad for Gordon's Farm Equipment.

I point to the mug. 'I understand you work for Gordon's.'

He looks at the mug as if he's never seen it before. 'Did. Just quit. I told them I was sick last week and couldn't come in, but they gave me grief. Didn't believe me. I got fed up with them.'

'How come they didn't believe you?'

He shrugs. 'I guess I've taken more sick leave than some people.'

Usually when I show up, people ask me what I want, giving me an opening. But he seems uninterested that he's got a police officer sitting in his living room. 'Let me tell you why I'm here. I understand you're related to Andy Eastman. Cousins.'

'That's right. What of it?'

'Andy told me that when he was a kid you were very supportive of him. Word was that his daddy was abusive and . . .'

His response is thunderous. His body jerks forward as if he's ready to spring to his feet. 'Who told you that?'

'Well, Andy did. Said his dad hit him.'

He blinks. 'Oh, OK. Yeah, Tolleson hit him. Often.'

'How did you know that? You were young. Did he tell you?'

He shakes his head. 'I don't remember how I knew. I think the whole family knew.'

'Your brother?'

'Eddie? Probably. I don't remember if we ever talked about it. I was more worried for Andy than Eddie was. Eddie was always kind of more self-centered.'

'What did you think when Andy's dad took off?'

He takes a sip of coffee and stares at me, as if he's trying to figure out what I'm after. Or maybe trying to frame the response. 'Like everybody else, I wasn't sorry to see the son of a bitch go.'

'Did people in your family discuss it? Wonder where he'd gone?'

He frowns. 'I don't remember. Why are you asking these questions?'

'Did you hear about the body that was found in the feed store under the floorboards in Jarrett Creek?'

'No, when did this happen?'

'Last week. Funny, I thought most people had heard about it.'

He shrugs. 'I don't watch TV news and I don't read the paper, and like I said I was sick with Covid, so I didn't go out. I guess the news passed me by.'

'Well, at any rate, I'm investigating it, and I think the body might be Lamar Tolleson's.'

He sits back, crossing his arms across his chest. 'Really? What makes you think that?'

I pause, weighing my answer. 'Too big a coincidence that Andy's daddy disappeared the same time this body seems to have been hidden. I guess if we lived in a big city, the coincidence wouldn't be that noticeable. But Jarrett Creek is a small town. Gotta consider that the body is Tolleson's.'

'Disappeared or dead, you're not going to hear me or anybody else mourn him. I'd give up on it if I were you. Let sleeping dogs lie and all that kind of stuff.' Another admonition to forget about this crime.

'Can't do that.'

'You're the lawman. Guess it's up to you.'

'Your brother Eddie was working as a carpenter with two other boys renovating the store around the time the body was buried under the floor.'

'Are you suggesting that Eddie had something to do with it? If so, you're way off base. He was always a straight arrow. He'd never have a hand in either killing a man or hiding the body.'

'How about the other two? Paddy Sullivan and Jonas Miller? You think they were capable of doing that?'

He's chewing his lower lip. 'I couldn't tell you.'

'You didn't know anything about the body from thirty years ago, but did you hear that Paddy Sullivan was murdered?'

'That I did know.'

'How'd you find out?'

He shrugs. 'Probably at work. That was just before I got sick.'

'You were the same age as Paddy. How well did you know him?'

'I didn't know him at all. I mean, except at school. He was popular and I didn't run with that crowd.'

Funny he calls it a crowd. Jarrett Creek is a small school. When you have forty kids in a graduating class, it's pretty intimate.

'Your brother worked alongside him all summer. Did your brother ever talk about him? Did they get along?'

'Eddie and I didn't have that kind of relationship where we'd talk about stuff like that. I don't remember him ever saying anything bad about Paddy or Jonas. Except he did say Jonas made him laugh.'

'Different subject. You weren't close to your brother, but did you get along well with your daddy?'

'Daddy? Sure. What does he have to do with this? He's been gone for fifteen years.'

'Well, he was still alive when the guy was killed. I heard that your daddy took you to the Two Dog bar. Did he do that often?'

He looks startled. 'Kind of question is that?'

'Indulge me.'

He gulps down the last of his coffee. When he sets it down, it slips from his hand and clatters on the table next to him. He glares at his hand and shakes it as if he hurt it. 'We went a time or two. But Grant wouldn't serve me, so I didn't see the point.'

'I want to think back to a time when you were there with your daddy and a man named Gil Webb. According to Webb, you and your daddy had an argument.'

'Probably. We were always ragging on each other. We argued about football teams, politics, whatever.'

'I understand. But this sounded like it was a lot more heated, and I wonder if you were arguing because you'd just found out about the abuse and maybe you wanted your daddy to make it stop.'

He sneers. 'If Webb said that, it must be true. Damn gossip.'

'No, Webb didn't say that, I'm just speculating.' It makes sense, but I need to have him say it.

He shifts in his chair. 'Look, I was a kid. You know, I thought there was a way to solve anything. I thought my daddy ought to confront Tolleson and get him to stop.'

'Did your daddy tell you he was going to take care of it?'

His expression is outraged. 'He might have gone to Tolleson and told him to cut it out, but he wouldn't have hurt him. If you think that body is Tolleson's, it has nothing to do with my daddy.'

'So when Tolleson disappeared, there was no discussion in your family about it? Seems like your mamma might have mentioned it. Or maybe you would have talked to Andy. I understand you were protective of him.'

'You've been busy with the gossip machine.'

'Trying to do my job.'

'Well, if it was a subject of conversation, I don't recall. Could be that Mamma and Daddy discussed it, but not with me. As for Andy, as you might imagine, he wasn't upset that his daddy

was gone. More like relieved. I didn't see any reason to make
a big deal out of it.'

The fact is that even if Dylan knows who killed his uncle,
how am I going to get him to admit it? There are no apparent
clues to tie anyone in the family to it. Just coincidence. An
argument at the Two Dog. Dylan's moodiness and inability to
move on. As long as they all stonewall, there's no way to prove
who did it.

I get to my feet. 'Well, if you think of anything that might
help me figure out what happened back then, I'd appreciate a
call.' I hand him my card. He doesn't glance at it, just tosses
it on the coffee table on top of a stack of books.

THIRTY-ONE

On the way back to headquarters in the afternoon, I
mull over my options. I'm stuck. Even if the body
under the floorboards turns out to be Lamar Tolleson,
I haven't found any evidence that could point the finger at who
killed him. As for Paddy Sullivan, why was he killed? Did he
know who killed Tolleson? Was someone worried that he'd talk?
Was he killed to prevent that?

The only tenuous connection between Sullivan and the
Tolleson family is the clipping I found in Sullivan's belongings
about Andy Eastman's business opening. 'We done good.' Did
Sullivan and someone else kill Lamar Tolleson?

I wish Maria was here to bounce ideas off. I've come to
depend on her, and for the first time wonder if maybe I'm slipping. I feel like I ought to have gotten farther along, made better
intuitive leaps, understood more of the connections.

Calling her to discuss the case isn't an option. She'll be back
soon enough. Meanwhile, I'm on my own and I have to dig a
little deeper.

I think back to my various conversations and wonder if I'm
leaving someone out. I spoke with Marsha Berry, Sullivan's
high school girlfriend, and she gave me nothing. But I never

questioned Marsha's mother. Maybe, like Reanna Barstow's mamma, Lucille might remember more than her daughter does.

There's one other question that puzzles me. Why was Mark Granger attacked just before work started on the feed store? He had been talking about his plans for a few weeks. Why did whoever attacked him wait so long? Did they think he wouldn't go through with it? Maybe his attacker was somebody who doesn't live in Jarrett Creek anymore and who couldn't get away earlier. Somebody like Eddie Polasek.

Another loose end is why Melvin Granger paid so little for the fine deck at the back of his house. It seems like a small thing, but it nags at me. I should go back through Granger's receipts to see if anything jumps out at me.

When I get back to headquarters, Brick says things have been quiet.

I go over to Town Café and grab some lunch and then, on the spur of the moment, decide to go back to the feed store and take another look at the crime scene. Sometimes refreshing my look at the scene sparks ideas.

A crew is back at work on renovations. Mark Granger is behind the counter looking frazzled. 'So many little decisions to make,' he says.

'Did you and Chelsea ever find your daddy's will?'

'We did.' He shakes his head. 'Daddy had it stuck in a magazine. Chelsea found it when she was cleaning out the office.'

'Any surprises?'

'No, thank goodness. He split everything between Chelsea and me. Not that there was all that much, but at least it's the way we thought it would be, so there was nothing to argue over.'

'You and your sister still at odds?'

He sighs. 'We're all right. She had a contract drawn up specifying how much we'd each pay for the store renovation and what we'd each get out of it. It was a fair contract.'

I tell him I'd like to look at the back room again where all the action took place. He walks back with me.

The entire floor has been ripped out by now and some of the joists replaced. 'At least we didn't find any more bodies,' he says dryly.

I try to picture how the body was brought up the steps and stuffed in between joists. Grisly work, since it would have been decomposing. It also would have stunk, unless they poured the shellac over it before they carried it up. Somebody was determined to hide that body. I remember Jonas Miller's daughter telling me the story of Jonas and the others coming back to work and finding some of the floor work done. She said Jonas said nobody would admit to doing it. Whoever did that must have known something about carpentry. I wonder if the boards were already cut or if they had to do that? And if they did, was there sawdust left from the cutting, or did they clean up afterwards? The only person who would know that is Eddie Polasek. The other two are dead.

And then I think about Sullivan coming here last week, right into the place where the body was hidden. Was he blackmailing someone? Did he know who had killed the man thirty years ago and said he was threatened to tell? Was whoever he was meeting waiting for him? Why did they meet here? Maybe they had planned to extricate the body, and something went wrong and Sullivan got killed.

This room isn't going to divulge that information.

Marsha Berry asked me to look in on her mother, Lucille, so that's a good excuse to drop over to see her. She isn't in good health. She's a spindly woman, not that old, but frail-looking. She tells me she's diabetic. 'I got the Covid before there was a vaccine and it almost killed me. They told me somebody my age with diabetes was at high risk, but I had no idea.' I remember her quavery voice from last time I talked to her.

'I told your daughter I'd stop by and check in on you. How are you doing?'

'That's kind of you. I'm getting better, but it's sure taking a long time.' We're sitting in her claustrophobic living room, filled with too much furniture and too many knick-knacks. Not a hoarder, exactly, but somebody who holds onto things. I'm hoping she holds onto memories as well.

'Marsha said you wanted to know about Paddy Sullivan. I wish she'd married him, then she would have stayed around here instead of flitting all over the country.'

'Did you like Paddy?'

'He was a nice enough boy. Done all right for himself as I heard it. I have to say the boy she married has done well, too, though. And she seems happy.' She dabs at her mouth with a handkerchief.

'Do you remember the kids your daughter hung around with in those days, besides Paddy?'

'Let me think. There was the Polasek boys. Eddie was the younger one. The other boy, the older one, what was his name, Ryan? Something like that.'

'Dylan.'

'That's right. I heard that Hazel named him after Bob Dylan. I thought that was funny.' She chuckles.

'So both the Polasek brothers and Paddy Sullivan were friends?' Dylan said he barely knew Paddy Sullivan.

She frowns. 'Oh, yes. You know it's a small school and everybody knows everybody. All of them hung out together. Did anyway, until . . .' She stops, frowning. 'There was something that happened.' She takes her glasses off and rubs her eyes. 'My memory. Hasn't been the same since I was sick.' She stares at me as if I could conjure up her memory.

I wait. Then she nods. 'I remember. Paddy and Dylan had a falling-out. I tell you why I remember. Marsha was gone all summer at that camp she went to, and when she got back, she wanted to have a farewell party before everybody went off their separate ways to college and whatnot. Anyway, somebody told her that those two boys wouldn't both come to the party because they had a problem with each other. She wasn't happy about that.'

'Do you remember what the problem was?'

'No, if I ever did know, I've forgotten. All I know is that Marsha decided not to have the party. She said she didn't want to stir things up. She had broken up with Paddy by then anyway. So she and her girlfriends got together one night to celebrate, and that was it.'

'I wonder who might know what the boys fought about?'

She blinks. 'I don't know. Why would you want to know that?'

'Seems odd that they held a grudge.'

'Well, boys and their rivalries. It's always something. Probably over some girl. I suppose Missy Lockwood would know. She knows everything.' She lifts an eyebrow to render judgment.

So it's back to Missy Lockwood. This time I'll talk to her in person. And when she's not watching her grandkids.

I phone, and she tells me she doesn't have the kids this afternoon, but that she has to be somewhere at three o'clock. If I can come by now, she'll talk to me.

THIRTY-TWO

M issy answers the door wearing black yoga pants and a knee-length T-shirt. A social person, she chatters as she leads me into her living room, telling me more about her grandkids than anyone needs to know. According to her they are smarter and cuter than any kids ever born.

Her living room is a riot of color, and surprisingly tidy for someone who tends to two young children several times a week. 'Thank goodness I've got a lot of energy,' she says. 'Otherwise the kids would kill me.'

When we're settled with coffee and a massive plate of brownies on the coffee table, she says, 'OK, shoot. What more can I tell you?'

'I have a question about Dylan Polasek and Paddy Sullivan.'

'Dylan. Huh. Him and Paddy were in the class above me, so I didn't know them very well. But Dylan was interesting. He was a hottie. All the girls had a crush on him. He was a brooding sort of guy. We all thought he was like Heathcliff. You know, in *Wuthering Heights*?'

I remember the book vaguely, but Heathcliff is a character everybody remembers as brooding. Seems to suit Dylan, now that I've met him. 'Did he date anybody in particular?'

'Oh, let me think.' She looks off in the distance, her bright eyes alert, searching. 'I don't think he had anybody special, but I could be wrong.' She grabs a brownie and takes a bite.

'Apparently Dylan and Paddy Sullivan were good friends, but they had a falling-out. Do you have any idea what it was about?'

She brushes crumbs into a pile on the table and frowns. 'Oh, my, I remember people talking about that. I wasn't there so I only know what I heard.'

I nod. 'What did you hear?'

She leans forward, as if it's a confidential matter. 'A bunch of kids were out at the lake. This was like sometime in the summer. And Dylan and Paddy got into a fistfight. Nobody could tell me why they were fighting. But then it's as if Dylan dropped off the face of the earth. I think he moved to Bobtail right after that.'

'He didn't go to college?'

'That's the crazy thing. He was really smart and I think he got into college, but he didn't go.'

I feel like I'm following a slim thread that could lead to a dead end, but every time I think the thread has played out, there's one more extension. 'Who would likely have been at the lake?'

'Oh, gosh. Let me get my yearbook. I hauled it out after we talked the other day.' She leaves and I eat a brownie while I wait for her. She comes back, plops down next to me and opens the yearbook to the senior class. She runs her forefinger along the rows of kids. 'Let's see. This was the in-crowd. There was Molly Gillespie. She lives in Houston now. And there's Burt. He lives over in Austin.' It's like she's talking to herself. 'Wait a minute. I know who would have been there who's still here in town. Barbara Barrett. Married Mike Barrett, but they divorced a good while back. He ran around on her. Anyway, she works at the Bobtail Junior College. I think she's some kind of administrator. Got a good job anyway. I see her every Saturday at our yoga class.'

'Yoga class? In Jarrett Creek?' Wendy takes yoga classes in Bryan, but I didn't know there were any such classes around here.

'Yes, even little ol' Jarrett Creek has yoga. Jolinda Guthrie runs classes out of her house. Well, her garage. She got it fixed up so she can hold yoga classes there. She's a good teacher.'

'Anything else you can remember about the business with Paddy and Dylan? Was Dylan's brother Eddie involved?'

'No, I don't think Eddie and Dylan were ever close. Eddie was more serious. He made good grades and had some ambition.' She laughs. 'I hear he's got a good job at a bank in Dallas.'

Happily, Missy has someplace to be at three o'clock or I might have been there listening to her dish gossip until midnight. I'm not sure Oscar is right that men are as gossipy as women. Although Missy doesn't seem to be a mean gossip. Just far-ranging in her interests.

I can't help wondering if all this meandering from one bit of information to the next is actually going to get me anywhere. But I remind myself that the murder I'm concentrating on at present happened thirty years ago. Of course the leads are going to be tenuous.

I go back to the station and put in a call to Bobtail JC to make an appointment to see Barbara Barrett, who may or may not have been at the lake thirty years ago when Paddy Sullivan and Dylan Polasek got into a fistfight, and may or may not know what their fight was about.

I'm told she's in a meeting but, 'She always returns her calls,' a crisp-voiced secretary informs me.

It occurs to me that Eddie Polasek might remember something of the fight. I could ask Dylan directly, but without some background, he'll likely stonewall. In fact, if I were someone who was involved in a murder thirty years ago, I'd do exactly what everybody I've questioned has done – given me nothing.

I'm ready to place a call to Eddie when I get a call from Sergeant Reagan. 'Wondering how things are going in your little town. Any more murders?'

Is that an actual bit of humor?

'Not this week. But I have to tell you, I'm not getting very far. The leads are cold on the old murder, and nonexistent on the current one.'

'Well, I have a couple of things for you. I don't know how useful.'

'Sullivan's cell phone?'

'Yes. Techs were able to retrieve the information from his damaged phone. Turns out the call he took at home the evening he was killed was made from the phone at Granger's Feed Store.'

'So whoever called him was already at the store.'

'Seems like it.'

'Fingerprints on the phone?'

'Too smudged to be of any use. Looks like lots of people used the phone. We surmise that the firefighters who showed might have used it. There was a call to you and to the Bobtail PD.'

'I'll ask if they used the landline. Seems like they would have used their cell phones. You said there was something else?'

'Yes, again I don't know that it means anything for you. I had somebody do a routine check on everybody involved, including Granger's kids.'

That's something I should have done myself. It's where having a bigger police department comes in handy. 'Anything interesting?'

'Granger's son had a problem last year. His business went belly-up and he had to declare bankruptcy.'

'He mentioned that.'

'Did he also mention that his business partner skipped out on him?'

'No. Did he make off with funds or anything?'

'The officer I had doing the background checks didn't dig into it too deeply. Just a little information.'

'I'll keep it in mind. I appreciate the heads-up.'

'That's all I've got. You need anything?'

What I actually need is a real lead, but that's not anything I can ask for. I tell him I'll let him know if I do.

In the back of my mind, I'd hoped that something would come of Sullivan's phone. It would have been convenient if Sullivan's murderer had made an error of judgment and called from their own phone. But nothing is ever that easy.

Reagan has no sooner hung up when Barbara Barrett calls me. 'I'm leaving the office soon. Why don't you come to my house and we can have a glass of wine?'

'That sounds like a good plan.'

She says she'll be home a little after five.

While I wait, I call Eddie Polasek again.

This time, he's clearly annoyed. 'I don't know what else I can tell you other than what I told you last time you called.'

'This won't take long. Apparently, right after school was out, the summer you were working on the feed store renovation, your brother and Paddy Sullivan had a falling-out.'

He snorts. 'You've got to be kidding. You think Dylan killed Sullivan because of a fight they had thirty years ago? That's digging pretty deep, isn't it?'

'I just want to know why they were fighting.'

'I couldn't tell you. My brother and I were never all that close. Like oil and water.'

'You know anybody who might know?'

He exhales an impatient breath. 'I suppose Mamma might remember, if she ever knew. Craddock, you're talking young people. If everybody has changed as much as I have, they're not the same people they were back then. Honestly, I don't see why you're even bothering. Whoever killed that man might be long dead themselves.'

'You mean like your daddy?'

'What?' An explosive sound. 'My daddy wouldn't have hurt a fly. And even if he did kill whoever that is you found, Daddy's been gone for fifteen years. What are you going to do, dig him up and stick him in jail?'

I'm determined to ignore his attitude. 'Your daddy who wouldn't hurt a fly threatened to kill his brother-in-law.'

Silence. 'When?'

'Right before his brother-in-law disappeared. Don't tell me you didn't know that Lamar Tolleson abused his wife and son.'

More silence. 'We all knew that. We just didn't know how bad it was.'

Now it's my turn to think before I speak. 'What do you mean?'

'If you don't know, I'm not the one to tell you. If that body is Tolleson's whoever killed him did the world a favor.'

'You're not the only one who's told me that. The problem is, even if I could let the old murder go, I can't do that with the one last week.'

He sighs. 'Well, that one I can't help you with.'

*　　*　　*

Barbara Barrett has an air of command. She ushers me into her house that evening as if she's ready to take me over and set things straight. I can see her as a college administrator.

She gets me settled in a comfortable chair and says, 'Red or white?'

'Red, if you've got it.' I don't usually have a glass of wine with someone I'm questioning, but I don't have the slightest suspicion that Barbara Barrett was involved in either death I'm investigating.

She brings me a glass of good pinot noir and sinks into her sofa with a sigh. 'I love my job, but some days it's hard.'

'Every job has those days.'

She grins. 'I expect yours has a lot of them. But that's not why you're here. You said you had a question about Paddy Sullivan? That's ancient history.'

'I hope you can help me. Missy Lockwood tells me you were part of a bunch of kids that hung out together back in high school.'

'Those were the days! When I was a size six and cute as a button. And I could wear a bikini and go out to the lake every day.' She laughs.

She's still attractive, even with a little more weight on her.

I tell her the specific incident I'm interested in, the fight between Dylan and Paddy.

She nods, becoming serious. 'I remember that. But what I mostly remember is nobody knew what the heck they were upset with each other about.' She squints and takes a sip of wine. 'I'm trying to think exactly how it happened. We had all been in the water and were lying around and all of a sudden Dylan said something and Paddy jumped to his feet and said something like you better keep your damn trap shut. And Dylan jumped up and said it wasn't himself he was worried about, it was Paddy.' She shakes her head. 'We were all kind of like, hey guys, what's going on, and telling them to cool it. But before we knew it, one of them took a swing at the other one.' She shakes her head. 'Oh, wait. I know what it was! Paddy said something like, you always were a mamma's boy and I'll bet you can't keep your mouth shut. And that's when Dylan took a swing at him.'

'Any idea what it was about?'

She laughs at that and takes another sip of wine. 'I'd say it was the usual. Probably testosterone at work.'

'Except that apparently they never got over it, and shortly afterwards Dylan moved out of town.'

She frowns. 'I guess I never connected the two things. I didn't know Dylan that well. I'm not sure anybody did.'

'Later in the summer, Marsha Berry was planning a party and decided to ditch the idea because those two guys were still on the outs.'

'Ha! I went to the girls' party and all I have to say is we had a lot more fun than we would have if the guys had been there. No offense.' She grins.

'None taken.'

'But you're right. If they were still mad at each other, it might have been something more. I just don't know what it might be.' She gets up. 'I'm starving. You want a snack?'

It's tempting, but somehow I'm enjoying this young woman's company so much that it feels like I'd be cheating on Wendy. I bow out and thank her for her time.

The little bit that she told me makes me think it's time I talk to Eddie and Dylan Polasek's mamma Hazel again. If she's smart, she'll stonewall me. But if I'm lucky, she might want to get something off her chest.

THIRTY-THREE

I'm at the station by eight the next morning. Something has been nagging at me and I need to sort it out. Dusty has come with me and he immediately goes to Maria's desk, disappointed when he sees yet again that she isn't there. 'She'll be back before too long,' I tell him. And then I realize she never called last night. I had told her I wanted to hear from her every night. I hope she hasn't gotten herself into trouble.

I need to go back through the papers we got from Melvin Granger's office to find out if there's anything else that Sullivan did for Melvin Granger. The deck is sticking in my mind as an oddity. But just as I haul out the box of papers, Brick comes in, smelling like aftershave and looking like he could run ten miles without breaking a sweat.

'Let me ask you something,' I ask when he gets settled with a cup of coffee. 'How are you with details?'

He eyes the receipts I've taken out of the box. 'You mean like financial stuff?'

'Something like that.'

'Pretty good. It's not my favorite activity, but I'll do what's needed.'

I tell him the issue, that Granger hired Paddy Sullivan to build a deck, when he claimed he didn't remember him. 'And he didn't pay much for the deck. I'd like to find out if there were more bills for the deck that I missed, and if Sullivan did any more work for Granger.'

'I got you. Let me see what I can find.'

When he's started, I call Dylan and Eddie's mamma, Hazel Moore, and tell her I'd like to talk to her again.

She sighs. 'I figured you would. Come on over.'

Hazel is no longer using her walker. 'My hip is pretty good. I was worried at my age that it wouldn't heal well, but I'm good. Not going dancing anytime soon. But I probably wouldn't have anyway.'

Before I can ask anything, when we're seated she says, 'I hear you've been busy getting our family tree organized.' There's a sharp edge to her tone.

'It was a surprise to me to find out that Cheryl Eastman is your sister-in-law.'

'Why should you have known that?'

'No reason. But I've put together some interesting connections and I'd like you to tell me if I've missed something.'

She waits like a deer alert to a hunter in the distance.

'This is about Andy Eastman, Cheryl's son.'

She blinks. 'He's my nephew. Nice boy. Does my taxes for free.'

'Your boys were a little older than Andy, and Dylan was fond of him. Took Andy under his wing. Then your husband Tim found out that Andy's daddy was abusing Cheryl and Andy. Hitting them. Have I got that right so far?'

'Approximately.' Her voice is steely.

'When the abuse came to light, your husband threatened Lamar Tolleson. Told him if he ever touched Cheryl again, he'd kill him. And right about that time, Andy's daddy disappeared.'

She's watching me.

'You can see where I'm going with this.'

'Not exactly.'

'Well, I think the body we found at Granger's store might be Lamar Tolleson.'

Her laugh is artificial. 'I don't think so. Cheryl said he'd gone to Colorado. He called her.'

'Someone called her, but I don't think it was Tolleson. I called the number he gave her where she could reach him, and back then it belonged to a grocery story. And they'd never heard of Tolleson. And there are no records of him in Colorado.'

'Huh. That may be, but whatever happened to him, it had nothing to do with my husband. Tim wouldn't have hurt a fly.'

'Yeah, that's what your son Eddie said.' Those exact words, in fact. Family lore. I hunch forward. 'It's too much of a coincidence to think that Lamar Tolleson disappeared at the same time his family found out he was beating up on his wife and kid.'

'Coincidence or not, that's what happened.' She's defiant.

'Except now we've found that body in the floorboards in Granger's Feed Store. We're checking the DNA, but my suspicion is we're going to find out that the body is that of Tolleson.'

'That doesn't mean my husband had anything to do with it.'

'Maybe not, but meanwhile, your son Eddie, Jonas Miller, and Paddy Sullivan were renovating Granger's Feed Store.'

'Yes, so what?'

'So they had the perfect opportunity to stash a body there.'

'Oh, my Lord. You are fishing, that's all. Neither one of my sons would have killed their uncle.'

'Maybe not, but they might know who did.'

She shrugs.

'There's another thing. Paddy Sullivan and your son Dylan had a falling-out that summer. They came to blows in front of some of their friends. One of them heard Paddy say he was worried that Dylan had blabbed something. To you.'

'Blabbed to me? Is that what has you all in a lather? I'll tell you what he blabbed to me.' Her expression is stony. 'We had heard that Lamar was hitting Andy. But Dylan told me it was much worse than that.' She shudders. 'Dylan told Andy he knew his daddy was beating up on him.' She gives a little whimper. She's near tears. 'He told Andy that Tim was going to talk to his daddy and make sure it didn't happen again. Andy trusted Dylan. Thought he was a god. So because he thought he was finally safe, he told Dylan the whole story. His daddy hadn't just been beating up on him, he'd been . . . oh, I can't even say it.' She groans and when she speaks, her voice has gone high with emotion. 'He'd been messing with the boy. You know what I mean. With sex.'

I fall back in my chair and blow out a breath. If there was ever a reason for someone to kill a man, that was it. But which one of them did it?

'That's terrible. And Dylan told you?'

She nods.

'But Hazel, I don't think that's what the boys argued about. Why would Paddy Sullivan care if Dylan told you about the sexual abuse? No, I think Dylan told you something else.' I pause to give her a chance to catch up. 'You knew that body was Tolleson's, didn't you?'

She's frozen, her eyes pleading with me.

'Hazel, who killed Tolleson? Was it Dylan?'

She brings her hands to her mouth as if to hold back her words. 'Suppose I told you it was my husband who did it.'

'That would certainly tie things up nicely. Your husband is dead and he can't speak for himself. And nothing could happen to him. Except his good name would be dragged down.'

She gasps. 'Tim was a good man.'

'Who did it, Hazel? How did it happen? Was there a fight? Was it an accident? If so, the sentence might be light. Whoever did it would go to prison, but a lot of people wouldn't blame them. Tolleson was a bad man.'

Desperation lights her eyes. 'It was Paddy Sullivan. He killed Lamar.'

'Why? What was the connection between Sullivan and Tolleson? I know your family was glad to see the last of

Tolleson, but what did Paddy Sullivan have against him? And who told you Sullivan did it?'

She's trapped. She sits mute, her mouth trembling. There's no reason for me to prolong her pain. I have to confront her sons. They know more than they are saying. I get up to leave.

'No, please, leave my son alone.' For a moment I'm not sure which son she means, but then she continues, 'He's had such a hard time. When his daddy died . . . Listen, wait a minute. Listen to me.'

I sit back down.

She takes a shaky breath. 'When Tim died, Dylan blamed himself. They'd been arguing. It was a long-standing problem between them. When Dylan didn't go to college, Tim wanted him to go to work at Gordon's, and Dylan didn't want to. He had some hare-brained idea that he was going to go into business for himself. But it was obvious to us that it was a dream and he was never going to make much of himself. Didn't have the initiative. Tim persuaded him to try out a job with Gordon's, but Dylan hated it and he and Tim were always arguing about it. Anyway, one day they'd had a big blowup and Tim ended up making a mistake and he was killed on the job. Dylan felt like it was his fault because he'd upset his daddy and Tim was distracted.'

'That's why Dylan works for Gordon's now.'

'I think he's been doing penance. He works there but his heart has never been in it.' She grabs a tissue from the table at her side and blows her nose.

A sad tale, but it still doesn't answer the question of who killed Lamar Tolleson.

'Did Dylan tell you what happened to Lamar Tolleson?'

She groans. 'It was so long ago. Why did that damn Granger boy have to get that idea of fixing up his daddy's feed store? If he'd left well enough alone, none of this would ever have come to light.'

'Well, it has come to light. What happened, Hazel?'

'All I know is that Dylan told me Sullivan did it. I didn't ask why.'

I don't bother to ask if she believed her son. Of course she believed him. But why would Sullivan kill Tolleson? And if he did, why did someone kill him? I had assumed he was black-mailing someone who was involved in the murder, or had threatened to tell. So what am I getting wrong?

'Hazel, I'm going to have to ask Dylan about this.'

'Be my guest.'

I call Dylan and when he answers I tell him I need to talk to him again. He doesn't ask why.

I can't leave Hazel alone because she'll call him the second I'm out of her sight to warn him about our conversation. I call Brick at headquarters. 'I need you to come sit with somebody.'

Hazel understands and she doesn't like it one bit. 'You don't need to do that. I won't warn him.'

I tell her it's protocol.

Brick is there in ten minutes. I introduce him to Hazel and tell him I need him to make sure Hazel doesn't make any phone calls until I OK it. He turns his dazzling smile on her, and by the time I leave she doesn't seem quite as upset.

THIRTY-FOUR

On the way to Bobtail mid-morning, my mind is buzzing. If Hazel is telling the truth and Sullivan landed the blow that killed Tolleson, I need to know why he was involved in the first place. What did Tolleson mean to him?

I think back to when Mark Granger was attacked. His attacker warned him not to continue the renovation. If Sullivan did kill Tolleson, it makes sense that he would be the one who warned Mark Granger to forget about renovating the feed store. But that still doesn't explain why he killed Tolleson in the first place. And doesn't explain who killed Sullivan. What makes more sense is that Hazel was lying, that it was Dylan who killed Tolleson, and then killed Sullivan to keep him from revealing it.

If Dylan Polasek has killed two men, he might think nothing

of killing me. I take the Colt out of my glove box and strap it on.

'What brings you back so soon?' Dylan asks when he opens the door.

I ask if I can come in.

His eyes go to the gun that I haven't bothered to cover up. He steps aside to let me in, but I tell him to go first. We sit in the same places we sat before.

'You have reason to think I'm dangerous?' He nods to the gun.

'I talked to your mamma and I need to corroborate some things she told me.'

He flexes his shoulders as if they're tense. 'I see.'

'Why don't you tell me what you told her about who killed Lamar Tolleson?'

He takes a sharp breath that ends in a coughing fit. 'I don't know what you're talking about.'

'The man we found in the floorboards is likely Lamar Tolleson, and she told me you revealed to her who killed him. I want to get your side of the story.'

He hunches over, hands clasped between his knees. 'What did she tell you?'

'You first.'

He shrugs. 'Paddy Sullivan killed Lamar Tolleson. Or at least I think it was him.'

What does that mean, he 'thinks.' 'Why? What kind of connection was there between those two men? Sullivan was twenty years old and Tolleson was a good fifteen, twenty years older. Tolleson was abusing his wife and son. The son you were close to. It makes more sense that one of Tolleson's relatives killed him. So what was Sullivan's connection?'

Dylan stares at me.

'And another thing. How did you know Sullivan killed him? Were you there? Did he tell you?'

His stubborn expression settles in.

'You told me you barely knew Paddy Sullivan. But that wasn't true, was it? You and Sullivan were actually good friends in high school. Why lie to me about that?'

He shakes his head, looking down at the floor.

'According to people I've questioned, you had a falling-out with Sullivan right after Tolleson disappeared. What was all that about?'

As I've fired questions at Dylan, he's grown pale and sulky. 'I think I'd better get a lawyer.'

I raise my hands in surrender. 'Say no more. I'll take you over to Bobtail PD and they can put you in a cell while we wait for your lawyer.'

'Put me in a cell? Why?'

'Son, I'm not sure I believe your story. But if nothing else, you're a material witness and I need to make sure you won't disappear on me before your lawyer has time to get to you.'

He stares at me.

'But I'll tell you what, you can call your lawyer now and the lawyer can meet us at the station.'

'I'm not going anywhere with you.'

'Then I'll have to call Bobtail PD to get some backup.'

'Hold on! What's the damn hurry?'

I take a good look at him. 'I've got two murdered men, that's what's the hurry. One of them used to be a friend of yours, Paddy Sullivan. You say he killed Tolleson, but there are too many holes in your story. I need you to come straight with me, but now that you've stated that you want a lawyer, I have to comply.'

'Well, just wait a minute. Let me think.'

'Take your time. While you're at it, I'm going to make a call.'

I step into the kitchen, which is as much of a nightmare as I remembered, crusted dishes in the sink, and a smell that could be rotting vegetables or meat. I call Sheriff Hedges at Bobtail PD and tell him I need some backup. He says he'll send officers right away.

When I go back into the room, Dylan is sitting with his head in his hands. This is not the position of someone who is sure of his next move.

It has been my observation that although people who have committed crimes don't want to lose their freedom and go to prison, being caught and admitting what they've done sometimes frees them psychologically. Dylan Polasek looks and acts like a man who is tormented. If he murdered Tolleson and Sullivan, his guilt will never let go of him.

'Bobtail PD officers will be here soon.'

He groans.

'Are you going to call your lawyer?'

'Chief Craddock, I don't have a lawyer. And even if I did, I don't think I need one.'

I consider whether I ought to get him to sign a waiver, but I don't want to interject a formality into the moment.

'Dylan, as I understand it you were a promising young student in your teens. You got into college and didn't go. It seems that something happened. What was it?'

He sits back and looks at me with weary eyes, but stays quiet.

'I think something happened that made you feel guilty and the guilt has eaten at you ever since. It has blighted your life, made you unable to move on. I think if you gave up that guilt, you'd clear the way for a better future.'

He laughs, and it isn't a pleasant sound. 'I'm fifty years old. How much of a future have I got?'

'Twenty-five, thirty years?' I'm not going to mention that if he murdered Tolleson he's likely to spend most of those years in prison. He knows that.

A minute ticks by.

'Dylan, did you kill Lamar Tolleson?'

He drags a hand across his brow and looks around the room as if he's pondering seeing it for the last time. 'Let's see if the truth sets me free. The answer is I don't know.'

'You want to explain?'

'I don't know what good it's going to do anybody, but I can tell you the circumstances.'

I wait while he nods to himself and folds his arms across his chest, as if protecting himself.

'I don't know if Mamma told you, but Lamar wasn't just hitting his kid, he was diddling him.' He and I both flinch at the word.

'How did you find this out?'

'I heard the whole story from Andy, eventually. But I first heard about the abuse from a friend of Daddy's, Gil Webb. Gil told Daddy he needed to talk to him, and Daddy wanted me to come along. Maybe he had some idea what Gil was going to say. I don't know. Anyway, Gil told us that Andy showed up at

school with a black eye. Gil's sister was a school nurse and she got Andy to talk to her and he said his daddy hit him. Often. My daddy had a fit. He told me he'd already suspected Tolleson was hitting Cheryl, but that confirmed it. He told me he was going to put a stop to it.' He nods to himself. 'Daddy was a good man. Strong.'

'Are you saying your daddy had something to do with Tolleson's death?'

He looks startled. 'No, not at all. I'm just giving you the background. Daddy told me he went to see Lamar and told him if he ever heard of Lamar touching either Cheryl or Andy again, he'd turn him in to the cops.'

'Your aunt Cheryl said your daddy threatened to kill Tolleson.'

'Could have, I guess. Anyway, I had a soft spot for Andy. He was a cute kid, but I'd always known there was something sad in him. I guess that's why I took to him. I thought he needed somebody to be nice to him. After what Webb told us, I took Andy out for an ice cream and told him I knew his daddy had hit him and that it wasn't going to happen anymore. And then he said . . .' His voice cracks. 'Oh, Lord.' He takes a shuddering breath. 'He said, "And what about the other stuff?"' Dylan swallows and wipes his eyes. 'I asked what other stuff and then he told me his daddy had been coming into his room at night and . . .' He clenches his fists. 'If I'd had Tolleson there at the moment, I would have killed him. What kind of man does that? To his own little boy.'

I shake my head. What punishment is right for someone who kills a man who assaulted his son? I know whoever killed Tolleson shouldn't have taken the law into his own hands, but dragging the boy into the legal system would have been another piece of torture. 'So what happened next?'

'What Andy told me ate at me. One evening after work, Paddy Sullivan and I got drunk and I told him about it. He was more of an action person than I was. He said we ought to teach Lamar a lesson. That we should beat him up the same way he beat on his family. We worked each other into a state.'

'Did you go to his house?'

'No, I didn't want Andy or his mamma to know what we

were up to. I called Lamar and told him I had a problem and needed to ask his advice. The son of a bitch loved to hand out advice like he had all the answers, and I knew he couldn't resist. I asked him to meet me at the park out at the lake. He said it was late and could we meet the next day and I said it was kind of urgent. I hinted that I'd gotten some girl in trouble.'

'So he arrived and you and Sullivan were waiting for him.'

He closes his eyes and takes a deep breath. I'm hoping the backup police officers don't come right now. I need to hear Dylan out. 'That's right. And we lit into him. First, we told him what we thought of him. He denied it. And then one of us, I don't remember which one, hit him. He didn't fall so we both started punching him. And then he fell. And he hit his head on the concrete picnic table. It was a terrible sound.' He shudders.

'That's what you meant when you said you didn't know if you killed him.'

'Yeah. Like who threw that punch that knocked him back. I don't know.'

'But you told your mamma it was Sullivan.'

He sighs. 'I suppose I did. Or maybe she decided to blame him instead of me.'

'What happened after he fell?'

Dylan doesn't speak for a minute, lost in his memories. 'When we realized he was dead, I threw up. I was a wreck. Sullivan was stronger. He said we had to get rid of the body. We put it in the trunk. God, that was awful, hauling a man's body into the trunk of a car.' He shakes his head hard, as if to get rid of the image. 'I was scared to death somebody was going to come by and ask what we were doing out there.' He jumps up, startling me. 'I have to get some water.'

'I'll get it. You sit still.' In the kitchen, I rinse out a glass and bring back the water. He's sitting with his eyes closed, breathing hard. I hand him the water. He gulps it down.

'You got the body in the trunk. Then what?'

He swipes his hand across his mouth. 'Then we had to figure out where to take it. We didn't want to drive too far because we were afraid we'd get pulled over by the highway patrol for drunk driving and they'd find the body. Paddy had some bourbon in the car and we drank the rest of that, for courage.' He huffs a laugh. 'I haven't been able to stand the taste of bourbon ever since.'

'So where did you take the body?'

'Sullivan's daddy owned a lot across the railroad tracks and we took it there.' He drops his head into his hands. 'It was horrible.'

'How did Tolleson's body end up under the floorboards in Granger's place?'

Dylan lifts his head and has a half-smile on his face. He looks like he's aged ten years in the last few minutes. 'Stupid. Ignorant. Fools.' He spits out each word as if to rid himself of them. 'I told you we buried Tolleson on a lot that Sullivan's daddy owned. Well, a few weeks after it happened, Sullivan called me in a panic. He said his daddy had decided to build a house on the property. That meant digging a foundation.'

'So you had to move the body.'

'Yeah. Thought we did, anyway. Turns out that later that year, his folks split up and nothing ever got built there. And of course if Mark Granger hadn't gotten the bright idea to modernize the feed store . . .' His voice trails away.

'So why did you choose the feed store?'

'You know they were working on renovations there, and they were ready to lay the floor back in. The boards were cut and ready. Paddy figured that if we hid it in the floor, nobody would ever find it. One big fiasco after another,' he mutters.

'What do you mean?'

'When we dug up the body, it stunk to high heaven. We were both puking. We knew we had to cover the odor or Granger would have smelled it and made us tear up the floor. Paddy thought of pouring shellac on it. You know, shellac has that strong odor and it dries hard. We figured when it hardened it would seal the whole thing. Actually worked pretty well.'

'Where did you get shellac?'

'Damnedest thing. Sullivan's daddy had built a den onto their house and shellacked the floor, so they had some left over. A lot, as it turned out. Enough for our purposes anyway.'

I hear a car pull up outside and I know the interview is over, for now. But it's really only beginning.

'Dylan, the cops are here and they're going to take you in. I need to talk to you further.'

'I've told you all I know.'

'There are details I'll need to get from you.'

At least now I don't have to worry about the DNA test. I know who the victim is.

THIRTY-FIVE

On the way to the Bobtail station, I stop to pick up a sandwich lunch for Dylan and me.

While I wait for the food, I call Brick and tell him he can leave Hazel Moore's house.

'We have to finish our Scrabble game,' he says.

'If she wants to know what's going on, tell her to call me.'

She calls me within a few minutes. 'Your deputy is a very nice man. If I had to be penned up, he's at least nice.'

'Hazel, I've talked to Dylan and he told me some of what happened.'

'So you know he didn't kill anybody.'

'We'll see.'

'What do you mean we'll see? He didn't kill Lamar Tolleson!'

'I just need to clear up a few things.'

When I get to Bobtail PD, I tell Sheriff Hedges the gist of my conversation with Dylan and ask if I can continue my questioning. He's fine with that.

Dylan is in a cell, sitting on the cot looking defeated. I go inside with a folding chair, hand him the sandwich and sit down. He takes the sandwich but doesn't unwrap it.

'Dylan, I really appreciate the information you've given me, but I need to ask you a few more questions.'

He nods.

'Now you said you didn't want a lawyer before, but I'm giving you another chance.'

'I don't know what good a lawyer would do me now.'

'The questions I have are about after Tolleson died. I

mentioned that I heard you and Paddy Sullivan had a problem with each other that summer. A squabble in front of some of your friends. But you never told me what that was about.'

He begins to unwrap the sandwich, taking his time. 'It was strange. At first it bothered me a lot and Paddy was OK. But then it kind of reversed itself. What we did ate at Paddy. I was the opposite. I began to realize that regardless of how it ended up we'd done a fine thing because I knew Andy and Cheryl were safe. But Paddy got more and more antsy. He kept wanting to meet up and go over the details, make sure we had covered our tracks. Drove me crazy. And then he got the idea that I was going to blame him. He thought I'd tell Mamma that it was him that had killed Lamar. And he wouldn't let go of it. That's what we were fighting about.'

'Did he ever try to blackmail you?'

'No, in fact he was worried that I'd blackmail him. You know he left Jarrett Creek and wouldn't come back, right?'

'His wife told me that. Was it because of guilt, or fear of being caught?'

'Mostly I think it was because of me. He figured he'd be better off not being in my line of sight.'

'He never called you? Never arranged to meet?'

'No, to tell you the truth I was just as glad not to see him.'

'But you sent him a clipping with a note.'

He looks surprised. 'I'd forgotten about that. How did you know?'

'Found it in Sullivan's belongings.'

'I thought maybe it might ease things for him.'

'After he left town, things settled down for you?'

He sighs. 'Not really. I always felt the guilt, and I started doing some drugs to ease things up. Daddy forced me into going to work at Gordon's and then he and I didn't get along so well anymore. Then he had that accident . . .'

'Your mamma told me you blamed yourself for that.'

He shrugs. 'I don't know, maybe. She kind of does an armchair psychologist thing. But I do know that after he died, when Gordon offered to keep me on, I felt like I had to continue to work there. Make up for what happened.'

'But you quit a couple of days ago.'

'Knowing that the body had been found . . .'

'What difference did that make?'

He sighs. 'I guess I started thinking about all those years, thirty years since it happened, and realized I was pretty much in the same situation I was then. I've gone nowhere, and no future in sight that appealed to me. I don't know . . .' He shakes his head.

'Dylan, did you try to persuade Mark Granger not to renovate the feed store?'

'Never met the man.'

'Did you know he was going to renovate the store?'

'Mamma told me.'

'And that didn't make you nervous?'

'First of all, I didn't know whether they'd be tearing up the floor. And I figured that even if they found the body, after all these years, nobody would know who it was, and if they did, nobody would care enough to pursue it. I didn't count on you being so persistent.'

'Mark said someone called and threatened him. Was that you?'

'Not me.'

'Did you talk to Sullivan when you found out Mark was going to do the renovations?'

'No, sir, never.'

'Any idea who killed him?'

'All I know is it wasn't me.'

I leave the cell to go talk to Sheriff Hedges and ask him how we can charge someone with a crime that was done thirty years ago when your suspect swears he didn't know whether his was the deciding blow, and the only other people present at the time are dead.

He agrees that unless something else comes to light, it's not likely we'll be able to make a case against Polasek and we should cut him loose. 'I'll talk to the district attorney, but it seems like slim chance to me and they're not going to want to pursue it.'

But there's still the matter of who killed Paddy Sullivan. On the drive back to Jarrett Creek, I mull over the skimpy facts of the Sullivan case. The only way I'm going to charge

Dylan Polasek with anything that will stick is if I can prove that he killed Sullivan. The fact is, I believe him when he says he didn't. But if he didn't, who did?

Hazel Moore knew what happened – at least her son's version. She probably told her husband, Tim, and they might also have told Tolleson's wife Cheryl, so she'd know she was safe. They may have brought their son Eddie in on it, too. And what about Andy? Did he know? They wouldn't have told him initially, because he was a child, but it's possible he found out eventually. Did Cheryl's current husband know? Any one of them could have killed Paddy. But why?

Maybe Sullivan panicked when he knew the feed store was going to be torn up. He always suspected that Dylan would tell Hazel and maybe he worried that Dylan had told her it was him who dealt the fatal blow. Maybe he called Hazel and told her he wouldn't put up with being accused. Maybe he told her he was going to blame Dylan and she killed him. But with her hip, how did she get up those stairs?

The call to Sullivan the night he was killed was made from the feed store's landline. Had he spoken to that person before? Did whoever called him ask him to meet to discuss the body and how to keep it from being discovered? For the tenth time in this case, I wish Maria were here to bounce this off.

And then it occurs to me that I haven't heard from her in two days. I know I've been completely immersed in solving two murders, but when did I stop being able to multitask? I should have called this morning when I didn't hear from her last night.

When I get to headquarters, the first thing I do is call her cell. She doesn't answer. I leave a message for her to call me as soon as she can. I get a mental picture of her in a cell alongside Allison Gleason.

Brick has left a message that he's gone home to get lunch. Unlike the rest of us on the force, Brick is very particular about what he eats. No hamburgers or enchiladas for him. He said he goes home and makes a salad and has a piece of chicken with it. No wonder he's in fighting trim.

I'm glad he's not here, though. I want to be alone for a few minutes to think. Driving back I got more and more frustrated by my circular ideas. Who killed Paddy Sullivan? I have been lazy, thinking that once I knew who killed the man hidden under the floorboards, the recent murder would fall into place. But it hasn't.

I sit back, hands folded behind my head, and stare out at the front parking lot. What am I missing? Somebody called Paddy Sullivan from the feed store and said something to him that sent him flying out of the house and headed for Jarrett Creek, a place he hadn't been back to in years. At least to his wife's knowledge. And shot him in the very place where he'd helped bury a body thirty years ago.

There are minor questions I've put to myself that haven't gotten an answer. Why did whoever threatened Mark Granger wait until just before renovations were to begin before they warned him not to proceed? Then, there's the matter of timing. Why was Sullivan killed at exactly that time?

Another matter I keep coming back to is Melvin Granger muttering, 'Poor woman.' Maybe he meant Cheryl. Is it possible that Paddy Sullivan or Dylan Polasek told Melvin what they'd done? That it had been an accident, that they had killed a man who abused his wife and son? Would Melvin have agreed to keep quiet about the body hidden under the floor in his storage room? He might have if Sullivan and Dylan Polasek made him a deal to provide various services in return for keeping his mouth shut. Sullivan might have provided that deck for next to nothing. But what did Dylan do for him?

Brick shows up from his lunch and I ask him what he's found in the papers I gave him. I hope there's some explanation of why Sullivan charged so little for the deck.

'Couple of things,' he says.

We sit down and he pulls over a short stack of bills that he has separated out. 'I don't know if this is the kind of thing you were looking for, but it struck me as odd. Here are some invoices for kitchen appliances at contractor prices. And there's a bill for a couple of different kinds of tile and some lumber. It looks like there must have been some remodeling going on, but I don't see any bills for labor.'

I pull them to me to look them over. I remember the modern kitchen in Granger's house. Sure enough, the appliances, tile, and lumber all went through Sullivan's account. At cost.

I sit back, my mind roiling. Clearly, Granger had some kind of deal with Paddy Sullivan. Was it because Granger knew what happened, and Sullivan agreed to provide building services to him as a sort of quid pro quo? If so, I wonder what kind of deal he had with Dylan Polasek?

Getting answers means another trip to Bobtail, but I don't want to ask Dylan on the phone. I call to make sure he's back home. He is, sounding tired. 'Dylan, I have one more piece of business I need to ask you about. I'd like you to stay put until I get there.'

'Can't you ask me now?'

'I'll be there in fifteen minutes.'

It takes me twenty, but he's still there. I noticed he's picked up the place a little. 'You want something? Coffee? Water?' he asks.

I shake my head. I want to get this over with. 'Dylan, I have one more question for you. Did Melvin Granger know that body was buried in the floor?'

He's as still as a deer for several seconds. 'Listen, he didn't have anything to do with Tolleson being killed.'

'But he knew the body was there.'

He sighs and runs his hands through his thinning hair. 'Yeah, he knew. The shellac wasn't quite enough to cover the smell. When it started smelling, he called Sullivan and told him he thought we'd trapped an animal. He wanted us to tear up the floor and get it out. We decided to tell him.'

'Why would you do that?' I'm thinking about young men and the impulsive decisions they make. If Granger had turned them in, they'd have been in deep trouble.

'You sure you want to know?'

I'm startled, but I tell him I do.

'We had something on Granger. Something we thought was funny when we first found out, but when Granger started in on us trying to get us to tear up the floor, Sullivan realized that we could use it to keep him quiet.'

He's right. I'm not sure I want to know what Melvin was doing. But I have to. 'What was it?'

'Granger had a lady on the side. Not such a big deal, but he sure as hell didn't want his family to know.'

The news makes me weary. Here was Melvin Granger, upright man with a sweet, attractive wife and a good family, and that wasn't enough for him. I don't want to know who the affair was with.

'How did you find out?'

'That's the ironic part. The night we brought the body to hide it in the floorboards?'

I nod.

'We had just gotten the body hidden, got most of the boards nailed down, when we heard somebody coming up the stairs.' He spits out a short laugh. 'Scared us half to death. We figured we were going to be caught. We hid in that back room, but we heard when Granger came into the store with this woman. They were making out in the front room. We almost died. Sullivan was bolder than I was. He peeked out and saw who she was. We didn't figure to say anything about it. But it came in handy when Granger confronted us. We told him if he ratted on us, that we'd tell his family that he had this woman on the side.'

'It's still hard for me to imagine him being OK with you killing somebody and hiding the body in his place.'

'We told him it was an accident and we told him what Tolleson had done. He didn't like that. Funny that he was running around on his wife, but he didn't like the idea of somebody hitting their wife.'

'So over the years, you and Sullivan did little favors for Granger, too.'

'Well, after a while we figured he wasn't seeing the woman anymore and his reasons for keeping quiet might ease up.'

'I know that Sullivan did some work on Granger's house for him. What did you provide?'

'My mamma is a champion quilter. She kept his family in quilts.' I remember the quilt on Granger's bed.

I can't wait to get out of Dylan Polasek's place. The whole story of Tolleson's abuse, the young men's drunken rage resulting in his death, and Granger's cheating, leading to mutual blackmail, has brought on a headache, and I'm not prone to headaches.

People often kill in order to keep a secret under wraps. A secret that will destroy their standing in the community. Before

I knew the identity of the man killed thirty years ago, and what happened to him, I thought it was his death that was the relevant secret. But even if the cover-up was wrong, people will most likely think the boys who killed Tolleson were heroes for saving his wife and child from his abuse. So the relevant secret lies in the second murder. Who killed Paddy Sullivan? And why?

It's five o'clock, and on the way to Jarrett Creek I call Brick to find out if anything has come up. He says it's quiet, so I head home. I can wait for Maria's call just as easily from there.

On impulse, I stop by to talk to Mark and Chelsea Granger. I want to see how they're doing after the funeral. I hope they're getting along better.

Chelsea opens the door, grim-faced. Her frown deepens when she sees it's me. 'Chief Craddock, is anything wrong?'

Strange question. 'No, just came by to see how you two are doing. You've had a traumatic couple of weeks, what with two dead bodies found in the store and your daddy dying.'

She ushers me into the living room and asks if I'd like a drink. 'People left enough alcohol here to last us the rest of the year. I don't know why people think drinking is the proper approach to tragedy.' She shrugs. 'That doesn't mean I haven't taken advantage, though. How about a glass of wine?'

I tell her a glass of red would be good. She brings a glass of dark, rich-looking wine that turns out to be a good zinfandel. Thirty years ago, when I was a new chief of police, there was a big brouhaha about wine-drinking at parties. The town has eased up in all those years.

'Mark around?'

'No, he's gone to Bobtail. Said he was going to see a friend for dinner.'

'Has your husband gone back to Lubbock?'

'Yes, thank goodness. I still can't believe he didn't bring the kids. I don't care what Mark said, I think he was punishing me by not letting me see them.'

'He really wants you back.'

'I want to go back for the sake of the boys, but the marriage is not working. I don't completely trust him.'

'You think he's having an affair?'

She grimaces. 'I don't know. I just sometimes think he's not telling me the whole truth. I shouldn't complain. He's really generous with me. But I have this uneasy feeling he's lying about something.' She laughs wryly. 'Same complaint I have about my brother. It's probably me, not them.' She gives herself a shake. 'But you didn't come here to give me marriage counseling.'

'Don't know that I'd be all that good at it anyway. No, I was just wondering how you and your brother are doing after the funeral. I know it's hard to lose your dad.'

'Honestly, it's also something of a relief. He hated being bedridden. After Mamma died, he was never the same anyway.'

'They had a good marriage?'

'They seemed to. Better than mine, for sure.'

'Your mamma was happy?' I'm curious to know if there was ever a hint that she knew Melvin had an affair.

She cocks her head. 'I never heard her say a word against Daddy. Well, that's not entirely true. They had their spats like anybody does.'

'Anything in particular set them off? Money? Politics? Religion?' I don't mention flirtation.

She looks at me with curiosity, as well she might. It's an invasive question. 'They agreed on most everything. Daddy didn't go to church a lot, and Mamma would like for him to have gone with her more, but I don't think either of them cared much about politics. Money? I mean, sometimes it was an issue. Like, they had a problem when Mamma wanted a new kitchen and Daddy said he couldn't afford it. But he must have figured out a way, because she got it. Why are you asking these questions?'

'Just making conversation. Are you and Mark getting along any better? He told me you two signed a contract about the store.'

Now she's decidedly uncomfortable. 'We get along fine.' Terse.

'It's good to have a contract, though. Too many siblings have problems because they made assumptions or had vague expectations.'

'Let's just say I have no expectations where Mark is concerned.'

'You think he's a bad businessman because of the bankruptcy?'

She nods.

'You said you didn't entirely trust him. Is it that you don't trust him to do right by you?'

She levels her gaze at me, as if speculating. 'He'll do the best he can.' She shakes her head. 'The problem is I've been lending him money. I know I shouldn't, but I hate to see him in financial trouble. I felt like I had to help him get back on his feet. And that's why I wanted a contract.'

'Sound like you're doing the right thing.'

As I'm walking to my car, I get the feeling I've missed something, but what?

THIRTY-SIX

B y now I'm truly alarmed that I haven't heard from Maria. Last night I had a long conversation with Wendy on the phone, trying to assure her that things are fine. And trying to assure myself at the same time.

Loretta eases my mood by coming over mid-morning with coffee cake. 'I haven't seen you in a few days. Have you made any headway on those two murders? And where's Maria?'

We're sitting on my porch. With the weather cooling off, it's pleasant. In fact, she's wearing a sweater, although she wears a sweater when it gets cooler than seventy-five degrees outside.

'Well, we cleared up the question of the body hidden under the floorboards. It was Lamar Tolleson.' I assume everybody knows by now the way the grapevine works. I'm baffled how selective the grapevine is. Seems like it would have been in high gear when Lamar Tolleson went missing.

'I heard that. People say it was no great loss, although that isn't a Christian thing to say. Do you know who killed him?'

'I do. It was basically an accident. And no, I'm not going to talk about who it was. That will come out eventually. But for now, I'm working on how his death ties in with Paddy Sullivan's murder.'

'Poor Paddy's wife. She must wonder what goes on here in Jarrett Creek. Her husband gets a call to come over here and next thing she knows, he's dead.'

I'm trying to figure out how to phrase my next question, and I decide the best thing is to swear her to secrecy. No matter how much she likes gossip, if she gives her word she'll keep quiet, I know she'll do it. 'I need to ask you something. But I need it to end right here. Nobody else needs to know that I asked.'

She blinks and rears back in her seat. 'Say no more. I'll keep your confidence.'

'Did you ever hear a rumor that Melvin Granger had an affair?'

I don't know what question she was expecting, but it wasn't that. Her mouth falls open. 'Never. Who was he supposed to have an affair with?'

'I don't have the answer to that. Don't want to know, to tell you the truth.'

'Well, who told you he did?'

'I have to keep that information to myself.'

I can see the wheels turning. 'What does that have to do with Lamar Tolleson being killed?'

'It's subtle.' I get up from my chair. 'Anyway, I have to get to work.'

'Wait. You still haven't told me what you heard from Maria.'

I don't want to worry her, but I have to tell her the truth. 'I haven't heard anything for a couple of days. If I don't hear anything today, I'm going to have to phone the authorities in Monterrey.'

'You should have done that yesterday!'

'Maria can take care of herself. I'm sure she's just busy.' I hope I'm right.

I've been pondering the information Sergeant Reagan told me about Mark Granger's bankruptcy. My talk with Chelsea last night is nagging at me. I feel like I'm missing a piece of the story having to do with Mark's partner skipping out after the bankruptcy. Where did he go? Has anyone heard from him?

At headquarters, I put in a call to the federal court that

handles bankruptcies in Houston. I talk to a clerk who tells me he can get me the information I need. 'It will take a couple of hours, and I'll send you the results.' He hesitates. 'OK if I send a PDF?'

I laugh. 'Son, I may be old, and I may only be the chief of police of a small town, but I do know enough technology to be able to open a PDF.'

He mutters an apology.

Now it's a waiting game. I'm wondering if there's more I can do, when the phone rings. It's Sheriff Hedges from Bobtail. 'Thought I'd better give you a call. There's been an incident.'

I don't like the tone of his voice. 'What happened?'

'Dylan Polasek was found dead this morning. Looks like suicide.'

The bottom drops out of my stomach. My first thought is that I should have given him more encouragement yesterday. But he didn't seem all that distressed.

'How?'

'Shot himself.'

I ponder that. 'You sure it was suicide?'

'Craddock, he was still holding the gun. Look, his killing himself wasn't a stretch considering what he was going through lately, people finding out he was responsible for a death all those years ago. He didn't seem like the most stable guy in the first place.'

'Maybe. But it still seems odd.'

'What are you thinking?'

'I saw him yesterday afternoon, and he said he felt better after confessing his part in Tolleson's death. Didn't seem all that distraught to me. Was he drinking?'

'I don't know. Forensics is still processing the scene. I'll get back to you.'

I don't ask if there was a suicide note. It's a myth that most people leave one.

'Have you notified his family?'

He draws a breath. 'That's why I called. I wonder if you'd mind doing that.'

'I'm on it.'

The hardest part about having to tell Hazel Moore that her

son is dead is wondering what part I may have played in it, and whether I could have said something to stop him.

I don't call Hazel in advance. If she isn't home, I'll call and tell her to let me know when she's home. But she is there, and by that telepathy that I've seen before and never understood, she sees me and immediately claps a hand to her mouth and moans, 'No.'

'Hazel, let's go inside.'

I tell her what Sheriff Hedges told me and she shakes her head. 'No. He would never do that. Somebody killed him just like they killed Paddy Sullivan.'

'I'm not arguing with you, but why do you think that?'

'I talked to him yesterday after you left. He said Sheriff Hedges released him and he thought things were going to be all right. He said he felt better than he had in a long time. Like he had some hope for his life to get better.' She breaks down, weeping. 'I'm going to have to call Eddie. It will just about kill him, too.'

I don't know if I should tell her that Hedges is looking further into Dylan's death. Which is worse, knowing your son committed suicide, or knowing that someone killed him? Either way, her life is blighted. 'I'm so sorry, Hazel. If I'd had any inkling that he was so upset, I would have taken steps.'

'Listen to me, Samuel. Somebody needs to investigate this. I know he didn't kill himself.'

'It could be that he got to thinking, and went into a funk. It happens.' But I'm with her. I have my doubts. We'll find out.

I wait while she calls a friend to come and be with her.

News of the death has shaken me, and I go back to headquarters considering whether I ought to go to Dylan's house to take my own measure of things, when a car swings into the parking lot with two people in it.

Dusty leaps to his feet and charges toward the door, but it takes me a second to register that it's Maria's car. Relief courses through me and I hurry over to open the door. Maria has Wendy's daughter with her. They both look bedraggled.

'Get in here and tell me what's going on,' I say, holding the door open.

Maria prods Allison, to precede her. Allison jerks away from her and stomps into the office.

Dusty is beside himself with delight, leaping and yelping. Maria crouches down and rubs his ears until he settles.

I can't help scolding her. 'I've been calling you for two days! Why didn't you answer? I've been worried out of my mind.'

She looks up. Her expression is sheepish. 'Either lost my phone or it was stolen. Anyway, I couldn't find it. I intended to buy a cheap one, but never found the time. I've been busy.' She rolls her eyes in Allison's direction.

'Well, I'm glad you're back.'

When she stands up, she says to Allison, 'I'll take you back to your cell.'

Allison whips her head toward Maria with a furious look. 'Oh, come on. You don't really mean that.'

'I do. I take my promises seriously and I promised the judge I'd lock you up until you're cleared.'

'That's ridiculous,' Allison says.

Maria gives her a stone face. 'You think so? That's the attitude that got you in trouble in the first place. Thinking rules don't apply to you.'

Allison turns her attention to me. 'Do you believe this? I'm the victim here, and everybody acts like I'm a criminal.'

I'm glad Wendy isn't here to see her daughter defying Maria. And me. 'What I believe is that if Maria says you need to get into a cell, she's got a good reason. So let her escort you in, and then I'll listen to the full story.'

'I got railroaded, that's the story,' she says.

'And you still need to be locked up until I hear otherwise,' Maria says.

'Who's going to know?' Allison demands.

'I am.' Maria points toward the door that leads to the cells. 'If you need to use the facilities, they're on the right. I'll wait.'

Maybe it's because I'm feeling frustrated that I can't solve Sullivan's murder, but Allison's attitude has riled me. I'm usually pretty mild-mannered, but I think about the pain she's caused Wendy, and I'd like to shake some sense into her. I figure I'd better wait a few minutes before I talk to her, so I'll have a chance to calm down.

Maria comes back out and I can see by the look on her face

that she's as disgusted as I am. 'Have you talked to Wendy?' I ask.

'I haven't done anything but keep my eye on her. She's a handful. She actually had the nerve to ask me to take Allison to a friend's house.'

'Tell me what happened in Mexico. How did you manage to get her out?'

'You know I told you my friend knew a judge. Turned out the judge didn't have a lot of respect for Señora Rojas, the legislator's wife. She demanded that Allison be put on trial, but he said she's well known for stirring things up. Still, the police were scared of her, so they weren't too big on letting Allison go. When I told the judge what witnesses to the accident had told me, he said he'd fix things with the police, though. I told the judge that, as a deputy, I'd see to it that she was jailed here in the States until they got Señora Rojas to admit her driver was at fault. I had to sign a bunch of papers in front of a representative from the US consulate.'

'You did an amazing job. Wendy's never going to let you forget what you've done.'

She blushes. 'A lot of the success is due to you.'

'Me?'

'Yes. You suggested that I find out what happened to the car Allison was driving. It wasn't hard to find where it had been towed. And it was clear from the damage that Allison hadn't rear-ended anybody. The car was damaged from the side. I took photos.'

I laugh. 'Of course you did. And I want you to take credit.'

'I'm glad it worked out, but I'm not happy with that girl. She never admitted that she put herself in a tight spot by not getting insurance, and then lying about who was driving. And she didn't thank me, either.'

The last part rankles me, but I'll take care of that. 'Did you get her to tell you who the guy was who was driving the car?'

'Only that it was somebody she knew. She said they weren't doing anything, they'd just gone down to Monterrey on a whim.'

'And you believe her?'

'Yes, I do. She doesn't seem like a bad person, just careless.'

I suspect she's giving Allison the benefit of the doubt because of Wendy. 'You must have gotten an early flight this morning.'

'Seven o'clock. I didn't want to hang around in case anybody changed their mind.'

'How long do you think we'll have to keep Allison in jail?'

'Not long. The judge said he'd have the authorities notify you as soon as the case was dropped, and it shouldn't take more than a few days.'

'You want to call Wendy and give her the good news?'

'You can do that. I'm going over to the café to get myself a hamburger. And fries. I'm starving.'

Before I call Wendy, I want to have a word with Allison. I walk into the back room where she's sitting on the cot with her arms folded and a pout on her face.

'I'm going to call your mamma. You want to talk to her?'

'And tell her you've got me in jail?'

'Never mind. I'll let her know you're safe.'

She snorts and I get out of there before I tell her what I think of her shenanigans and her attitude. She reminds me of my sixteen-year-old niece Hailey, who was here for a few weeks this summer, complete with a teenage attitude. But Hailey was sixteen. This woman is nearly thirty. And still acting like a brat.

When Wendy answers the phone, I don't prolong it. 'Allison is here,' I say.

'You mean back in the US?'

'No, I mean here at the station. She came back with Maria this morning. Maria didn't have time to call you and let you know.'

There's a beat of silence. Wendy knows as well as I do that Allison could have made the call herself, and didn't. 'I don't know what to say except thank you. I have to process this, it seems impossible. But why didn't Allison call me to tell me?'

'I'm not sure. I'll let the two of you work that out.'

'Can I come and get her?'

'There's a little problem with that.'

'What problem?'

I tell her that Allison has to be in custody until we get clearance. 'I'm sorry. I know that's tough to hear.'

'Are you kidding? It means that – for a while anyway – I'll know exactly where she is. But I can come and see her, right?'

'Of course you can. I think she'd like that.'

And I'm going to make sure that even if she doesn't like it, she's going to act like she does.

As soon as I hang up, I stick my head into the back room with the cells. 'You want anything to eat? Maria said you didn't have time for breakfast.'

'I'm not hungry.'

I walk into the room, carrying a chair, set the chair outside the cell, and sit down. 'Do you have any idea how much worry and pain you've caused Wendy?'

'Do you know how much worry and pain it caused me?' she shoots back.

'Caused *you*? The situation that *you got yourself* into? Are you kidding?'

She sits up straighter, looking outraged that I've challenged her. 'I don't see why you're so upset. It's between me and my mother.'

'I'm upset because I don't see any contrition. I also don't see any gratitude for the amount of time and effort that it took Maria to get you out of a problem that you caused yourself. Not to mention the amount of money Wendy has spent trying to save your hide.' I should probably shut up now, but I've had it. 'I don't see anybody but a spoiled, impulsive brat who thinks she can do exactly as she pleases and to hell with the law, to hell with common sense, to hell with people who care about her.'

'That's not fair! That woman lied! It was her fault.'

I ignore her whine. 'The accident may have been her driver's fault, but by allowing your friend to leave the scene of the accident, you let yourself get into a position to be accused. And on top of that, you didn't do what even the dumbest person knows to do – get Mexican auto insurance.'

She looks daggers at me. 'I didn't think I needed insurance. We only intended to be there for one night.'

'That was a mistake. Have you owned up to that mistake? Do you understand how much trouble it got you into?'

'Even if I'd had insurance that woman would have made trouble. It's all down to her. It has nothing to do with me.'

'It has everything to do with you! What happened to your friend who was driving? Have you talked to him?'

'That's none of your business. I'll deal with him. Once you get off my case and let me out of here.'

I stand up. I know I'm losing it, but I've had it. 'As far as I can tell you didn't thank Maria for figuring out a way to get you out of the jam that you got yourself into. And believe me, it took some fancy work on her part. You haven't thanked me for sending her down there when I could have used her here to investigate a double murder. You wouldn't give your mamma the time of day when she wanted to at least hear your voice.'

Allison's eyes have widened and two bright red spots have appeared on her cheeks. I don't know if she's mad or finally understanding the trouble she's caused.

'I called your mamma to let her know you're here. You could have called her yourself and saved her a few hours of agony. She's coming to see you and even if you don't give a damn about how much grief you've caused her, you'd better find some way to pretend you care, because if you don't I may find that I lose the paperwork when it comes through and you can spend time in jail until I decide you've learned a lesson.'

I stomp out of the room, not wanting to give her a chance to make me even madder.

THIRTY-SEVEN

I stare down at my desk, wondering if I've done the right thing, wondering if Wendy will be mad at me for lecturing her daughter. I hope not, but I've had it. I've been hearing tales of her daughter's stunts ever since I met Wendy, and it's high time somebody fed the girl a dose of reality.

But I don't have time to dwell on her self-inflicted woes. I have Paddy Sullivan's murder to investigate. And maybe Dylan Polasek's.

I open the computer and find that – as promised – the federal bankruptcy clerk has sent me a file. It details the boilerplate bankruptcy of Mark Granger's Urban Threads. The store is described as being in a large space in a commercial

area. Like so many other business owners operating on the
edge, when the pandemic hit, Mark and his business partner,
Cash Lowell, couldn't pay their bills. I look up information on
the store on the internet and find a brief article stating that,
after the store closed, its assets were bought for pennies on the
dollar, which didn't quite cover their expenses. Theoretically,
they still owe $50,000, but the article says that the principals
of the store are unlikely to pay, that Mark Granger has moved
out of the city, and Cash Lowell has disappeared.

I look up Cash Lowell's name and find a couple of articles
that mention him in connection with the store. Although the
article doesn't convey a sense of alarm, the word 'disappeared'
crops up again. It's sobering. No one raised the alarm when
Lamar Tolleson disappeared all those years ago, either.

Maria comes back from the café and I tell her that Wendy
will be here soon, and I describe my one-sided conversation
with Allison.

She grins. 'Good luck. I think it's going to take more than
one talking-to for her to understand that she's to blame for her
own mess. But enough of that. I'm itching to know what's
going on here. Have you figured out who the mummy was and
who killed Paddy Sullivan?'

I spend the next half-hour bringing her up to date about
Lamar Tolleson's abuse and how Dylan Polasek told me he was
accidentally killed. And finally, that this morning I got word
that Dylan was dead, and my doubts that it was suicide.

'So both of the men who killed Tolleson are dead now?'
She looks puzzled. 'What do you suppose that's all about? It
doesn't sound like Tolleson's death was worth anybody's
revenge.'

'Except there was another piece of the puzzle. Melvin had
an affair at the same time Tolleson was killed.'

Her mouth drops open. 'You're kidding. How did you find
that out? And what does that have to do with the murders?'

'I found out from Dylan Polasek. He said that when they
were hiding Tolleson's body, Melvin came into the store with
some woman and he and Sullivan heard them messing around.'

'Why was that important?'

'Dylan told me that his and Sullivan's attempt to cover up

the odor of decomposition wasn't entirely successful and it started to smell. Melvin complained that he wanted to have the floor torn up to find the source. Polasek and Sullivan told him what they'd done. Melvin threatened to go to the police, but they told him they knew he was having an affair and they'd expose him if he told anybody about the body in the floor.'

'So it was blackmail?' Maria says.

'Not exactly. More of an uneasy truce. Sullivan and Polasek did a few favors for him over the years to keep him quiet.' I tell her about the deck and the kitchen Sullivan provided at cost for Granger, and the quilts that Hazel provided. 'Then Mark threw a wrench into the balance by deciding to renovate the store. They knew if the floor got pulled up, the body would be found.'

'So they called Mark and threatened him, and when he wouldn't back off, they beat him up?'

'Maybe. I've got another theory. I don't like it, and maybe you can poke holes in it.' I tell her how I've put things together. 'I had always wondered why Sullivan was killed at that exact time, and this explains it.'

'I can see why you don't like it, but it makes sense. What are you going to do now?'

'I'm going to wait until Wendy gets here. As soon as she's gone, I'm going over to talk to Carlton Jones.'

'I'm going to my place to change clothes, but I'll be back in a half-hour.'

'Take your time. It's good to have you back.'

'I don't want to miss anything,' she says. Dusty jumps up and starts after her. 'I'll take this mutt with me,' she says. 'I've missed him.'

I don't have long to wait for Wendy. She comes wheeling into the parking lot like she's being chased. I greet her at the door. She looks a little less tense than she was when Allison was missing, but she's still keyed up. I'm sure she's afraid that Allison will give her some kind of back talk. So am I. I don't want to lose my temper. Again.

When I take her back to see her daughter, I see the cells through her eyes. They look scruffy and not particularly clean. It's hard to keep them spotless when what we usually get in here are drunks sleeping it off.

Allison is lying on the cot with her arm over her eyes. 'Allison,' I say, trying for a friendly tone, 'your mamma's here.'

Allison sits up, blinking. Maybe she really was asleep. She glances at me and I see a little fear in her eyes. 'Oh, hi Mamma! I'm so happy to see you.' She grabs the bars and I can't tell if she's play-acting or really has had a change of heart. I'm fine either way.

'Can I . . .?' Wendy gestures towards the bars.

'Of course.' I open the door to the cell and Wendy rushes in and hugs her daughter tight. Allison closes her eyes and seems to return the hug.

'I'm glad you're OK,' Wendy says when she steps back. 'You look fine. So they didn't hurt you?'

'No, they were courteous. I'm pretty sure they didn't want an American girl to be all bruised if I had to go to court.' There's that hint of a whine.

'Did they let you have your things back?'

Allison shrugs. 'Yes. I didn't have much. We weren't . . . I mean, I was just down there for twenty-four hours.'

'I brought you a few things. A change of clothes, some toiletries. Make a list of what you need and I'll go into Bobtail and get it.'

'I would like to get out of these clothes.' She's wearing jeans and a gray T-shirt.

Wendy looks aghast. 'You've been wearing the same thing all this time?'

'No, Mom, I've been in their jail clothes. It was like a feed sack. It was horrible. But I'm glad you brought something fresh for me to wear.'

'I don't know if you'll like what I brought. I had to scrounge around into some things you left at the house.'

I could shake Wendy for being so obsequious with her daughter. The girl needs a dose of tough love. But at least Allison is treating Wendy with respect.

'Did you bring a toothbrush and toothpaste? If they let me brush my teeth.' She shoots a look at me.

'Oh, honey, I'm sure Samuel will do everything he can to make you comfortable.'

Now is not the time to tell her that I plan to take Allison to Bobtail where they have a better facility. And where I don't have to be in charge of her.

I leave them to have some privacy, and in twenty minutes I go back and tell Wendy I have somewhere to be. 'You can stay as long as you want. Maria is here now, and one of my other deputies will come in as well.'

'I think I'm going to go get the things Allison needs and come back. Is that OK?'

'Of course it is.'

As I close the door behind us, preparing to leave together, I see the distressed look on Allison's face. It's finally clear to her that she's stuck here for a while. In a cell.

Before I leave for Carlton Jones's place, I call Hedges. 'Did you ever tell me what kind of gun killed Polasek?'

'It was a Beretta. An old one.'

'Specific kind?'

'M9. You know the one. It was popular a while back. You can get them for not too much money anywhere. Is this important?'

'It might be. I'm on my way to find out.'

As usual, Carlton Jones is working in his garden with a complete view of the comings and goings of Granger's Feed Store. By now I guess he knows me, because he invites me into his kitchen for a glass of iced tea. For the first time, I meet the dog whose barking I've heard, although she was quiet this time. She's a dainty ball fluff with a bark much bigger than she looks. She dances around the same way Dusty does.

'Dahlia likes you,' Jones says. 'Always a good sign. She doesn't take to everybody.'

'Unusual name,' I say.

'I like to grow flowers and dahlias won't grow here,' he says, with as close to a smile as I've seen. 'So I figured if I was ever going to have dahlias, I'd have to name her that.'

I laugh. 'You've got a better reason than I have. I named my dog Dusty for no reason that I could think of, but after a while I remembered that Melvin Granger used to have a dog named Dusty, so I guess I wasn't very original.'

A companionable moment.

'You've got the glint in his eye of a man on a mission,' Jones says after he's downed half a glass of tea in one gulp.

'I am. I need you to think back to the night of the fire.'

'Let's sit down.'

We sit at the small chrome kitchen table. Dahlia flops down next to my chair, which I take as a compliment.

'That's almost two weeks ago now,' Jones says. 'I hope I can remember that far back.' I think he's joking.

'When I spoke to you afterwards, I asked if you'd seen anything unusual around the time the fire started, but now I want you to think back to a couple of hours before the fire.'

'All right.'

'Did you happen to notice approximately what time Mark Granger left the store that day?'

He pinches the bridge of his nose, closing his eyes to concentrate. 'You know, as it happens, I do remember. I never paid much attention to Granger's coming and goings before he was attacked, but afterwards I started keeping an eye out. I'm usually winding up work in the garden about the time he leaves, so if I'm not mistaken he left at the usual time. That would be six o'clock.' He stares at me, but I can tell he's not exactly seeing me.

That isn't what I was hoping to hear. But then he continues. 'But he came back about a half-hour later.'

That's more like it. 'How long did he stay?'

'I don't know for sure. I went inside to get supper.'

'You didn't mention this when I talked to you earlier. Why not?'

His gaze is troubled. 'At the time, I believe you asked if I noticed anybody who might have set fire to the store. The answer to that was no.'

'And you don't know if anybody else came to the store while Mark was there?'

He puts his hands on his knees. 'I see where you're headed. You sure you want to go that direction?'

I don't argue with him; I just keep quiet.

He sighs. 'Yes, somebody did. I was in the shower, and Dahlia kicked up a fuss. I had to stick my head out of the shower to tell her to be quiet.'

'Which means she heard somebody outside that she wasn't familiar with.'

'Yep.'

'When Mark Granger came back, she didn't bark, but later she did?'

'That's right.'

'Did you look to see who it was?'

'When I got out of the shower, I looked out back and saw a vehicle parked next to Granger's car. I don't know who it belonged to.'

He describes the vehicle, and I know I'm on the right track.

THIRTY-EIGHT

I pick up Maria and head for the Grangers' place.

Chelsea Granger looks wary when she sees me at her door for the second time in two days, especially since this time I have Maria with me. 'Now what?'

'Chelsea, we need to ask you some questions.'

She ushers us into the living room. Maria and I sit on the sofa and she perches on the arm of an armchair.

'You're scaring me. What is this about?' Chelsea says. Her eyes dart between the two of us.

'This is important. I need you to tell me the truth.' I look her in the eye.

'Of course I will. I've told you the truth all along.'

'Before your daddy died, did he say anything about the body that was found under the floor?'

She hesitates. 'Not to me, he didn't.'

'To your brother?'

She nods.

'What did he say?'

'Mark said Daddy told him he knew the body was there.'

I wait, but she seems to have stalled out. 'Did he tell Mark who put it there?'

'He said it was a couple of guys who were working on the renovations.'

'And did he tell Mark why the man had been killed?'

'I don't know if he did. You'd have to ask Mark. Honestly, I didn't want to know the details. I couldn't believe Daddy had kept that secret.'

'Why do you think he did?'

'I don't have any idea,' Chelsea says. 'I didn't want to hear anymore because I was afraid Daddy was involved somehow.'

'If it puts your mind at rest,' Maria says, 'he wasn't. He knew about it, but the man's death had nothing to do with him.'

'Then why didn't he say something? Why didn't he go to the police?' She's wringing her hands.

I don't want to hurt Granger's reputation with his daughter. There's no need to. 'Let's just say he had his reasons. He's not at fault. But I have something else to ask you.'

'OK.' She lets out a breath, relieved not to dwell on the subject of her daddy and the body. Her relief won't last long.

'On another matter, you told me more than once that you didn't trust your brother. You were vague about the reasons. I want you to tell me why.'

'Oh, just . . .' She waves her hand as if it was some casual reason, to be dismissed.

'No. I want to hear your real reason. It has to do with his bankruptcy. And the disappearance of his business partner. Am I right?'

She looks helpless. 'Sort of.'

'Tell me about the business partner.'

'Cash,' she says. Her eyes are haunted. 'I only met him a few times, but I liked him. I thought he was the brains behind the business. Mark could charm people, but Cash knew the business side. He was smart, and that's why I was surprised when they went bankrupt. But then Cash told me . . .' She takes a deep breath. 'He told me that Mark had been siphoning money away from the business.'

'And that's why they went belly-up?'

'Cash didn't say that directly, but I think that's what he meant. He said he had no intention of prosecuting Mark, but that he was going to ask him to make a plan to pay back the money.' A tear slides down the side of her nose and she brushes it away.

'You think this has anything to do with Cash's disappearance?'

She swallows. Her voice is small. 'I hope not.'

'When did Cash leave exactly?'

'I don't know. I wasn't there when he left. I'd gone back to Lubbock. I was only there for a few days to help them with a closeout sale.'

'How did you find out Cash was gone?'

'Mark told me. He complained that Cash had left him high and dry.'

'Did Mark say whether Cash confronted him about the missing money?'

'He told me Cash had accused him of skimming money. He admitted he had taken some funds, but he insisted that he intended to pay it back, and he said he and Cash had worked out a plan for him to do that.'

'You believe him?'

Her answer is a long time coming. I wait. 'I wanted to. I mean, he's my brother.' She squeezes her eyes shut and takes a shaky breath. 'Is that all?'

'Not quite. Let's go over details of the night Paddy Sullivan was killed.'

Her eyes fly open. 'You mean about the fire and all that?'

I nod. 'You remember what was going on here at the house that night?'

'Like what?' Wary as a cat.

'Were you taking care of your daddy before you got the call about the fire?'

'No, he was always asleep long before that.'

'What were you doing when the call came in?'

'Cleaning the dishes.'

And then I remember what it was that didn't fit. I had thought Chelsea said she and her brother were just finishing dinner when I called them about the fire. But that's not what she said. 'When I called you to tell you about the fire and the body, you said that Mark was finishing dinner. You didn't eat together?'

She looks trapped, but doesn't speak.

'Did he sit down to eat with you?' I ask.

'He didn't, did he?' Maria asks.

Chelsea shakes her head.

'Do you know where he was?' I ask.

She clutches the arms of the chair as if it might levitate. 'I was almost done cooking when he came in from work. But then he left again. He said he needed to pick up a few things at the grocery store. I told him not to be long because we'd be eating soon.'

'Did he come back right away?' I ask.

Her eyes widen and she puts a hand to her mouth as if to hold back words. She's beginning to see where this is going. When she speaks, it's in a whisper. 'No. He was late. Supper was cold by the time he got back. We had a big fight and I told him if I was going to cook, the least he could do was show up on time.'

'Did he say why he was so late?'

She draws a deep breath. 'No.'

'Did he have groceries with him?'

She shakes her head. 'I asked him if he'd left them in the car, and he told me he'd gotten sidetracked and didn't go to the grocery store. That's when we got the call about the fire and I never thought about it again.' I don't believe that. I'll bet she's thought of it twenty times.

'Chelsea, do you mind if I take a look at your daddy's desk again?'

She's almost in a trance and doesn't ask why. 'Go ahead.' She waves me away.

I head back to Melvin's office again. Sure enough, the Beretta is missing.

Back in the living room, I ask her if she knows what happened to the gun. She shakes her head.

Maria speaks to Chelsea. 'Do you have any friends here in town you can have come over and keep you company?'

'I don't feel like seeing anyone right now. I may call my husband. I don't know.'

She looks worn out, and there's more to come if her brother did what I think he did.

THIRTY-NINE

Outside, Maria and I sit in the car and discuss the implication of what Chelsea told us.

'Of course Mark would have been late to supper that night,' I say. 'Not only did he have to meet Sullivan at the store to kill him, but he had to hide Sullivan's car so he needed to wait until it was dark enough to drive it to the lake and dump it.'

'I'd forgotten about the car in the lake. Seems like I was gone a month dealing with Allison.' She frowns. 'Why would he go to the trouble of driving it into the lake? Why not just keep it hidden somewhere?'

'I wondered the same thing, but then I think he figured the water would wash away any trace evidence. He was right. There aren't likely to be fingerprints or DNA since it was submerged in water. But if Granger got back into his car right after he dumped Sullivan's car, there might be trace evidence from Sullivan's car in Granger's.'

'What I don't understand is why Mark killed him. Mark knew nothing about Sullivan or the body.'

'I'll tell you what I think. When Sullivan found out Mark was going to renovate the store, he panicked. I suspect he called and threatened Mark, and then when he found out Mark was going ahead with the project anyway, he called again, this time to tell him there was a good reason not to tear up the place. He likely told Mark about the body, and also about the affair, and that if Mark didn't stop construction, he'd reveal the whole story.'

'It's even possible that Paddy Sullivan tried to blackmail Mark,' Maria says.

'Maybe. Either way, Mark probably figured he'd get away with killing Sullivan. He was a stranger to town, and for all anyone knew, he didn't know Sullivan.'

'But saving his daddy's reputation doesn't seem like motive enough to kill somebody.'

'You're right. I think it's more than that. I think Mark wanted to save his own reputation. That was more important than his daddy's.'

'He didn't want people to know he was a failure?'

'Ever since his sister got here, she's been criticizing him for his poor business decisions. He was sinking money into the feed store project that he didn't have. He told me he couldn't ask his sister for help, but Chelsea told me she was lending him money. I think he felt desperate to prove he could make a go of it. When the business with the body came up, he was afraid it would shut down his plans entirely. Killing Sullivan may have seemed like an easy fix.'

'Easy fix? I mean killing a man? That's easy?'

'You remember what Chelsea said, that Mark's partner said Mark had been skimming money? Mark said he and the partner worked out a way for him to pay the money back, but then the partner disappeared.'

She lets out a breath. 'And you think Mark killed him, too.'

'I think we have a killer on our hands. Let's go pick him up and hear what he has to say.' I start the car.

I get two calls on the way to the feed store. One is from Hernandez, the lawyer, wanting to talk to Maria about the details of Allison's release. I tell him she's busy and that she'll call as soon as she can.

The second call is from Houston, from a detective there who had worked on Cash Lowell's disappearance. He said he'd given up finding Lowell, and he was interested that I brought up questions about him. 'His folks have been after us, but there was no indication that he had come to a bad end,' he says. 'For all anybody knew, he just went off to lick his wounds after the bankruptcy. But I'm open to hearing your concerns.' He's a slow-talking, deliberate man, but sounds like the deliberation is carefulness, not disinterest.

I tell him I'm looking at Cash Lowell's business partner as a suspect in another matter. 'I'll get back to you after I question him.'

* * *

At the feed store, Maria and I find Mark Granger in the back room conferring with a carpenter, poring over architectural plans laid out on a table. The place is half torn up.

Mark straightens when he sees us. 'Hey, Chief, sorry I missed you yesterday afternoon when you came by.'

'Chelsea said you were in Bobtail visiting a friend.'

'That's right.'

'Mind if we go outside for a minute? We've got a couple of questions to put to you.'

He puts on a puzzled look. 'Sure.'

We go down the steps and into the back area, where there's an old wooden table with a couple of benches. Carlton Jones is in his garden. Either he doesn't see us or he ignores us. Mark sits across from Maria and me.

'What's this about?' he asks.

I take out my black notebook and a pen. 'Can I get the name of the person you were with in Bobtail yesterday?'

'What? Why do you need to know?' An annoyed expression.

'Answer the question.'

He hesitates. 'His name is John Baker. But you won't find him in Bobtail. He's a friend of mine from Houston. He was passing through and called to ask if I wanted to have a bite to eat.'

'Good. Then you've got his phone number on your cell phone so I can check it out.'

He blinks. 'I may have deleted it.'

'Why would you do that?'

'I didn't think I'd need it again.' He's fidgeting.

'Let's take a look. You want to get your phone out?'

'I, uh, left my phone upstairs.'

'Maria can go get it. Where'd you leave it?'

Maria hops up, looking expectant.

'Is this really necessary?' Now he's indignant, but his eyes are calculating. 'Oh, wait, I do have the phone.' He slips it out of his pants pocket and makes a show of glancing at his recent phone calls. 'Let's see. I made a couple of calls this morning and then, yep, I deleted it.'

'Mind if I take a look?'

He hands it over with a smirk. He's so cocky that he has no

idea what I'm really looking for. I see a familiar number on the recent calls and I hit dial.

When someone answers, I say, 'Good afternoon, Sheriff. It's Craddock. Where are you?'

'I'm at Dylan Polasek's place. There's been a development. How did you get this number? It's Polasek's phone.'

'I'll tell you when I see you. I think we've got what we need. Can we meet at your office?'

'I'll be waiting. You need any help?'

'I don't think so.'

Mark is frowning. I slip his phone into my jacket pocket.

'Hey! What are you doing? That's mine.'

'You mind coming with us?'

'Where are we going?'

'Taking you in for questioning.'

'Questioning about what?' His voice is raised and I see Carlton Jones come to attention to watch us.

'A man named Dylan Polasek was found dead this morning and I need to question you pertaining to that.'

'I never heard of him.'

'Then you've got nothing to worry about.'

'I can't leave right now. I've got the store to tend to. And decisions to make about the renovation.'

'I'll call your sister. She can take care of it.'

'She's not here. She's gone to Bryan.'

'She must have gotten back, because we just left her.'

I make the call and Chelsea answers the phone. Mark is looking at me with fury in his eyes.

I tell Chelsea I need to discuss a few things with her brother. 'Can you come down and tend the store for a while?' Her voice is brittle when she tells me she'll come right away.

Meanwhile I call Brick and I ask him to mind the station. He'll be entertaining for Allison, if nothing else.

It only takes Chelsea ten minutes to get to the store. We meet her at the bottom of the stairs and she hurries past us, avoiding her brother's gaze.

When we get in the car and head toward Bobtail, Mark says, 'Where are we going? I thought you were taking me in to ask questions.'

'We're doing that at headquarters in Bobtail,' I say.

'Why not here? I don't have time to be traipsing all over the county.'

'It's better if we meet with the sheriff.'

He's silent the rest of the way, and we make no attempt to engage him in conversation. I'd like to know what's going through his head.

When we arrive, I ask if he wants a lawyer present when he's questioned.

'I have nothing to hide. Why should I need a lawyer?'

He does need one; he just doesn't know it yet.

Hedges is waiting for us and takes us into an interrogation room.

'Can I talk to you and your deputy for a minute?' Hedges says to me when Mark is seated. 'You don't mind if we step out for a minute, do you?' he says to Mark.

Mark shakes his head. He doesn't realize this is standard procedure, giving a suspect time to stew and worry.

Outside, Hedges says, 'Why don't you go across the street and get a cup of coffee. Give it twenty minutes.'

FORTY

When we're hunched over cups of coffee neither of us is in the mood for, Maria says, 'One thing we haven't discussed. Why did Mark kill Dylan Polasek? How did Mark even know who Dylan was?'

'I imagine Sullivan told him.'

'But why kill Polasek now?'

'I suspect I know the answer. A few days ago, Polasek quit his job. He said it was because he was tired of it, but I figure Polasek decided to try to get some money out of Mark. Blackmailing him with information about his daddy having an affair. Polasek figured in a small town like Jarrett Creek, Mark wouldn't want people to know his daddy had been fooling around. But instead of paying, Mark decided one more murder would tidy things up.'

Maria sighs. 'Polasek wasn't too bright, was he?'

'He might also have figured out that Mark killed Sullivan and tried to blackmail him about that. We'll try to get that information from Mark.'

'What's your approach going to be?'

I tell her I don't have a set plan. 'I'll see what his responses are when we get started. Feel free to butt in.'

We get a call that Sheriff Hedges is ready for us to come back, but instead of taking us to the interrogation room, he ushers us into his office. 'Forensics has established that Polasek likely didn't kill himself. The gun was positioned in his right hand. But we checked out what you said about his right hand being a problem for him after he had a motor-cycle accident. According to the people he worked with, he could use the hand for general things, but not for something precise.'

'Like using a gun on himself,' I say.

'Right.'

We head for the interrogation room. I've got a knot in my stomach. I know why people are sometimes driven to kill. Often it's an impulse born to satisfy some basic need: greed, revenge, fear, hatred, or momentary rage. The more difficult question is why someone *plots* to kill? In this case there was no revenge factor, no hatred. There was desperation about money, but mostly just plain old ego and fear of exposure. Determination to avoid exposure. Determination to save face.

When we get to the interrogation room, Mark is an unhappy man. He's had an hour to enjoy the dingy, smelly room, and he's full of bluster. He demands to know what he's being held for and when he can get out of here. I apologize profusely for keeping him waiting for so long.

'We had some loose ends to tie up,' I say. 'Mark, I have a few questions to ask you.'

'I've got a business to run,' Mark says, 'so I'd appreciate it if we could get on with it. I don't know what you think I've done, but we ought to be able to clear it up fast.'

I've been thinking hard about how to approach Granger. If

he did, in fact, kill his business partner, he thought he got away with it. He thinks it was cleverness on his part, when instead it was pure luck. But I'm not going to start there. I'm going to work backwards.

'I agree. Let's get right to it. Why did you lie when you said you didn't know Dylan Polasek?'

'I don't know what you're talking about. Who is he?'

'You told me you didn't know Polasek, but when I called the last number on your cell phone, it went straight to his phone, so you had called it before.'

He forces a chuckle. 'Oh, that. He must be the guy who called me yesterday. I was just returning the call. I wanted to find out what he wanted.'

'And what did he want?'

'Nothing. It was a wrong number.'

'I see. Well, how come that wrong number had called you twice in the last couple of days? And how come those calls lasted at least five minutes?'

Mark is able to look amazingly relaxed. He shrugs. 'He was trying to sell me something. I didn't want to be rude. I've been in sales myself. I know it's a tough business.'

'You said it was a wrong number, and now you're telling me he was trying to sell you something? What was he trying to sell you?'

'I don't really remember. I wasn't paying a lot of attention.' He's playing it cool, but sweat has collected at his brow below his hairline.

'OK. I want you to think back to the night Michael Sullivan was killed and the fire started.'

He's startled at the abrupt change, but he recovers quickly. 'Hell of a night.'

'Your sister tells me you came in from work, but you left right away again and came in late for supper. She said you argued about it.'

'She has a little control issue. I told her I was going out to have a beer. I needed to unwind.'

'Where did you go for a beer?'

'Bought a six-pack at the convenience store and took the beer out to the lake and sat out there in my car and drank it.'

Cagey. He didn't name a place where I could have checked to see whether his story checked out.

'You drank the whole six pack?'

'I had a couple.'

'What did you do with the rest of it?'

'Took it home.'

'Your sister said you claimed you had gone grocery shopping, but you came in empty-handed. So how'd you get the beer home without her seeing you?'

'Oh, come on. It's not like she was at the door checking me in. She just didn't see me put it in the fridge, that's all.'

'Where were you at the lake?'

'What do you mean where was I?' Impatient.

'I mean, were you in the park? Did you get out and walk to the beach? Sit up on the bank?'

'That's it. I parked up on the bank at the side of the road.'

'Then I'm in luck. We found a car upside-down in the lake. You were in the perfect position to see whoever had that accident. That must have been some spectacle.' I know he must have waited until dark to dump the car, but I'm thinking this line of questioning might unnerve him. So far, he's kept his cool.

He licks his lips. 'Yeah. Quite a sight. Thing went over and I thought it must have killed whoever was inside, but then he climbed out and seemed to be OK.'

'What did he look like?'

'It was dark so I didn't see him very well.'

'Dark? Hm, it wasn't that late. When the fire got reported, it was barely dark.'

'It was dusk though. You know how things get shadowy at dusk.' He's picking at his nails.

'What direction did he go when he took off?'

'That . . .' He stalls out, and I can see his mind racing to keep up. 'Somebody came and picked him up.'

'In what kind of vehicle?'

'Some kind of pickup.'

'Color?' I'm writing all this down as if I think he's telling me something real.

'Dark.'

'Who was driving?'

'I don't know. All I saw was that the guy who had the accident climbed in and they took off.'

'You must have gotten a look at the guy who had the accident when he opened the door of the cab and the light came on?'

'It happened so fast. I guess he was a medium-build guy, youngish. Dark hair.'

'Clothing?'

'You know, the regular. Jeans. T-shirt.'

'And you called the police to say you'd seen an accident?'

'Called? No, I didn't make any call.'

'Why not?'

'Why didn't I call you?'

'Yes, it seems like that's what most people would have done. They see a car go into the water and somebody gets out. I mean, there might have been somebody in the passenger seat who was trapped.'

He blinks. 'I thought I should mind my own business.'

'I wish you'd made the call because that car belonged to the guy who was killed in the store, Michael Sullivan. Whoever ditched that car probably killed Sullivan. Might have given me a lead.'

He shrugs, but there's a hint of worry in his eyes.

'We'll leave the lake for now. But let's talk more about Michael Sullivan. Paddy, they called him.'

'I didn't know him.'

'No? Odd. When I had a chance to take a look at the calls Sullivan made from work, lo and behold I found that he had telephoned you a number of times in the week before he died.'

'Oh!' He looks triumphant. 'He must have been the guy threatening me with those anonymous phone calls.'

'Could be, but he didn't just call out, he also received calls from you.'

'I must have misdialed.'

'I don't think so. The calls lasted a few minutes. So what were you discussing with him? Did he tell you about the body he and Polasek hid in the floorboard? Did he tell you your daddy knew about it?'

He's frozen, unexpectedly at the end of his ability to dissemble.

'Did you meet with him before the day he was killed?'

'Of course not.'

'I thought he might be the man who roughed you up. You claimed it was two men who jumped you, but I wonder if that was a story you made up, and you actually got into it with Sullivan.' It's just as possible that his wounds were self-inflicted and that we'll never know for sure. What I'm pretty sure of, though, is that his story was bogus.

He sneers. 'I'm telling you I never met the man.'

'Mark, I'm going to put to you what I think actually happened.'

He stays still while I lay out my theory that Michael Sullivan heard that he was planning to renovate the store, and he called Mark and threatened to reveal certain facts about Mark's daddy if he didn't abandon the idea. And that to shut him up, Mark lured him to the store to talk things over and shot him instead. And then later dumped his car in the lake.

'That's preposterous. I didn't kill Michael Sullivan. I don't even own a gun.'

'Your daddy did. I found it when I was going through his belongings. It didn't occur to me at the time that it could have been used to shoot Sullivan because your dad was an invalid. But the gun is missing, and I believe if we check, we'll find it was the same gun found in Polasek's hand that he supposedly shot himself with.'

'Polasek must have stolen it.' He's sweating profusely now, his face pale.

'Now Mark, you know that's not likely. You know exactly what happened. You used that gun to kill Michael Sullivan, and then you put it back in the desk drawer, where it was when I saw it. Last night, when it came time to kill Dylan Polasek, you took it out again.'

'That's not true. I don't know anything about that gun. Or any gun. And I didn't kill anybody.'

'Mark, give it up. You've left too many things to chance. And your luck has run out.'

'Listen, I didn't do this. You can't prove a thing.' The words of every arrogant killer, ever.

'Unfortunately for you, I can prove it. Somebody saw you come back to the store the night Sullivan was killed.'

'Who? There was nobody around.'

We all freeze. He's tripped himself up, and he knows it. 'I mean, he couldn't have seen my car, because I wasn't there.'

'You thought there was nobody. But there was.'

Carlton Jones was being a good Samaritan, keeping an eye out for Mark's safety after he was supposedly attacked. And that's why he saw Mark go back to the store to meet Sullivan.

I'd like to say I feel satisfied when I join Hedges in his office to put together the facts and the theories, but I don't. Three local men are dead, leaving shattered families in their wake. Tolleson's wife Cheryl and son Andy will finally have closure. But having his body found will reopen old wounds that they had worked to heal.

Sullivan's death leaves a family in mourning, now having to deal with the fact that thirty years ago he had a hand in killing a man and covering up the deed.

As for Dylan Polasek, my only regret is that I didn't put the facts together soon enough to save him. He may have had to reckon with a blighted life, but his mamma will mourn him for the rest of her life.

The whole thing is such a waste. Mark Granger could have been part of the community. He could have ignored Sullivan's threats and let the body be exposed. It's likely Sullivan and Polasek would have kept their mouths shut. And if they had, there's a good chance I would never have found out who the body belonged to anyway. It was Sullivan's death that triggered me going down the path that led to Tolleson. All Sullivan and Polasek would have to have done was stonewall. *'Don't have clue who that was in the floor. Nothing to do with us.'* Like Loretta and Oscar Grant said, I could have walked away at that point and figured it was too long ago to bother.

I have no doubt that eventually the cop I spoke to in Houston will track down what happened to Cash Lowell. And it won't be good.

I liked Mark, and I'm sorry he couldn't let well enough alone.

He might have even gotten away with killing his partner if he hadn't decided murder was an easy way out.

I'm sorry about what Chelsea will go through. When someone commits a violent crime, it affects everyone. His sister will have hard decisions to make. On top of whether to go back to her husband and try to work things out, she'll have to decide what's to become of Granger's Feed Store. Will it remain part of the town, or will it be sold and torn down? I have a hunch she won't want to see that happen. We'll see.

FORTY-ONE

A week later, Wendy and I are having dinner at our favorite steak restaurant in Bryan. We're celebrating Allison being released from jail. It took a week, but the Mexican authorities finally gave the go-ahead. I have to credit Sergeant Reagan for his part. He put in an official request through Wendy's lawyer, Chuck Hernandez, that the case be dropped, and it went through.

I also gave him credit for doing a routine check on Mark's background and alerting me to the sinister disappearance of his business partner. Even though I was already suspicious of Mark, the information from Reagan pushed me forward. Maria found my praise of Reagan hard to take. She hasn't gotten over being grumpy about his initial insults.

I've got something to say to Wendy about her daughter, but I'm not sure how to bring it up, so instead I've been answering her questions about the aftermath of Mark's arrest.

'Chelsea has decided to take over the store herself,' I say. 'She's made a deal with her husband to let the boys visit once a month.'

'She must be so sad about her brother.'

'I think she had a suspicion that he wasn't the greatest person, although having it confirmed was hard. Especially after losing her dad.'

We're quiet for a minute, thinking our own thoughts.

'Samuel, you've been itchy ever since we got here. Why don't you tell me what's up?'

'It's hard. I don't want to jeopardize our relationship, but I have to talk to you about Allison.'

She dips her head and stares into her wine. When she looks back up at me, her eyes are filled with tears. 'I know she was rude to Maria. Was she rude to you, too?'

It's the opening I need. 'I can take that. So can Maria. What I can't take is the way you let her walk all over you.' As soon as Allison was released, instead of going to Bryan to see Wendy, she had a friend pick her up and left for parts unknown.

'I don't know what to do. She's hurt me too many times, but I can't stand to cut her out of my life entirely.'

'Do you have any idea why she treats you so badly?'

Wendy toys with her wine glass. In the candlelight, her hair and face are glowing, but her expression is grim. 'She blames me for her daddy's death.'

'Why? I thought he had a heart attack.'

'He did. But we had a fight just before that, and she thinks I was too hard on him. And she may be right.'

I start to say something, but she holds up a hand. 'When we were arguing, I told him I was leaving him.'

This is new information. We've been seeing each other for a couple of years, but she never mentioned this. 'Was he surprised?'

'Surprised? I don't know. Angry, yes. He thought I was having an affair.'

I'm not going to ask if he was right. I don't want to know.

'Would you have left him?'

'I don't know. It wasn't the first time I threatened to leave. I've told you he wasn't the easiest man to live with, but that's not really fair. I wasn't easy, either. I wanted a more adventuresome life than he did. I wanted to travel and go out, like this . . .' She waves a hand around the restaurant. 'He hated to eat out, wanted me to cook. He hated traveling and didn't like it when I went anyway. He would get angry and pout. And,' she draws a deep breath, 'he bad-mouthed me to the girls when I was gone.'

'I'm sorry. You never told me.'

'I've always felt guilty and Allison feeds that guilt. You know what's funny? Allison is the free spirit, and yet she blames me for wanting to have some fun, to enjoy life. Jessica is quiet. She's a homebody, but somehow she never blamed me for wanting more.'

'Have you and Allison discussed this?'

'A few times, but we always end up fighting.'

I hesitate. Do I have the right to give her any advice? Yes, if only because I love her and want her to stop letting her daughter hurt her. 'Don't you think you've punished yourself enough?'

'I don't know. Maybe. But what does that mean? It's not as if I can pretend she doesn't exist.'

'Of course not. But maybe you can try to accept that she's got to work this out for herself. Maybe limit the time you spend with her and not let her make you feel guilty.'

'Ha.' She takes a sip of wine. 'Easier said than done. Every time she shows up, I start off hoping that she's changed her mind about me. And then she starts in.'

'Is there anybody who could talk to her? Your sister?'

'You're kidding, right?'

I can't help chuckling. 'Seems to run in the family.' Her sister's daughter, Tammy, spends half her time with Wendy, because she can't get along with her mother.

Somehow, that lightens the mood and we drift to other subjects. I don't want to press too hard, but I've got an ulterior motive. I think it's time we talked about our future. Will we marry? Live together? What will that mean for her relationship with her daughter?

But she's laughing about something, and I leave it for now.